Hring caught the first cut and replied with a thrust. His sword was shorter than most, as handy for a jab as for a cut. The point sank deep into the berserker's chest, an automatic counter to the wild, swinging attack. Hring withdrew his point, twisting the sword to make a large wound, and the blood came spurting after it. Had it been any other man, the fight would have ended then. The berserker seemed not to notice the wound, but continued his attack. Hring kept his shield busy defending himself as he tried to find an opening for counterattack. The berserker drove him down the length of the hall, then back up toward the dais again. Hring saw that each blow his foe delivered was the same, only the speed with which they were delivered made them confusing. The berserker's sword came down once more, and sword and hand flew free of the arm, cut off clean at the wrist. Hring slammed his shield into the man's face, knocking him over onto his back. He thrust his sword point into the berserker's open mouth, then leaned his full weight onto his sword pommel. He waited until the body had stopped jerking before he withdrew his blade and wiped it off. He was conscious of a great deal of cheering going on. Yngva was looking at him with a wild glitter in her eyes, her face flushed to the upper surfaces of her breasts where they showed above her bodice. To Hring, the fight had been worth that look.

King OF THE WOOD

JOHN MADDOX ROBERTS

A TOM DOHERTY ASSOCIATES BOOK

KING OF THE WOOD

Copyright © 1983 by John Maddox Roberts

Reprinted by arrangement with Doubleday & Company, Inc.

First Tor printing: April 1986

A TOR Book

Published by Tom Doherty Associates
49 West 24 Street
New York, N.Y. 10010

Cover art by Kirk Reinert

ISBN: 0-812-55206-7
CAN. ED.: 0-812-55207-5

Library of Congress Catalog Card Number: 82-45335

Printed in the United States

0 9 8 7 6 5 4 3 2 1

For Hank Reinhardt,
known to all true men as Ulric Greywolf

Skaal, Wolfbrother!

Chronology

995 A.D.   The pagan followers of Ironbeard flee Norway to found settlements in Treeland (eastern North America) to escape forced conversion by Olaf Tryggvason's Christians. Settlements begin from Maine to Virginia, continually pushing southward.

1014 A.D.   Pagan Norsemen fleeing Ireland after the Battle of Clontarf arrive.

1067 A.D.   Saxons fleeing the Norman Conquest arrive and settle in the North, bringing strong Christian church.

1120 A.D.   Treeland splits into Christian North and pagan South. The pagan South assumes the name of Thorsheim. The Saxon house of Godwinson assumes the crown of Treeland. The Scyldings rule in Thorsheim.

1125 A.D.   Florida peninsula colonized by Muslim Spain.

1190 A.D. The Battle of Helgi's Steading defeats encroachment of the Onondaga League into Treeland. Most Skraelings (Indians) in Treeland converted. Mining of iron in Treeland releases Newlanders from dependence on Europe for iron.

1380 A.D. King of Norway claims suzerainty over Treeland and Thorsheim and sends a naval expedition. Norwegian fleet trapped in Bjornsby Harbor (New York) and utterly defeated by combined fleets of Treeland and Thorsheim.

1392 A.D. First war between Treeland and Thorsheim ends indecisively.

1400 A.D. Church of Treeland breaks with Rome.

1425 A.D. Second war between Treeland and Thorsheim ends indecisively.

1450 A.D. The present.

Prologue

In the beginning were the trees.

When Ironbeard's followers fled the persecution of Olaf Tryggvason's Christians they boarded their knarrs and sailed West, searching for the isles rumored to lie there, near the world's Edge. Many days they sailed, with the storm at their backs, before they sighted land. They came ashore where there was fresh water and it was then that they saw the trees: oak and ash and new trees for which they had no names, tall trees as ancient as gods that stood like the pillars of a temple, blocking the sun and allowing no lesser growth within the fastness of their domain. After the barrenness of the Northland, it was like a land of heroes, and when some ships went back to the Northland for supplies the word spread that there was a land in the West where a man could wear the hammer around his neck or sacrifice to Odin or perform the planting rites in the fields without being burned or flogged or hanged by the followers of Christ. More Norsemen came.

There were other men there, black-haired savages the

Norsemen called Skraelings. There were many of them, but their weapons were of flint and wood, and the less powerful tribes became slaves or serfs, or else they fled. The Skraelings taught the Norsemen how to grow the fruits of the new land. The harvests were richer than any in the Old World, and in gratitude groves were set aside in stands of the sacred trees, and sacrifices were made, and the branches of the oak and ash bore the bodies of men and women hanged by their necks at harvest time, or by their feet with their throats cut at planting.

The traders and explorers and trappers ranged far. In the West they found herds of beasts that seemed to be the flocks kept by giants. In the South were Skraelings who lived in cities of dazzling splendor, and the Norsemen looked upon their gold with envy, but these Skraelings were very numerous, with vast armies of warlike men. But they were eager to trade gold for iron and horses, and soon the southern Skraelings held an empire as vast as that claimed by the Pope.

The Christians came when the Saxon nobles fled England, their lands usurped by William the Bastard. First a trickle of them, then a torrent, and they struggled with the pagans for control of Treeland, until fought to a standstill at Bjarni's Stream, and there the border stabilized. The Muslims came from Spain and took the southern peninsula and built their bright cities, lured by the trade with the old southern Skraelings and with the rising new power, the Azteca. The Norsemen knew these Muslims of old as Bluemen, and so the southern peninsula became Bluemensgard.

And so they struggled and fought, explored and traded, worshiped and sacrificed, lived and died, in the new land for four hundred and fifty years. Over all brooded the forest, so vast that there seemed no end to it, and it became the source and focus of life, gigantic, dark, vital, caring nothing for any of them.

Book One

The Wolf's-head

Chapter 1

The snow had stopped falling when the mounted men reached the rune-stone border. They stopped at the stones and leaned easy on their saddle pommels, and the horses pawed at the thin layer of snow, looking for grass. Three men rode a little ahead, close to the line of tall stones that marched along the bank of the river, one every hundred paces. The rest of the men wrapped themselves in their cloaks and waited.

One of the three, an old man with a scarred, fierce face, a dented iron cap atop his head, addressed the other two. "You know the King's law and sentence well enough, but the custom says I must tell you here, before you leave. You, Hring, are declared outlaw for the crime of kinslaying. For seven years you must be exiled from Treeland. If you return before seven years from this day, the ninth of November, the year of our Salvation fourteen hundred and fifty, you may be slain out of hand by any man, and no man may claim vengeance for your blood."

The man thus addressed was Hring Kristjanson, son of the thegn of Long Isle. His eyes were blank and impassive as he heard the sentence yet again. He was remembering the day on the practice field in the shadow of the castle wall, when his half brother Hake had struck him with the blunt practice sword when his back was turned. He had seen red then, and the next thing he knew, Hake was stretched stark on the ground, his helm smashed in like a drinking horn under a man's foot at an oath-taking. This same fierce old man, Gudmund the housecarl, had pried the practice sword, now clotted with Hake's blood and brains, from Hring's stiff fingers.

Then there had been the court, his father the thegn sitting bowed and miserable, his stepmother's eyes glowing with triumph. His full brother Hroald was dead two years past in a brush with the Skraelings; now Hring would be exiled. Now her own offspring would rule. It had cost her a son, but Hake had not been her favorite. That was Thorkel. Always Thorkel. He would be thegn as soon as Helva could contrive it.

Then there had been the bishop, pronouncing him excommunicate, beyond the pale of Christendom, forbidden the sacraments. Then the King's decree, which was only form, since everyone knew the punishment for a kinslayer. Seven years an outlaw, a wolf's-head with every man's hand against him. An ordinary murderer only got three. It made little difference, since outlawry for a year was the death of most men. His friend Halvdan the skald had chosen to share his exile. Halvdan was a pagan from the south, but immune like all skalds.

"Now that's done," continued Gudmund, "I'll speak my own mind. Come back when your outlawry's done. If

your father lives, you'll be reconciled. If not, then we'll
see you made thegn. You'll still have friends.''

"Thorkel's heir now," said Hring.

"My loyalty's to the thegn, Kristjan, not to Thorkel.''
He spat to leeward.

"My advice to you, Gudmund," said Hring, "is to take
your gear and find another lord as soon as you can. By this
day twelvemonth no friend of mine, no man loyal to my
father, will be alive in the thegndom, mark me.''

"All the more reason for a loyal man to watch out for
the thegn's interests, a thing he seems little inclined to do
for himself of late." He turned to the third man. "And
you, Halvdan, will you not reconsider? You could be
living in the hall, eating at the thegn's table and sleeping
warm. You well know his liberality. There's good meat,
and barley beer and clear wine and fine wheaten bread.''

"Without me, Hring wouldn't last a month across the
river." The young man grinned. His blond hair was clipped
short and there was a gap between his front teeth. "Besides,
I long for a visit to my old home.''

"A man's loyalties lie where they will," said Gudmund.
To Hring he said: "Your mail and helm are in the saddlebag.
I saw to their cleaning and oiling before we left. I charge
you to put them on when you've crossed. Don't come back
for seven years, but come back then without fail." With
that, the old man wheeled his pony and left them.

On the bluff above the ferry, Hring and Halvdan studied
the rune stone that stood by the path. Gray and old, it
towered ten yards high, its north side green with moss. The
south side was carved with a likeness of the crucified
Christ, so entwined in interlace design that he appeared to
be drowning in a pit of serpents instead of hanging on the

cross. This was the boundary between Treeland and Thorsheim. Between Christian and pagan.

They walked the horses down to the ferry. The ferryman came out of his hut. He was a Skraeling. No Northman could live in the land flanking the river that the Northmen called Bjarni's Stream and the Skraelings called Po-to-mak. The Skraeling guided the horses to their places on the raft and the men followed.

"You are lucky to be crossing now," said the Skraeling. "In a month, there will be too much ice in the river to risk crossing."

"No man is lucky crossing this river at any season," said Hring grimly. They said no more until they reached the other shore. Hring gave the ferryman a quarter mark and the two men trudged their horses up the southern bank. Another row of rune stones lined the southern bank. These bore the likeness of a squat god who bore a stylized hammer that looked almost like a cross with bent arms. It was primitive and ferocious and Hring found it stirring in a disturbing manner. He made out the archaic runes haltingly, but some of the words he was unfamiliar with. "Halvdan," he said, "what say these runes?" His friend scanned the jagged marks in the stone for a while, his head bobbing as he caught the rhythm of the words, then his voice broke forth in the deep, singsong cant of a skald using the Cursing Voice.

> *Swift fall the hammer*   *On him who crosses*
> *No joy of living*   *No honor in death*
> *He that trespasses*   *Damned be forever*
> *Feast for the ravens*   *Who honors not Thor*

Hring dismounted and opened his saddlebag. From it he took the rolled-up shirt of mail and slid it on over his head.

The rings were cold, but the weight was reassuring. Around his waist he buckled the sword belt, drawing it tight. On his head he placed the helm, turned so that the nose guard was to the rear, where it would not interfere with his vision. If a fight were imminent, he would reverse it. His round shield hung from his saddle, its snarling wolf's mask proclaiming his new status.

"Your fine gear will avail you little if we're attacked in this land," said Halvdan.

"At least they'll know me for a thegn's son," retorted Hring.

"Or a man who's robbed a thegn's son," replied Halvdan. "As I understand it, that's as great an honor in these parts."

"That is so," said Halvdan, laughing. "But here's honor greater than that." He patted his harp where it hung across his back. "No lord has glory without a skald to put it in verse and spread it about."

"In the North, the histories of kings are written in books."

"Where nobody ever sees them again. And no scribbling monk is sacrosanct anywhere that I know of, while a skald is welcome at any hearth." This was an old game of theirs, arguing the respective merits of skald and prince, letters and runes, prayer and poem. It was always friendly, for neither took himself seriously enough to care much.

They rode until the sun was westering in the far mountains. There were no villages this near the border, though they passed the remnants of several that had been burned in the wars between Treeland and Thorsheim in the last century. In one of these they bedded down for the night, where a hut still had its roof, patched over the years by travelers. They hunted up dry wood and started a fire

with flint and steel. In a bronze kettle Halvdan heated
water. When it was boiling he poured some into a bowl
which held ground maize, to make porridge. Into the rest
he crumbled a cake of chokoatl, to which he added some
syrup of the sugarcane.

"It would be better if we had some milk to put in it,"
said Hring.

"Better yet if we had great joints of beef, cooked with
those hot peppers the Skraelings of the South raise, and
mugs of ale. We've left those things behind."

"Forcibly, in my case. You made your own choice."
Hring took a stick from the fire and applied its smoldering
end to his pipe. Halvdan did the same. Soon the clearing
before the hut was misty and fragrant with the smoke of
tabac and cherry bark.

"I follow my own wyrd," said Halvdan at last. "You'll
not hear me complain. The gods don't like that." When
they had finished, they rolled into their blankets and slept.

Hring was not sure what woke him. He listened for
out-of-place sounds, but heard nothing. He tried to move
but found he could not. Had he been bound in his sleep?
He tried to call out to Halvdan, but he could not speak.
Then he knew that this must be a dream. The fire had
burned to embers, but the clearing was bright with the full
moon reflected from the snow. He saw a stirring among
the trees. Two figures came walking, almost gliding, sound-
less across the glade. When they were near, he saw that
they were women, both tall. One wore a long cloak, a
cowl hiding her features. The other was young and
bareheaded. Her fair hair fell below her waist in two plaits
as thick as a child's arm. Her deep-shadowed eyes regarded him with icy detachment.

"Will he do, Mother?" said the fair one.

"He will do marvelous well," said the other. Her hand rose, and she bent to touch Hring. Her finger traced a design on his brow, and where the nail touched, his skin was so cold that it burned.

"The seal of our wyrd is upon him now," said the cowled one. It was the second time he had heard the old word this night. Christians weren't supposed to use it. But then, he thought, he was no longer in Christian land, and the church had done with him. The fair one pointed at him.

"Sealed to me are you, wolf's-head, to do my will. It may be soon or it may be late, but your wyrd and mine are entwined like mating serpents." Then the women faded back into the trees.

On the next day, Hring told Halvdan of his vision, and asked what it might mean. To his surprise, Halvdan turned most serious.

"A witch may ensorcell a man and subdue him to her will," he said. "This may be done a number of ways. She might cause you to eat enchanted food or drink, or obtain some cast-off bit of you—a nail paring or a lock of your hair or the like. Or she may trace a sign on your brow." The two searched the clearing, but there were no tracks in the snow other than their own.

"Perhaps it was just a dream," said Hring. "Why should a witch want me to do her bidding, in any case?"

"Your god has withdrawn his protection from you. This is a land of the old gods, and you have none to shield you here. Such as you would make a fitting tool for the workings of a witch."

They saddled their horses in silence, the dank fear of

sorcery adding to the chill of the air. As they rode the southern coastal trail, the woods seemed to Hring to darken, the black, twisted, bare trees stark against the leaden sky.

"Halvdan," said Hring, to break the uncanny silence of the wood, "what are the witches of the pagan lands like?"

"Oh, there are many kinds. Some are harmless; fortune-tellers, runecasters, the spaewives, who sell winds to the sailors. A few are evil in a small way. They sour milk and make burrs to grow in their neighbors' fields. The priestesses, though, they are another matter."

"Priestesses?"

"They are women consecrated to the old gods—Frey, and Freyja, and others. The gods who reigned before Thor and Odin, the dark ones of the earth and the trees. Their worship is grim and bloody."

Hring began to cross himself, remembered it would do no good, and let his hand fall. "Why do men worship such dark ones?"

"Because they bring fertility to the fields, and to the flocks and to the herds. But they yield their favor grudgingly. Their price is blood. Odin inspires men to verse, and he receives the slain in battle into his hall. Thor brings the good rain and the terrible lightning. But it is the gods of the earth who say whether whole populations starve or have bread.

"The bright gods of the sky are worshiped in the temples, and men are sacrificed to them but rarely, since the dead of battle please them well enough. The old gods take their worship in dark groves and deep caverns, and they must have blood on their feast days, and it must be the blood of strong men and fine women."

Hring shivered, though his wool cloak kept him warm enough. He felt alone and alien in this dark land of blood and savagery. He almost felt that he should have taken his chances with the Skraelings of the West. "And these priestesses?"

"Odin, Thor, and the others of their families are served by priests and skalds and chieftains, but the old ones are tended by a line of women. The rites are passed down from mother to daughter, and no man may witness the great services save those who do not return from them."

These words cast Hring into a deep gloom. He was a big youth, but new come to his full growth, heavy of bones and large-handed, and he was armed as befitted a chieftain's son, but here he felt small and defenseless. Halvdan struck his harp and began a song to lighten his mood. As the day brightened a bit, the evils of the night seemed to recede, leaving only a vague, bitter aftertaste.

The town was called Tyrsby, and it stood where two roads met at the shore. It had a fine shelving beach where the smaller vessels could be dragged ashore, and a wooden stockade surrounded it for protection from the Christians of the North, the Skraelings, and the bandits and pirates who abounded everywhere.

Odd the gatekeeper saw none of these. Instead he saw two mounted men approaching from the north. That road was so seldom used these days that grass grew on it, and in the spring it took a man as sharp-eyed as Odd even to see it. He studied the two. Both were young men, but one was the older by a few years and wore a harp across his back. The other was little more than a youth, though bigger than most, and shaggy locks of fiery red hair hung below his steel cap. Odd climbed down from his tower and bade his son keep coast watch for ships. He went to meet the strangers.

Hring and Halvdan saw the old man striding importantly through the gate, holding a great ax. When they came even with him they halted and waited for him to speak first, which was the custom.

"I am Odd, gatekeeper of Tyrsby, appointed by the Thing. I would ask you who you are, and what is your business, but I can see a good deal already." He regarded Halvdan. "Your harp proclaims you a skald, and the gold rings on your arms say you're a good one. You bear the sword of a warrior, yet you have no byrnie nor helm. Such rings as yours could buy fine armor, but you wear none. Therefore you must be Odin's man." Now he turned to Hring. "You wear the arms of a noble, yet you travel with no following save a skald. Your shield proclaims you a wolf's-head and you've come down the northern road. You wear no hammer, but you wear no cross either. You are an exile from the Christian lands, and you must have the blood of a man on your hands, for no noble would be sent hither stripped of his god's shield for a lesser matter."

"You've sharp eyes and a keen wit, my friend," said Halvdan.

"A man with my duty has little enough to pass the time save trying to read men by what can be seen. As long as you mean no mischief, you may have freedom of the town. A skald is always welcome, and as for your friend, no man here seeks vengeance for a slain Christian, and since he's a Christian no longer, his origin will not be held against him, as long as he is not disrespectful of the gods here."

"I would insult no god," said Hring. "I am a stranger here, and would stay on good terms even with the fairies and trolls."

"You speak wisely for a young man," said Odd. "The

Small People should always be honored. There is an inn in the town where you may rest. They will be glad of a skald who has been traveling in the North. We've had little news of those parts of late." The two thanked the gatekeeper and rode through the stockade.

The inn was a low building, built like every other structure in the town of logs. The bark had been trimmed from the doorposts and they had been artfully carved with serpentine designs and images from the adventures of Sigurd. The two young men unsaddled their horses and turned them loose on the common, then went to the inn, carrying their gear.

Inside, their eyes took a few moments to adjust to the dim, smoky interior light. The long room had a bed of coals in the center, over which joints of meat turned on spits tended by an old Skraeling slave woman. There was a long table down the middle of the room, with a gap for the fire. Along the bench sat a company of men: Norse woods runners, a few Skraelings, even one or two dusky men from the Moorish kingdom to the south. An innkeeper came up to greet the new arrivals.

"Greetings and welcome, gentlemen," he said. His eyes flickered over Halvdan's harp, Hring's wolf shield. "You seem to have fared far, and I warrant you're hungry."

"Lean road fare has been our lot for many days," said Halvdan. "We're of a mood for some proper man's fare."

"You'll find that here, in plenty. We have venison, fat bear, boar, mutton, beef, horse, even dog if you've been living among the Skraelings and taken to it. There's wild fowl, too."

"A joint of venison and a pheasant for me," said Hring,

his mouth watering at the smells coming from the fire. "And red wine."

"I'll have boar and a capon and ale," said Halvdan. "Is there a bathhouse near? This time of year, we've been shy of water in our travels."

"Through the hanging down at the end of the hall," said the innkeeper, pointing. "Go there and be comfortable while your supper's preparing." The old Skraeling thrall brought the customary guest cups—hot spiced wine at this season. Hring and Halvdan carried their cups through the leather hanging, and the heat and steam hit them as they entered the wooden shed built onto the inn. There were no other men inside, but two girls in thin, damp shifts stood by the great tub, attending a brazier where stones were heating. The two men stripped quickly and lowered themselves into the scalding water. The girls flogged them liberally with willow twigs to get their blood circulating, then scrubbed them with sponges. As their ministrations proceeded lower, Hring began a rough jest concerning the relative size of his and Halvdan's members, but his friend cut him short.

"You must never joke about such matters here," he said urgently. "The genitals, whether man's or woman's, have great magical significance. It can offend the gods to speak lightly of them." Halvdan spoke in the northern dialect, which the bath attendants probably would not understand. "You northern folk have been influenced by the Saxons, and most of their humor involves the genitals in some way or other, but here a joke that wouldn't raise an eyebrow up North will get you flogged or even killed."

"So many new rules to remember," said Hring, shaking his head. "Will I ever learn them all?"

"There aren't many others of great importance," said

Halvdan. The two dressed and went to seek their dinner. They found it laid out on bread trenchers. Next to the trenchers stood two pitchers, one of ale and the other of red wine. They sat down, drawing the folding eating knives from their pouches, and began carving.

When their hunger had abated somewhat, the two young men leaned back, picking their teeth with straws from the floor. They cleared their trenchers by tossing the bones to the dogs that rooted about beneath the tables. They were refilling their cups when they saw that they had a visitor.

"May I join you gentlemen?" he asked politely. Hring gestured for him to sit and studied the man. He was tall, with dark hair and beard, and he wore a cloak of beautifully dressed beaver skins. There were fine bracelets of wrought gold on his wrists.

"I am Dieter Vidfaring, a trader. You gentlemen have recently come from the North?" Hring confirmed this and introduced himself and Halvdan.

"I meant to speak to you when you came in," said Dieter, "but I waited, for you looked like men who had better uses for your mouths than speech, so now you've had your dinner I'll make a bargain with you. I'm headed for the fairs in the summer, and need news of the North. If you'll give me the news, I'll buy your wine and ale."

"Fair enough," said Hring, but Halvdan interrupted. "I am a skald and must sing the news for any man that asks, while I'm taking hospitality."

"That's understood," said Dieter. "I would just like to ask my questions first." The two young men assented. "First, what's the situation with the Onondaga League?"

"They tried a foray in the fall, after the harvest was in," said Hring. "We beat them back across the border, and most of the mountain trappers got in safely."

"That's good," said Dieter. "I'll be trading for furs at the Herring Isle fair." The summer fairs were held on neutral islands where Christian and pagan could meet and trade safely. Dieter continued his questioning, his many shrewd queries richly interspersed with anecdotes from his wide travels. The two younger men found him to be a witty and entertaining companion, even when his mind was on business. By and by the host came to their table. "You've had them long enough, Dieter," he said. "Everyone wants to hear the skald." Halvdan took a last swallow of ale and pulled the cover from his harp. It was an ancient instrument, its black wood polished to a fine luster by the hands of generations of skalds.

There was instant silence as Halvdan sat before the fire and began tuning. Silently, the old Skraeling woman put a full tankard of ale on the hearth next to the skald. The room was packed now, for the story had spread through the town that a skald had arrived. Hring saw Odd the gate-keeper there with his son, their duty ended with the closing of the gate at nightfall.

Halvdan broke into song, using the News-Spreading Voice, high and clear, and its attendant meter, telling of the latest doings up North, much of it secondhand from other skalds, but reasonably reliable for all of that. Hring noted that Halvdan discreetly omitted any reference to the story of the son of the thegn of Long Isle. If any man asked about that subject, he would be obliged to sing of it, but no rule of the skalds said that he had to initiate the tale.

When the news was over, Halvdan took requests. Most wanted to hear hero epics and sagas, and Halvdan obliged, singing a few of the most exciting parts of each, since the entirety of any of them would have consumed several long evenings. The audience sat in rapt attention, and no man or woman took so much as a drink except when Halvdan laid aside his harp for a moment to take a draft himself. Hring noted that even the worldly Dieter was as enthralled as the others, and his heart swelled with satisfaction, for he was proud of his friend, who was more like a brother to him than any of his own kin.

Halvdan finished with the battle scene from Ketil's Saga, describing the naval battle of Bjornsby Harbor in 1380, when the king of Norway's fleet had been annihilated utterly by the combined fleets of Treeland and Thorsheim, the last time that the two enemies had united to protect their independence from the suzerainty of Europe. When the song ended, Halvdan replaced the cover of his harp and returned to his table.

"I'd hear more of such harping," said Dieter. "Have you two younkers a destination, or are you free?"

"We're as free as any man may be, and the gods allow," said Halvdan, knocking the table to signify acknowledgment of the gods' superiority.

"My pack train is heading south tomorrow," said Dieter. "We already have a full complement of packmasters and guards, but a certain Lady Yngva has joined us, desiring an escort to her home in the South. The roads are dangerous this time of year, but the sea-lanes are even more so. She is willing to pay for the hire of extra guards. Would you two be interested? The work is light and the pay acceptable."

"It sounds good to me," said Hring. "We were headed South anyway, and it's safer traveling in company than alone. Who is this Lady Yngva?"

"I've never seen her," said Dieter. "She sent a

thrallwoman to bargain. But she pays good gold, and that's good enough for me.''

"For me too," said Halvdan. "Southbound with Dieter's train it is, then.'' The three men shook hands on the bargain.

The next morning, Hring and Halvdan rode from Tyrsby to the field where Dieter's train was assembled. There were more than two hundred pack mules, and for every ten mules there was a packmaster. There were some twenty guards and a pack of thralls owned by Dieter who performed the menial tasks. In the midst of the train was a single wagon, pulled by mules, in which rode the Lady Yngva. Hring found himself mightily curious to see this lady. The wagon was driven by the thrallwoman, a half Skraeling named Bluefeather. Hring and Halvdan were assigned watches and positions on the march. Dieter told Hring to stay close by the wagon, though he would not explain why. The position suited Hring well enough, since he would be neither courting ambush at the front nor eating dust in the rear.

The first days, the train shook down until every man knew the routine and camp could be made or struck in the minimum time. Hring and Halvdan fell easily into the routine, and life was agreeable for them as the train progressed into the warmer climes of the South.

Still, they had had little sight of the mysterious Lady Yngva. Halvdan said that he had seen her once, wrapped in shawls and veils as she went into the woods during a break to answer a call of nature, but no part of her face had he seen. She was the subject of much speculation among the trainsmen, but she had paid good gold, and Dieter would not have her spied upon.

On an afternoon two months after Hring and Halvdan had joined the train at Tyrsby, the thrallwoman Bluefeather came to Hring. All were relaxing, for the train took one day in twelve to rest. They were just north of the border of the Moorish kingdom on the southern peninsula called Bluemensgard. In the North, the weather would still be bitter, but here it was balmy, and the dogwood was already in bloom, and it was fatiguing to wear mail.

"Young red-haired master," said Bluefeather, "my lady wishes your attendance, and that of your friend the skald."

Hring and Halvdan looked at one another in puzzlement, but got up quickly to follow the thrall. She led them to the wagon, which was close-curtained as usual. "There is a warm spring nearby," said the thrall, "and my lady wishes to go there and bathe. She must have an armed escort. You two wait here."

Bluefeather went into the wagon and the two men looked at one another and shrugged. Bluefeather emerged a few moments later, followed by Lady Yngva, who was so swathed in cloth as to be invisible. The two women set off from the glade where the train was camped toward the surrounding hills, and the two men followed hastily. They climbed the slope of a hill, covered with the new growth of the premature spring of the South. Beyond the crest, they descended into a small valley, noticeably warmer than its surroundings. Here the foliage grew thicker, and the smell of growing things was almost a reek in the nostrils.

They came to a small clearing. Lady Yngva halted and turned to face the men. She lowered the cowl and shawl that hid her face. Hring felt a hollowness in the pit of his stomach. It was the woman of his vision.

Lady Yngva had the thick yellow plaits he remembered.

Her eyebrows were thick and straight, her cheekbones broad and high. The long, straight nose was flanked by eyes of the palest gray, as gray as the North Sea in winter, and as cold. It was such a strong face that many would have considered it homely, but the force that came from the woman made her beautiful and desirable.

"You," she said, pointing at Hring, "follow me to the spring. You, skald, stay with Bluefeather until I return." Her voice was deep and furry.

"It shall be my pleasure, my lady," said Halvdan, and Hring looked at him sharply, wondering that his friend could take so light a tone with so queenly a woman. Yngva took a trail downhill and Hring followed, and the air grew warmer. She stopped at a pool lined with stones and turned to Hring. She walked up to him and looked up into his face, so close that he had to rest his hand on his sword hilt.

"You remember me, don't you, Red Man?" The bodice of her dress exposed the cleft of her breasts, and Hring, who considered himself knowledgeable where women were concerned, was struck dumb. She wore no artificial scent, but the smell which rose from her body and clothes, musky and a bit acrid, set his knees trembling as if he were a boy stealing his first kiss from a milkmaid. It was a strong, feminine scent, as ancient as the earth.

"I remember you, lady," he said, inwardly cursing at the shaking in his voice.

"Good," she said, beginning to unlace her bodice. She stripped off the outer garment, then pulled her undershift over her head. She stood naked in front of him, her eyes as chill as steel. Her body was whiter than any milk, laced with a network of blue veins, like some fine marble. Her shoulders were broad, her waist narrow, swelling downward to wide, womanly hips. Her thighs and calves were powerful, and the sun behind her shone through a covering of fine white down, surrounding them with a pale halo. Her belly was rounded, swelling out from below the deep, wide navel into a double curve, cleft by a line running from the crotch upward. Her pubic thatch was a dense tangle of dark-blond curls writhing upward almost to the navel and coating her thighs on the insides for a hand-breadth toward the knees. Hring was grateful that his mailed codpiece hid his reaction.

Without a word, she turned and walked down to the pool, and Hring trembled at the sight of her buttocks, smooth arches of muscle, bunching and relaxing alternately beneath the sheath of velvety white skin. Many would have considered it a peasant body, more fit for a farm woman than a fine lady, but Hring, who had known many women of many degrees, was as overcome by desire as a boy of fourteen with his first willing maid.

She stepped into the water, waded out knee-deep, then turned to him. She drew one plait over her shoulder and began unbraiding her hair.

"Cool yourself, Hring," she said. "I am a priestess, and a woman such as I does not spread her thighs for any wandering wolf's-head, nor lightly for any man."

"Then your behavior is puzzling, my lady," said Hring, proud that he could keep his voice from shaking, at least not much.

"Puzzling?" she said, with a silky laugh. "I am showing you what may be yours someday, if you prove yourself. The gods will it, but you might fail them. Then I would need to find another. That would sadden me, for I have searched long."

"Searched for what, lady?"

"That you shall know, perhaps sooner than you like."
The wild glare lurking in her eyes made him shiver as
much from fear as lust. When both plaits were unbraided
the hair fell in shaggy waves to the backs of her knees.
"Give me the soap from my bag," she ordered. Hring
found the soap ball and threw it to her. He tossed it
slightly to one side, to make her reach for it and lose a bit of
her dignity. She caught it, making the move with such
fluid animal grace that Hring felt ashamed of his trick.
Clothed or naked, this one was a queen.

She waded into deeper water, scrubbing at her body and
hair with the soap. Hring walked to a large, flat boulder by
the water and sat, toying with his dagger to give his hands
occupation. "Is this wise, lady? There could be Skraelings
about."

"They would not touch me. Neither would outlaws,
unless they were ignorant, and few are in these parts."
Nothing seemed to shake her confidence. Yngva emerged
from the water and sat on the boulder next to Hring. Her
buttocks did not spread when she sat, and she began
wringing the water from her hair.

"Why do you call me Red Man?" Hring asked.

"For your hair, of course. It's seldom seen down here."
Hring thought, and realized that he had seen few men or
women with red hair since coming South. It seemed odd.
She spread her hair over her shoulders until it almost
covered her body, letting the sun dry it.

When it was dry, Yngva drew her hair over her shoulders and began working it into braids again. "Few men
have seen me thus, Red Man," she said.

"I shall try to be worthy of the honor, lady," he
replied, maddened by the woman's teasing. No, he told

himself, whatever her intent was, it was too serious to be called teasing.

"Is that what you really want?" she asked, her cold eyes as blank and enigmatic as ever. Without giving him a chance to answer, she rose and began to resume her clothes. Hring forbore to say anything more, for fear of being further humiliated by this fearful woman, whom he desired more than any other woman he had ever encountered.

Chapter 2

The fire crackled merrily, and the pot bubbled with a porridge of maize meal cooking with sugar and chopped dates, for they were now within the borders of Bluemensgard, and the Moors had transplanted many of the crops of their homeland in the New World colonies. Hring could now eat oranges, tangerines, and pomegranates every day, luxuries he had enjoyed only a few times in his life before, at great feasts.

The people they had seen since crossing the border had all been Skraelings or Moorish peasants, all of whom had the peculiar habit of dropping all labor at certain times of the day and prostrating themselves in prayer, which the Norsemen found most odd. "My father would've had them flogged back to their plows," Hring remarked.

"A Thorsheim peasant would've split your father's skull, then," said Feng, a rough guardsman of Dieter's train. "Peasants of Thorsheim are free men, not slaves." Hring had lapsed into silence. He had long ago determined not to speak of his past life, but self-discipline had never been his strongest quality.

Hring now was sipping from a cup of the drink brewed by the Bluemen from the coffee bean, which tasted acrid and bitter at first, but which was acknowledged by all to be the best of all drinks for keeping sentries awake and alert. He sprang to arms instantly when one of the men on outpost called out the approach of a rider. All the other men snatched up weapons and Dieter came up to the fire, his hands bloody from the lancing of a pack mule's inflamed withers.

"A rider comes!" shouted one of the men watching the trail. He was a Blueman, hired since they had crossed the border, and his voice held a slight quaver.

"That man is a coward," said Hring, readying his sword.

"I've employed Abdullah before," said Dieter, "and seen him fight. He's no coward. The one who comes must be more formidable than most." The master signaled to two good bowmen to go back out of the firelight and prepare their weapons. The men slunk away, notching arrow to string.

They heard the clops of a horse's hooves first, then saw the vague outline of beast and rider. "He must be a hardy man to travel alone at night like this," said Halvdan. "I would care to meet such a man." The firelight revealed such a man as could ride alone at any hour and in any land.

From crown to toe he was swathed in furs, even though the men of the train had discarded all but light tunics in deference to the warm climate. He was as big a man as Hring had ever seen, and above the great yellow beard and

mustache shone a pair of oddly mild blue eyes. He wore
no sword, but a long sax knife hung from his belt at one
side, and a short-handled fighting ax was stuck in the
other. Across his back was slung a long Welsh bow, of the
type becoming favored by the adventurous men who trav-
eled far beyond the Blue Mountains, into the land of the
Great Rivers and the mountains far to the West called
Freyja's Breasts. Hring had heard of such men, explorers
and trappers, but he had seen none.

"Ragnar Hringsson!" shouted Dieter. "I've never seen
you so far east! Dismount and share our pot. How has the
season been?"

"It has gone well," said the trapper, in a voice so light
as to match his eyes. He swung down from his rangy
beast. Standing, he was a head taller than Hring, who was
himself taller than any other man in the train. The man
reached into the breast of his coat and drew out a wooden
bowl, which he dipped into the pot. "There's meat on my
last pack mule," he said, shoveling gruel into his mouth.
"You're welcome to cook it." The attendants rushed to
the last of the man's string of four mules and unloaded a
quartered deer carcass. The head cook began to season the
meat as his assistants built up the fire.

None spoke while Ragnar ate, as befitted the custom of
hospitality. When the meat was half done, he tore a joint
off the spit and drew his sax and began carving chunks of
half-raw flesh, knifing them into his mouth and thrusting
the joint back into the coals to cook some more. When he
had consumed what seemed enough for three men, Dieter
saw fit to question him further.

"What will you be trading for this year?" the master
asked.

"Spanish yew staves," said Ragnar. "All the mountain

men want bows like mine, and most of the plains chiefs also. Llewellyn the Welshman was a bowyer in his own land, and he says there's no proper wood for bows in this land. We need good yew bows from Europe. Can you bring them to us, Dieter?"

The master sunk his head upon his breast in deep thought for a while. "I can place an order with Achmed in half a moon," he said at length. "His ship will carry the order to Sampson the Jew in Toledo by early spring. Sampson can have as many staves as you need sent to the Herring Isle fair by late summer, shall we say two skins to the stave?"

"That would be fair," said Ragnar, "if you supply two silken strings to each stave."

"You are a hard bargainer," said Dieter. "Two skins of the first quality for one stave and one silken bowstring plus an extra string for each skin of exceptional quality."

"And who shall judge the quality of the pelts?" asked Ragnar.

"The house of Cohen on Long Isle?" said Dieter. "They are the greatest house in the trading of skins in the North, and known to be fair."

Ragnar thought for a while. "Agreed. It's best to let Jews or other outlanders judge these matters. I've dealt with the house of Cohen, and they've never dealt with me except fairly." The two shook hands on the bargain and all readied for sleep.

"I'd have expected more from his looks," said Hring to Halvdan. "These mountain men are supposed to be very trolls for ferocity, yet this one is as soft-spoken as a maid, for all his size."

"So he would seem," said Halvdan. The skald did not use his ordinary voice. Instead, he was using the voice of a poet describing a hero, so Hring listened the more closely, knowing that his friend had information of more than ordinary merit to convey.

"The breeze tonight is mild, is it not?" said Halvdan.

"It is," said Hring.

"It's from the south," continued Halvdan. "Yet this breeze can quickly become the hurricano of which the Caribs of the southerly isles sing so eloquently, the terrible winds that can flatten towns in an instant. So it is with this man. His quiet words can become the fearful rage of Odin, so do not be deceived. Such a man as this has no need of brag and bluster. When it comes to the splintering of spears, he will be in the forefront, never fear. Keep your weapon loose in its sheath, for he'll be ready to note those who stand in the forefront with him when the cleaving of helms begins."

Hring rolled into his blankets with some trepidation, for this was a new note he found in the words of his friend, something that had not been there when they had been youths together in the North. He rested his hand on his sword hilt as he composed himself for sleep.

Hring awoke with a hand muffling his mouth. He tried to jerk up, but the hand, big as a mule pannier, held him down as easily as Hring would have held a kitten. In the flickering of the firelight he saw that it was Ragnar, signaling silence with a finger to his lips. The trapper leaned forward and whispered: "Men all around the camp. Arm yourself." Then he glided away, silent as a shadow. Hring got up to his knees and slipped on his mail, his heart beginning to hammer. He could see other men arming. Where were the sentries? But he knew. If men had gotten close enough for the mountain man to hear, then the sentries were still at their posts, with their throats slit.

Hring clapped his helm on his head and his fingers fumbled tying the thongs beneath his chin. His bowels churned and for a terrible moment he feared that he would mess his breeches and disgrace himself. He was slipping his forearm through his shield straps when the attack came.

There was a chorus of high-pitched shrieks, then the clearing was full of armed men, Skraelings and Norsemen together, as one of Dieter's men threw an armload of brush on the fire and the flames leaped up. Two Skraelings in buckskin clouts with axes in their hands charged in ahead of the rest and suddenly Ragnar was charging to meet them. The first was caught by Ragnar's huge foot under the jaw and as the kick straightened him the sax in Ragnar's right hand flashed across his belly, spilling his guts. The other slashed at Ragnar's head, but the mountain man ducked easily beneath the blow and the ax in his left hand swung backhanded and caught the Skraeling where the neck joined the skull. The man fell forward, the force of the blow tumbling him in a somersault to lie twitching on the reddening grass. Then Hring was too busy with his own affairs to see how the fight was going.

The man who leaped before him was a Norseman in helm and mail gorget and shield and short sword, wearing little else besides a loincloth. The man thrust at Hring's belly and Hring turned the thrust with his shield, at the same time cutting low at the man's knee. The man fell howling and Hring put his point in just below the ear, above the gorget, just as Gudmund had taught him to do on the practice field. He twisted the point free and blood spurted over his shield and mail. He did not even see the ax that glanced from his helm and smashed into his shoulder above his shield but suddenly he was on his back in the grass and as he tried to shake the flashing stars from his eyes he saw a huge Skraeling raising the weapon for the kill stroke and he had an instant to wonder whether he would go to Valhalla or to the hell he deserved for killing his half brother. Then a pair of legs bestrode him and a sword swung two-handed chopped the Skraeling in the chest and the savage's heart in its last beating sprayed Halvdan with a heavy mist of the wound dew the skald had sung of so often.

Halvdan was stark naked, foam dribbling from his lips, his eyes rolling as wildly as a stallion's when it lusts after the mares. Three more sprang to meet him, and he chopped them down in turn, one slash for each man. Hring could swear that their weapons were striking the skald, but Halvdan showed no sign of receiving wounds. Then Hring had struggled to his feet and the two stood back to back, hewing at the encircling men. Hring's shield arm hung almost useless, and he ducked and twisted to avoid the weapons that sought his life, while dealing hard blows in return. The red mist descended before Hring's eyes, as it had on the day when he had killed Hake, and when it cleared, the attackers who could still move had fled back into the woods.

The glade was very quiet except for the groans of the wounded. Dieter came to where Hring and Halvdan stood and the merchant surveyed the ring of bodies around them.

"It looks as if there has been a fight here," he said. Dieter's hands were now stained with other than mule's blood. "Come over to the fire, Hring. The priestess will doctor your hurts, if any." Hring looked to Halvdan, who stood shivering, his eyes still rolling wildly. "Leave him for a while," said Dieter. "The spell is still upon him. It will pass by and by."

"I saw him wounded," protested Hring. Halvdan was covered in blood from crown to sole.

"The blood isn't his," said Dieter. "No weapon can injure Odin's man when he is on the berserker's path. Come with me."

The wounded attackers had been brought to the fire, where Dieter saw to their disposition. "Kill that one," he said, pointing to a man whose hand was off. "This one we'll keep. A strong rogue like that will fetch a good price from the Moorish galley captains." Hring suddenly leaned over and vomited in a long, gut-wrenching spasm. "A clout on the head such as you took will make a man heave his dinner every time," said Dieter. Hring hoped that the man spoke the truth and was not just trying to save his pride. He went to a mule and took a waterskin to rinse his mouth. He was aware of a burning thirst and sluiced his throat with swallow after swallow.

When he felt a bit more himself, Hring went to the fire, where he was helped out of his mail, wincing at the pain in his shoulder. Yngva was stitching a man's rent forearm with a needle and the long hair of a horse's tail. When his turn came, she examined his shoulder.

"The bones are not broken," she said, "but the flesh is torn where the ax drove in the links of mail. You fought well for a beginner, Red Man. I saw you kill three."

"Four," said Hring.

"Even better. Still, you have a way to go before you can fight like a hero. Now, this Ragnar, there's a hero as men reckon such things. He must have slain fifteen. And your friend the berserker did for at least ten. Still, four's a creditable score. You'll improve."

Ragnar came from where he had been rigorously questioning the prisoners. They had not screamed much, for they were hard men. "They know little," said the mountain man, wiping his blade. "Their leader charged them to slay all but the priestess and bring her to their cave. Who hired them, they know not. The leader was slain. They are common bandits: outlawed Northmen and Moors, Skraelings cast out from their tribes, a poor lot." He turned to Hring. "You did well, younker. You could make your way in the western mountains. If you should want to take up the trade, ask for Ragnar Hringsson when you get beyond the Manslayer River. Ask of me at Tosti's Holding, where the Manslayer and the Western Stream meet. I trade there every year. I'll see you fitted out well and guided to where the trapping is good."

"I thank you," said Hring. "I'll think hard on your words. It seems a proper life for a man."

"It is that," nodded Ragnar. "Weaklings die quickly among the high mountains, and out on the wide plains. But spend a summer among the Cheyenne hunting the Giant's Flock and other meat will soon lack savor." The mountain man clapped Hring's unwounded shoulder as he rose and wandered off to his bed.

"You've earned a friend," observed Dieter as he poked up the fire. "A friend like Ragnar is valuable to have should you find yourself out West. He's a mild and easygoing man, for a trapper. Most are solitary savages, more like the berserker bears than like men. It's a hard life, out in the wind and snow, with a rock for your pillow and fierce Skraelings all about. If I were you, I'd put a few more years' experience into my sword arm before taking such a course." The trainmaster got up and left, leaving Hring alone with Yngva, whose last patient had departed. Her smile was mocking and her eyes glowed weirdly.

"Dream as you like, Red Man, your wyrd is in my hands. You've the blood of a kinsman on your hands, and none of your affairs shall prosper until you've been purified."

A sudden chill ran over Hring. Was there any aspect of his life this woman did not know?

"How do you come to know of my past?" he demanded.

"It's written on your brow, Red Man." She leaned forward and touched his forehead, and for an instant he felt the same burning he had known when the older witch had traced the mark there.

Yngva arose, gathered her shawls about her, and returned to her wagon. Hring climbed shakily to his feet and sought his blankets. He found Halvdan nearby, cleansed of blood, his hair damp from bathing in the stream that flowed by the campsite. There was much that Hring wanted to discuss with his friend, but the bone-deep tiredness was too much, and he sank upon his blankets, reflecting that the blood of four strangers was a matter of little note, while that of a brother could drown a man, though it were but a few drops.

The port of Al-Sindar was pleasantly situated on the west coast of the southern peninsula. A long offshore island gave it some protection from the seasonal hurricanos, and the surrounding fields produced heavy crops of rice.

Hring looked about him with interest, for this was his first glimpse of a world even more alien to him than was the pagan South. The low stone or adobe structures with their white-washed walls and rounded domes were a decided contrast to the castles and timber halls he had known. In the center of the town stood the mosque with its tall minaret and the modest palace of the territorial emir.

Dieter's train entered through the North Gate and, after paying the usual fees, headed for the bazaar, near the docks. Ragnar had left them some time back, for he did not like cities, and having placed his order for bowstaves he returned to the woods. Before he had left, though, Hring had wrung from him many tales of the western Skraelings and the silvertip bears and the Giant's Flocks among which they hunted.

The city was spacious, and a wide common had been laid out where caravaneers could make camp and pasture their animals while transacting their business at the bazaar. Dieter's men pitched their tents and began to examine their animals for doctoring. Those not concerned with husbandry took the opportunity to see the town. Hring was among these.

Hring and Halvdan first sought out a tavern. Both had many appetites in need of slaking, and Dieter had told them that many of these appetites were to be satisfied at a reasonable price at Omar's Caravansarai, a venerable institution near the docks.

The two young men wasted little time in finding the establishment, and they had ordered wine before they had located a table. They also ordered food: fruit and bread and nuts and meats of many kinds. They eased their thirst while they waited. The dishes that began to arrive were most agreeable. There were birds and four footed-creatures of many sorts, together with flat, tough cakes of bread, unfamiliar but excellent. There were bowls heaped with rice cooked in various savory sauces and innumerable fish dishes. The only things absent were pork and strong ales.

The innkeepers stocked wines for unbelievers, but the hot climate made brewing impractical for catering to the infrequent unbelievers, and pork was unthinkable, for all that the northerners longed for it.

Hring tore a flat loaf into quarters and dipped the piece into a bowl of pungent paste. He had learned that the paste was made of boiled chick-peas and was called houmiss. For the first time in many a day, Hring was feeling relaxed and ready for a frolic.

As he ate, Hring admired the Azteca cloak of feathers that hung displayed on the wall opposite him. It was a riot of reds, greens, yellows, and blues in jagged patterns against the chaste white of the wall. Above it were a pair of the flint-edged swords the southern Skraelings had used before the Norsemen began trading iron in those regions, together with a feathered shield.

The wealth and splendor of the Azteca Empire was legendary among the Norse, and the few outlanders who had been allowed to visit the capital city of Tenochtitlán said the magnificence of its palaces, temples, canals, and floating gardens made the finest cities of Europe seem paltry by comparison. Even Grenada and Constantinople could not compare.

Hring saw that Halvdan had no eyes to spare for exotic weapons and garb. The skald was staring instead through the window by their table toward the house across the narrow street. On its balcony were lounging at least a dozen women. Hring examined them with interest. This, beyond a doubt, was one of the famous brothels of Al-Sindar.

There were Moorish women, plump and naked except for their veils, a few Skraeling women with the hairstyles of various tribes, a couple of yellow-haired Norsewomen, even a black-skinned African, one of the few Hring had seen. Those without veils were smiling at the men passing below. When a man showed interest, prices and conditions were communicated with a series of discreet hand signals. Hring was interested to see such matters conducted with absolutely no vulgarity.

"Which do you think?" asked Halvdan. "I understand the Moorish women are most skilled, but the black would be a new experience, and they are rumored to be endowed with great natural talent. Skraelings and Norsewomen are to be found at home. I see no eastern women, with the yellow skin and the tilted eyes. That's a pity, for they're said to be constructed differently from other women, and I would like to see for myself. Perhaps they've some inside. Shall we pay a visit after we've finished here?"

Hring was about to agree heartily when the now familiar chill settled around his vitals. He looked again at the women, and despite his long continence they seemed dull and uninteresting. The image of Yngva reaching for a flying ball of soap flashed through his mind. "No," he said at length, "I think not."

"What?" Halvdan was suddenly concerned. "That doesn't sound like the Hring that I know. Has that long-braided witch cast a spell on you?"

"I fear so," nodded Hring. "I didn't tell you before, but she is the woman of my vision on our first night south of the border." He told Halvdan something of the words that had passed between himself and Ynvga. The skald grew more and more grim as the recitation went on.

"This is more serious than I had thought," said Halvdan. "It's no mere love spell she's cast on you to rob you of your manhood with other women. I counsel that we consult with a sorcerer or witch. Perhaps there's a counterspell."

"Somehow I doubt that we'll find another as powerful as this one," Hring said gloomily.

When hunger was satisfied, Halvdan went to sample the delights of the brothel. Hring found a bathhouse and luxuriated in hot water and steam for the first time in many weeks, while his malodorous clothes were laundered. He lay on a table and a muscular masseur worked him over vigorously, then a barber shaved his thin beard, about which Hring was sensitive. He was impatient to sport the full beard of a grown warrior, which seemed to take an inordinate time to appear upon his face.

Washed and fed, massaged, shaved, and dressed in clean clothes, Hring felt like a new man as he wandered toward the docks to see the ships. The docks were redolent of tar and hemp, with the additional fragrances of foreign spices and the less agreeable odors of the slave pens. The ships were of many types: there were the broad, two-masted knarrs of the Norsemen, some of them with the new topsails above their main courses. There were the sleek, lateen-rigged three-masters of the Moors and the twin-hulled ships of the Azteca merchants. There were even three dragon ships, manned by a band of Vikings, taking on supplies before descending upon the Caribs or Arawaks.

Hring detected a commotion down one of the docks and went to investigate. He found a group of men trying to load a large cage onto a two-masted knarr. In the cage was a full-grown bison bull, from the Giant's Flocks of the West. Hring had never seen one before, only skins and pictures, and was mightily curious. As he went closer he saw that a tall, rangy man, red-faced and sweating, was cursing a pack of Moorish cargo men as they tried to hoist the cage into the ship's hold. The cage was being lifted by a large crane, and the men were struggling with guide ropes wrapped about the cage to coax it over the edge of the dock and down into the hold. The terrified beast was making a difficult task no easier by plunging about, causing the cage to sway dangerously. Of a sudden, the hoisting cable parted, dropping the cage at the edge of the dock, half off and half on. The Moors dropped their ropes and fled from the cage, for the bellowing beast seemed about to break through the splintering bars.

The cage began to tilt slowly over the edge of the dock, and would surely have dropped into the water between dock and ship, but Hring seized one of the guide ropes and quickly took a few turns with it about a big wooden bollard. The red-faced man did the same with another. When the worst of the danger seemed past, the Moors returned sheepishly and hauled the cage back to a more secure position.

"Dogs!" shouted the tall man. "Black-bearded sons of diseased whores! This beardless boy has more manhood than the pack of you. May fifty generations of poxed pariah dogs shit upon the graves of your ancestors! Nobody gets paid until that cage is repaired and stowed safely in the hold."

He turned to Hring, his face beginning to lose some of its scarlet color. "Many thanks, young friend. I'm Halbjorn of Laxdale, merchant shipmaster. Come aboard for some ale, it's the least I owe you for saving such an investment." Hring followed the shipmaster aboard and into the small aft cabin.

"My name is Hring," he said, "from north of the rune-stone border. I've just come South with Dieter's train."

"I've done business with Dieter," said Halbjorn. "He's a good man, brave and moderately honest." The shipmaster drew a pitcher of ale from a cask set against the aft bulkhead. He had no mustache, and his beard was trimmed short along the jawline, the neck and cheeks shaved, and his hair was close to his head in tight curls. He set the pitcher between two tankards on the table. "Drink all you like. I can't drink it all, and it'll go sour soon enough in this heat."

Hring poured himself a tankard and took a long swallow. It was the first ale he had tasted in a long time, and it went down sweetly. "Why do you carry such a strange cargo?" he asked.

"The beast is for the menagerie of the Azteca Emperor in Tenochtitlán. The trappers were supposed to bring me a calf, but the creature seems to have grown somewhat on the way here."

"That is the way of cattle," observed Hring. "I suppose it must also be true of the wild ones. Do you trade often with the Azteca? I've never met one who has seen their lands."

"I've been to the port at Tuxpan to unload cargo and take on more. They let few foreigners go farther inland. They let me see as much of their empire as satisfies me, though." He reached into his purse and drew out a coin and handed it to Hring. It was the biggest gold coin he had ever seen, as wide as the first three fingers of his hand held together, and very finely minted. One side bore a stylized but recognizable depiction of an eagle with a serpent in its beak, the other the head of a man in an elaborate feather headdress. It weighed at least three ounces.

"They learned to strike coins from some Moorish coiners less than a hundred years ago," said Halbjorn. "Now they make the finest coins in the world. That will buy about as much as a silver penny up North, so rich is their empire in gold."

"A man could become very rich trading with them," said Hring.

"They long ago learned how valuable their gold is to us. They are hard bargainers. Besides, voyages to their ports are hazardous, and the waters are alive with Carib canoes."

"Are the Caribs as fierce as I've heard?" asked Hring. Those canoes, the hatchlings of the dragon's eggs, as Halvdan's poems called them, were said to be the stuff of nightmares.

"They're that bad, and worse," said Halbjorn, lighting his pipe from a hanging lamp. "Fifty rowers to a side in those canoes, and the craft hung all over with skulls. They're man-eaters, you know. So are the Azteca, but for reasons of ritual. The Caribs just like human meat. It's good to have brave men along when you sail Carib waters. How about you? Would you be willing to sail those waters? I can always use a good man." His eyes were open and friendly. Hring was strongly tempted.

"I'd have to consult with my sword brother, Halvdan the skald," Hring said at length. "I've never been to sea before, and I don't think he has, either."

"You'd learn the trade quickly enough. Remember my offer, when you decide to leave Dieter's service." They talked on for a while, of one thing and another, then Hring took his leave.

New thoughts occupied Hring's mind. He now had two new futures offered him: trapping and trading in the western mountains, and sailing the southern sea. Both were attractive. He walked along the dock and saw two figures aboard a Moorish galley, and the sight drove thoughts of mountains and seafaring from his mind. One of the two was Yngva, the other some sort of Skraeling in a white cotton kilt. Following an instinct that he did not seek to question, Hring moved silently to the dockside and stepped behind a bale of cotton to listen.

". . . said you would have them for me," Yngva was saying.

"My master, the high priest of Xipe Totec, charged me to deliver this to you." The Skraeling spoke the southern dialect of Norse with a thick accent. In the dim light Hring saw the Skraeling pass a bulky bag to Yngva. She opened the bag and examined its contents.

"Very well," she said at length. "Tell your master that the years to come will be fruitful, that fertility is assured. Tell him also that at the end of the cycle, the world shall be made safe."

It made no sense to Hring, and he thought that this might be some elaborate private code. But what had Yngva to do with some Skraeling priest? He remained hidden until Yngva had left the dock, then he returned to the inn.

Halvdan was there, sipping thoughtfully at a cup of wine. "There was an eastern woman there," he said, "a Cathayan. I was somewhat disappointed to find that she was made like other women. Perhaps it is the Mongol women who are different, or the Nipponese."

Hring told Halvdan of his day's doings.

"The woman is no solitary priestess of some local cult," observed Halvdan when he had heard Hring's tale. "But what business she might have with the southern

Skraelings I can't imagine. I counsel that we accept this Halbjorn's offer and go sailing among the isles.''

''I don't think we'd escape her,'' said Hring moodily, not really sure that he wanted to escape.

''No man can avoid his wyrd,'' agreed Halvdan. ''Very well, we'll leave our next move to the witch, though it lead to a bloody doom for us both.''

Chapter 3

The court of King Sweyn at Mjolnir Sound was a wide timber hall atop a hill overlooking the bay. The bay itself was crowded with the barges that came every year down the Iron River, bearing the ingots of gray metal that would be taken south and traded to the southern Skraelings. A few trading vessels were already in the harbor, braving the storms of late winter for the sake of the extra profit that went to the first ships to reach the southern ports in the trading season.

The hall stood almost within sight of the border with Bluemensgard, and Hring admired it as he leaned on his saddle pommel. He had nothing to do just now, as the small party was being ferried across the bay on a wide barge. Hring and Halvdan sat their horses and the handful of Skraeling servants lounged about the wagon. Yngva was inside the wagon. She had been in seclusion for days.

They had left Dieter's train behind in Al-Sindar. Dieter

was heading north for the fairs, and Yngva seemed to take it for granted that Hring and Halvdan would accompany her to whatever destination she chose. She had directed their course for Mjolnir Sound, with no explanation. Hring had asked Bluefeather if Yngva's home was at Mjolnir Sound, but the half Skraeling had answered that the priestess's home was far to the north and east, in a place whose name was too holy to mention. What business brought her hither Bluefeather was no more willing to communicate than was her mistress.

There was a fine sea breeze blowing as they neared the far shore. Later in the year this stretch of coast would be stifling, humid, and pestilent, but it was pleasant enough now. The road from the shore wound upward through the bustling town to a high earthwork rampart that entirely surrounded the base of the hill. The gap through which the road passed was heavily guarded by armed men. A man who seemed to be in authority came down from a block-house atop the rampart to question the new arrivals, but when Yngva came from the back of the wagon to sit beside Bluefeather on the driver's bench, the guard captain held his clenched fist before his eyes and bowed, and the rest of the guard did the same, and they did not look up until the wagon had passed. Hring noted this gesture with interest. It was the first time he had seen a Thorsheimer bow to anyone.

The hall was built of huge horizontal timbers laid atop a course of rough-cut stone, its steep roof supported by gable beams that thrust far out from the walls, their ends fancifully carved into likenesses of grotesque beasts and dragons. Much of the woodwork was heavily carved with strapwork and relief pictures, and Hring had noticed that nearly every available wood surface he had seen since crossing the border had been artistically carved. It was an art that had fallen into decay in the North, since they had begun building in stone.

They alit in the courtyard before a wide double door. Yngva sprang lightly to the ground and strode toward the door, gesturing for Hring and Halvdan to follow. She did not spare a glance for either of them. The guards at the door gave Yngva the same gesture and bow of respect as those at the rampart and she swept inside.

Hring blinked as his eyes adjusted to the dim light. When he could see, he turned his attention to the far end of the hall, beyond the rows of benches and the walls hung with shields behind them. At the end was a raised dais, upon which was a great chair. In the chair sat a man, and behind him stood armed men. In the smoky light of the fire that ran down the center of the hall Hring could make out little more. An ancient steward came hobbling up to Yngva, leaning heavily on a staff.

"Greeting, priestess," said the steward. "It has been a long time since you have graced the King's court."

"Not as long as your lord had hoped," said Yngva. "Take me to the King, Unferth. These two with me are my champions. One is a skald." Hring and Halvdan glanced at one another. They had not realized that they were more than mere guards. Unferth looked them over.

"Skalds are always welcome at the King's court," said the steward at length. "As are champions. And both appear to be noble youths, though the red one's a wolf's-head. But have no fear, young man. An outlaw from the Christian lands is doubly welcome here, since it means a former Christian to strengthen Thorsheim, and a dead

Christian back in Treeland.'' He let forth a dry, rasping chuckle as he turned and led them to the throne.

As they neared the dais, Hring studied its occupants. In the chair was a tall, burly man with a dense brown beard, dressed in rich clothing, with many gold rings on his arms. The top of the throne was carved to represent the wild boar, the battle swine that was the emblem of the royal family, and his own namesake.

Behind the throne stood a line of armed men, bearing spear and shield and dressed in mail. But it was the guards standing to either side of the throne who drew Hring's amazed attention. There were two of them, and they were naked except for a few bracelets, armbands, and neck rings. Their bodies were completely hairless and tattooed all over, the one on the right with patterns of dots arranged in whorls and the one on the left with intricate strapwork and interlace. Tattooed blue serpents coiled up their arms. Their hair and mustaches stood out from their heads in spiky locks and were dyed bright orange. They had no beards and bore no shields, but long swords as naked as themselves were in their hands, and their bright blue eyes never strayed from Hring and Halvdan, and never blinked.

''Half Gaels from the Irish settlement at Llyr,'' whispered Halvdan from the side of his mouth. ''Berserkers dedicated to the death god.''

Unferth tapped his staff on the floor and said, ''The priestess Yngva and her champions crave audience with King Sweyn of the Royal Scyldings.''

''Will it be a good year, my lady?'' asked Sweyn, formally.

''As the gods will it, King,'' she answered.

"And what brings you to our court?" asked Sweyn, trying to seem uninterested. Hring, though, noticed a tension and even a furtiveness in the man's eyes.

"I found it more pleasing to come in my own way than across the saddle of some bandit," she said.

"Lady, your words mystify me," the King said, but they could see that the words had struck home. "However, enigmatic utterances are the privilege of those who traffic with the gods. Will you and your two"—he gestured offhandedly, as if searching for words—"two champions attend us at our board tonight?"

"Gladly," said Yngva with a derisive laugh. "You've learned to ape the manners of the Godwinsons in the North. Time was when the Scyldings were not so high and mighty." Hring tensed as the two naked berserkers began to tremble, their lower lips drawing away from their teeth. Sweyn calmed them with a gesture.

"Time was when the priestesses of outworn gods had more power than was meet. Until supper, then. The servants will conduct you to the baths, of which you no doubt stand in need." Without waiting for a reply, Sweyn stood and walked from the hall, closely followed by his guards.

Bathed and wearing clean clothes, Hring and Halvdan sat at the boards laid across trestles arranged down the center of the hall. They sat just below the high table on the dais, where Yngva sat at Sweyn's left hand, while his sour-faced queen sat to his right.

There was abundant meat, both domestic beef, pork, and mutton levied from local landholders and wild game found by the King's huntsmen. The court was but newly settled at Mjolnir Sound, and both kinds of meat were abundant. Later, when the landholders' stock became depleted and game scarce, the court would move on, progressing north as the season advanced.

Hring gnawed at a beef bone and spoke with the warrior who sat next to him. The man was a local landholder who was important enough to rate a seat near the throne. "It's good that the King lets me gobble this meat," he was saying, "since I supplied him with so much of it. Always trouble when the court's here, though, with his layabout guards and mad bare-assed berserkers killing any man they've a fancy to."

"Does he give them such rein?" asked Halvdan, biting off a chunk of sausage. "His father kept them in line better."

"This one's not his father," said the talker with a snort. "His backside's so insecure on the Boar Throne that he thinks the only way folk will respect him is for fear of those blue-painted Irish halfbreeds." Their attention was drawn by events at the high table. The King and Yngva seemed to be having high words.

"If your line is to prosper, King," Yngva was saying, "then you and your court must attend the sacrifice this year at Ash Grove!"

"Pox on your ceremonies, witch!" shouted Sweyn. "I know what you plan. In the old days you priestesses could stretch a king across the stone and cut his throat, and say that it was all to bring fertility to the fields and flocks. But if the truth were known, it was to get rid of kings before their power could challenge that of the priestesses! Those days are over, woman. You'll not see me presenting my throat for your knife. I have my own priest"—he gestured behind him, where stood a tall figure in a long robe spangled with mystic symbols—"and he tells me of the stars and what they foretell, and what sacrifices I must make that the kingdom may prosper. I have done with this domination of women and their witcheries. Give me a priest who knows the stars, and men who carry swords, and a few berserkers with the bodies of men and the souls of bears, and you may have your old gods of the groves!" There was silence in the hall, and many made signs against enchantment, for most men still dreaded the power of the priestesses. "The fool!" said the man beside Hring in a low voice. "She can shut off the sun and the rain, and bring the wolves to devour the lambs and the calves. Where will his Boar Throne be then?"

Yngva stood then, dressed like a peasant woman in her coarse gown with its laced bodice, and looking a hundred times the queen that the King's wife was, in her splendid silks and foreign furs. Slowly, she raised an arm and pointed at the King.

"Foolish man!" she said, her voice as chill as her eyes. "Your reign shall be short, and none of your seed shall follow you to the throne, if you reject the gods of your ancestors. Your eastern priest may know the stars, but he knows little. You are a man and born of the earth and you shall return to the earth like any other man! The stars care nothing for any of us. If men never looked at the stars their lives would go on as always. But insult the gods of the earth and men will eat dry dust and drink sand. Loins and wombs will shrivel and no living thing will come forth to keep life on the land. Earth buries all, King. Earth buries nations and dynasties and empires, and brings forth grass and trees in their place. Earth can bury you, Sweyn, and nothing will come forth from you but grass to be eaten by the forest deer."

Around the hall, many heads nodded at the wisdom of these words, for Sweyn was not a king well liked by his people. The King, though, was pale with anger.

"You presume much, priestess," he said. "Were you not protected by old custom, I'd order my berserkers to split you with their swords and throw your carcass to the hogs outside."

"More than custom stays you, Sweyn!" Yngva made no attempt to hide her contempt of the King. "Your berserkers are mad enough to attack me, but every other man in this hall, even your own guards, would fall on them with no more than their eating knives, and cut them to pieces!" Sweyn looked about him in wrath, and saw from the looks directed at him that her words were true.

"Besides," continued Yngva, her voice oddly changed, "you place too much confidence in your berserkers. My own champions, Halvdan the skald and Hring Wolf's-head, are a match for those two beside you."

"Easy for you to claim, Yngva," said the King, thankful to have a graceful way to back down from the priestess's challenge. "You know I can force no fight on them. The skald's sacred, and only need fight if he so chooses. The red one's a free man accepting my hospitality. Every god in the world would reject me if I forced a fight on them."

"Hring, Halvdan," said Yngva, pointing at the two guards flanking the throne, "kill me those two."

Hring's mind was whirling. What was the meaning of this? A moment before, the power of Kings had been challenged by the power of a priestess. Now there was going to be a mere fight between men. Already, men were grinning in anticipation and making wagers. Somehow, a terrible confrontation had become merely a bloody entertainment. He caught Halvdan's eye. "A man doesn't fight his wyrd," said the skald. As Halvdan helped Hring on with his mail, he whispered advice. "Remember, this is a berserker. A wound that would stop an ordinary man will not slow him. Try to cut off his sword arm. Beheading will do the job, or else cut a leg out from under him and stand back to let him bleed out. Don't bother to go for the heart or guts. Many a berserker has killed a dozen men with his heart spitted."

"Let the wolf's-head fight first," said Sweyn, smiling and rocking back and forth on his seat in happy anticipation, relief showing all over him. Yngva showed only a faint, frosty smile.

The two berserkers beside the throne were not the same ones who had been there earlier in the day. Sweyn gestured to the one who stood on the right. The man was tattooed a solid blue, every square inch of him, even his palms and the soles of his feet. "Niall," said the King, "kill him." The man grinned wolfishly, then he leaped high into the air, spinning his sword until it was a circular blur and howling like a demented spirit. When he came down, he charged Hring, white foam spraying from his jaws. Hring was caught by surprise and barely got his shield up in time to meet the first attack.

He caught the first cut and replied with a thrust. Hring's sword was shorter than most, five fingers wide at the hilt and narrowing to a long point, as handy for a jab as for a cut. The point sank deep into ther berserker's chest, an automatic counter to the wild, swinging attack. Hring withdrew his point, twisting the sword to make a large wound, and the blood came spurting after it. Had it been any other man, the fight would have ended then. The berserker seemed not to notice the wound, but continued his attack. His sword was the old type, long and blunt-pointed, designed only for slashing. Hring kept his shield busy defending himself as he tried to find an opening for a counterattack. The berserker drove him down the length of the hall until they rounded the fire trench, then back up toward the dais again. Hring saw that each blow his foe delivered was the same; the weapon raised behind the right shoulder, then coming down to the left. Only the speed with which they were delivered made them confusing. When Hring's back was almost against the dais, he saw the sword go behind the shoulder again. Hring merely held his sword before him, tilted at a slight angle over his head. The berserker's sword came down once more, and sword and hand flew free of the arm, cut off clean at the wrist. Hring slammed his shield into the man's face, knocking him over onto his back. He tramped on the berserker's genitals, and as the man began to scream thrust his point into the open mouth, then leaned his full weight onto his sword pommel. Hring felt the sword crunch through the neck bones, past the rushes and into the dirt floor beneath. He waited until the body had stopped jerking about before he withdrew his blade and wiped it off. He was conscious of a great deal of cheering going on. In a half daze, he looked up and saw that King Sweyn wore a sour scowl, while Yngva was looking at him with a wild glitter in her eyes, her face flushed to the upper surfaces of her breasts where they showed above her bodice. To Hring, the fight had been worth that look.

Now Halvdan stood before the dais. He was naked, as Hring had seen him on the night of the bandit attack. He held his sword and was trembling in an ecstasy of possession by his god, singing some wild chant in a tongue Hring could not understand. The berserker leaped from the dais to confront him. This one had serpent spirals tattooed around his body and all his limbs, and he held an ax. He stood before Halvdan a moment, shaking and frothing, then he struck. The action was so swift in the flickering light of the fire that Hring was unsure just what was happening. The weapons flashed, ponderous ax and heavy broadsword moving with the serpent swiftness of daggers, and soon the red firelight was gleaming from flesh ashine with as much blood as sweat.

The dizzying movement stopped for a moment and Hring saw that the weapons were on the floor and both naked men, now covered with blood, were swaying in a close embrace. The berserker had Halvdan about the waist, trying to hoist him off the floor and cast him into the fire. Halvdan's arms were pinned to his sides. With a massive effort, Halvdan wrenched his blood- and sweat-slicked arms free. He reached behind the berserker and grasped a double handful of the orange-dyed hair and yanked down. As the shaven chin went up, Halvdan twisted his head and sank his teeth into the exposed throat.

The berserker fell, with Halvdan on top, worrying his throat like a wolf with a downed elk. Suddenly there was a soft, liquid sound, and Halvdan's face was bathed in a red fountain. Although he was choking on blood, Halvdan did not relinquish his tooth grip on the berserker's throat until he was sure the man was dead. Then he arose and walked unsteadily from the hall, and men stepped quickly from his way as he went.

Hring's eyes went once more to the dais. With a curse,

Sweyn stood and stormed out, while Yngva's eyes followed Halvdan's retreating form, and Hring liked little the way her bosom rose and fell rapidly as she watched the skald.

Chapter 4

Hring awoke to a rude toe nudging him in the ribs. He looked up from the straw on which he lay and made out the dim shape of Yngva, dressed for traveling.

"Get up, Red Man, if you care to live out the night." He rolled over and pushed himself onto his knees, still groggy, beginning to stiffen from the exertions of his fight with the berserker. "We're guests," he protested, "even Sweyn wouldn't dare kill us beneath his roof."

"Why couldn't the gods have sent me a man instead of a child?" Yngva said, disgustedly. "If a few of his mad Irishmen decided to avenge their friends, the King wouldn't be held to blame, now, would he? He'll be putting them up to it before the night's over, so we'd best be on our way."

Hring gathered his gear and followed her into the courtyard. Halvdan and Bluefeather already had the beasts saddled and loaded. "What about the gate guards?" Hring asked.

"They'll not question me," Yngva said.

She was as good as her word. The two men at the gate had fallen back, making their obeisance, when they recognized the priestess. It was the same at the gate in the city wall, and soon they were on an obscure track leading to the north and east.

When dawn came, they were well away from Mjolnir Sound, threading their way among low, marshy fens.

"Will he follow?" Hring asked.

"He may try," Yngva answered. "Little matter if he does. His huntsmen and Skraeling trackers will lead him astray."

"Where are we bound?" said Hring.

"To my home, Ash Grove." She pointed northeast. "Some weeks' journey that way. We'll be there by midsummer."

"We're not provisioned for such a trip," Hring protested. They had abandoned the wagon in Sweyn's citadel.

"The Skraelings will provide for us. Now, be silent, Red Man."

The mountains rose high and steep on every hand, the woods clustered so dense on their sides that sunlight only reached the leaf mold of the forest floor in scattered yellow drops. By day the calls of the birds were riotous, by night the frogs held court, and both day and night the insects buzzed and clicked, called and sang. The trees were laden with blossoms and the woods so full of deer that they never lacked for meat, even when Skraeling villages were few.

Midsummer was no more than a half-moon away when they came within sight of Ash Grove. Hring had never dreamed that there were any Norse settlements so deep

within the mountains. In most places, settlement had penetrated no deeper than the first coastal ranges, the lack of
navigable rivers and the resistance of the Skraelings having
prevented further intrusion. Ash Grove was so far within
the mountains that Hring would not have been surprised to
find it buried within the hillsides like a fairy town.

They came upon the town abruptly. One moment they
were riding through the dense forest, the next they were in
a cleared area of well-kept fields and pastures. The town
itself was a small cluster of buildings, small, thatched
cottages of wattle and daub surrounding a turf-roofed,
timber hall. Hring wondered for a moment at the strange-
ness of the place, for it seemed like any other village, then
realized that there was no wall around it. What magic kept
it safe from attack?

A brown-bearded man met them as they entered the
village. He strode to Yngva and made the now-familiar
salute. "Welcome home, lady. Your mother will be happy
now, though she always says you're safe when you're
abroad. Truth is, we've all worried, with the Scyldings
growing so mighty, of a sudden."

"Peace, Gunther," Yngva said, with a smile. "Sweyn's
only a man, after all, and not much of one, at that. Take
us to my mother." Gunther took her rein and led them up
a muddy street with scarcely a glance at Hring and Halvdan.
They stopped before the timber hall and the man swept the
cowhide door hanging aside and bellowed: "Old woman,
the daughter's come home!"

A woman in a plain-gray homespun dress came out. Her
face was strong-boned and unlined, her hair in thick gray
plaits. Except for her leaner body, her gray hair and
slightly yellowed teeth, she might have been Yngva's
twin. Hring knew that this was the cowled woman of his

vision. Behind her came servants bearing oxhorns filled with ale.

"Welcome home, daughter," the old woman said. The faintest ghost of a smile twisted at the corners of her mouth, and Hring guessed that this woman smiled as seldom as her daughter. They were a grim lot, these priestesses. Hring had been long enough in the South, now, to know that he must not dismount before accepting the guest cup. To do so would be to reject the hospitality of the house, and be a deadly insult to his host.

As the two women exchanged greetings, Hring took notice of the servant who handed him the horn. She was a Skraeling girl of about fourteen and she wore a beaded buckskin dress. Despite her Skraeling features, her hair was a pale brown, and the eyes that regarded him shyly were deep blue. He smiled at the girl and she looked at him, nervous and uncertain as a young doe, and Hring knew that blows were commoner than smiles in her life.

"So, you've brought them," the old woman was saying, eyeing the two men. The pale, ice-chip eyes were identical to Yngva's. These women looked at him and spoke of him as if he were an ox they were buying at a fair, and for a moment he wished he were anywhere but here. The old one pointed at a small house of logs and m d. "You two may lodge there. You and you"—she pointed to a merry-faced Norse servant girl and the pale-haired Skraeling maid—"take their gear and see to their needs. Yngva, come into the hall and tell me your story. Did you find what we needed in Al-Sindar?" In answer, Yngva held up the bag she had taken from the southern Skraeling at the port. The old woman looked satisfied. Hring was mystified by the bag. On the journey, he had sneaked a look into it while Yngva was asleep. It contained nothing but dried mushrooms. The women disappeared into the hall, and Hring and Halvdan followed the two servant girls into their new lodgings.

"These priestesses," Hring muttered, "they turn a man's blood to ice and his loins to pudding."

"As luck would have it, there are more agreeable women about," said Halvdan as he grabbed a handful of the Norse girl's buttock. She backhanded him soundly across the face. "Save your hands for harping, skald." But her look was more challenging than forbidding.

"Didn't your mistress bid you see to our wants?" Halvdan protested.

"That she did," the girl said, "so I'll see about some hot water for your bath. The two of you need that more than anything else."

"Independent, these backwoods women," Halvdan said as he watched the waggling bottom disappear through the door hanging.

"And what do they call you?" Hring asked the Skraeling girl. Her huge doe eyes regarded him, unblinking.

"No one calls me by name here, master," she said, her southern Norse slightly accented. Hring felt a sudden kinship with the girl. She was as much a stranger here as himself.

"Then what were you called at home?" The girl seemed to have to think a moment to remember, then she spoke some words in a strange tongue, full of odd glottal pauses, somewhat like the Arabic Hring had heard in Bluemensgard.

"That's a long name," said Halvdan. "What does it mean, girl?"

"It means Hair-Like-Winter-Grass, master."

"The name fits," said the skald, nodding. "You look as if your mother shared her lodge with some Norse Trapper."

"Who are your people?" Hring asked, not unkindly.

"The Absaroka, master."

"Then you've come a long way, girl," said Hring. "Remember, Halvdan, Ragnar spoke to us of the Absaroka. Great warriors and horsemen, said he, who pitch their lodges on the great plains. Were you taken by slavers, child, or did your family sell you?"

"I was captured by Pawnee, master. They sold me to Norse fur traders, and I was taken by boat from post to post, then by mule train to many villages, until the train stopped here two years ago and the lady Gudrun bought me."

"I wonder that such a pretty lass took so long to be sold," Hring said.

"Use your eyes," said Halvdan. "The girl's not of an age to bed yet, though she will be soon."

Hring held his peace. In the North, there were plenty of lords who were not so scrupulous in their taste for young girls, or for boys either, if the truth be known. These Southerners, if not more moral, were at least more superstitious in such matters.

The yellow-haired girl returned to conduct them to the bathhouse next to the hall kitchen. Soon they were stewing in hot water and enjoying the savory smells coming from next door. The serving girls kept their cups filled with good ale. It seemed that they were to be pampered here.

Dressed in their best clothes, they went into the hall, where a feast had been laid out for Yngva's homecoming. The hall was unlike most that Hring had seen. There were no shields or mail shirts hanging on the walls, no helms or swords. The only weapons in evidence besides his own and Halvdan's were a few bows and boar spears and other such hunting gear. The walls and the dark beams were heavily carved and the carving seemed faintly disturbing but Hring could make out little in the flickering firelight.

A great tapestry was hung behind the dais where Gudrun and Yngva sat, and of its details Hring could make out little, save that there was a towering central figure that sometimes seemed to be a man, and sometimes a tree.

Hring and Halvdan took their places at the benches and began eating with good appetite. As his eyes adjusted to the dimness, Hring saw that stag's antlers were nailed to the smoke-blackened beams. As he raised his eyes, he saw that strange objects dangled by cords from the roof beam. His eyes strained in the gloom to see, then it came to him: they were the skulls of horses! There were hundreds of them, many so old that the smoke of the hearth had blackened them as dark as the overhead beams.

Hring started to ask a neighbor about this, but decided against it. He nudged Halvdan, and the skald's gaze followed his own upward. Halvdan's face was expressionless as he lowered his eyes to his heaped trencher. Hring drank deep. Of all the disturbing things he had seen since coming to this pagan land, those horse skulls were somehow the most unsettling.

Hring sat idly before the house he and Halvdan shared, polishing his helm. It was an idle task, for all his gear was mirror-bright, there being little to do here except care for it. Were it not for Halvdan's presence and his unabating lust for Yngva, Hring would have gone mad from boredom. There were no warriors here to talk with, and travelers never seemd to come through. There was hunting in the woods round about, but that was so surrounded with ritual that it was hardly worth the trouble. Gudrun always insisted that one of her huntsmen go with him to ensure that he not kill some sacred beast or violate one of the woodland sanctuaries of the gods or offend the Small People.

Just now, the village was in a fever of activity, making ready for the midsummer festival. All the houses were being draped with garlands of leaves and flowers, and a tall pole was being erected in the field of barley near the edge of the settlement. From its crowning crosspiece two gigantic wreaths were hung. When its wreathing and garlanding were finished, the pole would resemble a gigantic phallus plunged into the field, the sign of Frey, the ancient earth god, who reigned before the coming of Odin and Thor.

Many of these things were still done in Treeland, despite the occasional protests of the priests, and no harm came of it. But Hring knew that there were other things connected with this festival; dark, bloody things. Things that went on in those groves that had been forbidden him on his hunting forays. He didn't like to think about such things. A noise nearby made him look up. It was Halvdan, returning from a ride with a hawk on his wrist. A couple of geese hung from his belt and he tossed them with a laugh to the cook, who sat supervising a hog butchering outside the door of the kitchen behind the great hall. The cook praised the catch and promised to have them dressed for Halvdan's supper. Hring smiled. Here, as everywhere, Halvdan was popular.

The skald had been in demand since they had arrived. It was a rare event for a remote village like this to see a real skald, and he had been singing for them before the hearth fire every night. They would listen to everything with rapt attention, but they always asked for the ancient eddas, the stories of the gods and giants, seldom for the sagas of the legendary families and never for the heroic lays of more modern warriors. Simple stories of war, of feud, murder and revenge, which were meat and drink to other Norsemen, seemed of little interest to these people.

"You'll polish a hole in that helm soon," Halvdan said as he rode up, "and you'll whet your sword down to a bird spit." He dismounted and gave the hooded hawk to Gudrun's falconer. When they were alone, Halvdan squatted down beside his friend and spoke in a voice uncharacteristically low and serious.

"This is a bad place for us, Hring. Let's be gone."

"You were the one who said a man doesn't fight his wyrd," Hring noted.

"So I was. Still, if we get away, then none of this was in our wyrd after all, was it? If we stay, it will not end well for us."

"I want that woman," Hring said.

"There are more important things," Halvdan said, drawing his sax and whittling a willow stick. "If it means you're still useless to other women, well," he grinned and said with a bit of his former spirit, "when your outlawry's up, you can always go back North and be a Christian priest." Hring knocked him over on the ground and they tussled about for a while, until a sharp kick turned them both on their backs in the dust.

"If you two have nothing better to do," Yngva said, "go to Gunther's house and have him instruct you in the midsummer dance. You'll be needing to know it, three days from now."

"I don't suppose I'll be needing to know it, lady," said Halvdan, with a touch of his old arrogance.

"No, harper," Yngva said, with her terrible smile, "you'll not be dancing at midsummer. Not with your feet on the ground, at any rate." She turned and strode away, and began barking orders to some who were decorating the hall.

"How will you be dancing, then?" said Hring, and he was shocked to see his friend's face so pale.

"Well," said Halvdan, quickly gathering his composure, "then, as the coastal Gaels put it so well, I'll be dancing with ass to ceiling that night!" And the two were rolling on the ground again.

Gunther was a smith, and he emerged from his smithy doffing his leather apron at Hring's call.

"You'll be wanting to know the dance steps, then, eh, Master Hring?" he said.

"So the lady instructed me," Hring answered. "I've never taken part in something like this. Is it something important?"

"Why," said Gunther, "it's the most important festival of the year, greater than midwinter, even. And you're the most important part of it: King of the Wood."

"King of the Wood?" Hring said. "What's that?"

"Why"—Gunther threw up his hands, at a loss to explain anything so basic—"King of the Wood's what keeps the world whole. When the new leaves come out in the spring, and the birds build their nests and the little ones break out from their shells, that's King of the Wood's doing. It's the greening of the barley and the sprouting of the malt. King of the Wood makes the cows calve and the ewes lamb and the nannies kid. Without King of the Wood, the folk go without bread or beer, and the bees make no honey for mead. No, sir, it's a poor world without King of the Wood."

And so, through the long afternoon, the smith guided Hring through the complicated steps of the dance he must tread. The children of the village followed them, singing and playing, as the bearish smith and the red-haired warrior pranced and posed, pausing before certain doors, passing others. Now and then Gunther would break in with a special instruction: "Now, here, sir, you breaks from the dance line and grabs the nearest young lass you can find; you tosses up her dress and feels of her, you know—" The rough-hewn smith blushed and made gestures to make his meaning clear. Hring marveled again that these fierce people could not bring themselves to speak of something that a Saxon would name in a single, short word. "It's to help the lass to conceive, you understand," Gunther continued, "and to bear easily. Of course, there's no rule I know of says you can't enjoy it, too. So next, you hop from foot to foot, your knees high . . ." And so it went through that day and the next, until Hring felt he could do the dance in his sleep, and sometimes did.

On the eve of the festival, Halvdan came to him.

"You may stay here if you must," the skald said. "I'll not interfere with your wyrd. But I'm going to leave." His harp was slung across his shoulder, his sword at his side.

"Where will you go, then?" Hring asked, saddened. They had not been separated for many years.

"I'll go to Al-Sindar. That shipmaster, Halbjorn, seemed a good man. I'll wait until his ship arrives again. Then I'll sail. There should be good makings for verses among the Isles. Join me there when you've had a bellyful of this priestess and her witchery. I don't think it will be long." Hring stood and embraced his friend.

"I've a strange wyrd to work out, Halvdan," Hring said, "but I feel it's coming to an end. I'll join you there soon. Now take my horse, it's the faster, and fly from here.'' Before another drop could fall from the candle, Halvdan was gone. Hring lay back on his bed, and he knew that he would have little sleep that night.

The morning was bright, with no trace of rain to begloom the prospect of midsummer festivities. The air shrilled with the sound of flutes taking up the song of the cicadas that made the air riotous.

Hring sat alone in his hut, naked and still sweating from the purifying bath in the sweat lodge. The old woman came in, bearing a steaming bowl in her hands.

"Drink this, Red Man, and be King of the Wood." Hring took the bowl from her hands. The bowl steamed slightly. There was a pungent but not unpleasant aroma of herbs from the thin broth, in which floated chunks of grayish matter. He knew that these were the mushrooms that the southern Skraeling had given to Yngva. What were they for? Under the glittering eye of the priestess, he drank the mixture down. The priestess took the empty bowl and left.

The hanging was swept open again and a group of solemn young women entered, bearing his regalia. A glance told him that all the women were pregnant. First they tied on his legs breeches of woven green vines, thick with fresh grass. Next came the jacket of braided wheat and barley, the new, green ears making him as furry as some strange green animal. In front they tied a great erect phallus of wicker, stitched all over with red-and-white petals of the wild rose. Over his face went a mask of holly leaves, trailing a long, gray-green beard of moss. In his red hair they wove bright-flowered tendrils and blooms of the coocoopint. Over all went the giant cape of leaves of oak and ash, of maple and locust, of all the great green giants of the forest. Into his left hand was put the staff of holly, into his right the staff of oak. As he touched them, Hring knew that his fingertips had gone numb. His feet seemed oddly far away and he was grateful for the support of the staves. The fruitful women left, and through the hanging Hring saw that the people outside were drinking the mushroom brew from the wooden bowl he had used.

"King of the Wood, come forth and bless your people!" It was Yngva's voice and Hring, moving slowly and stiffly in his cumbrous divine regalia, pushed out of the hut and into the sunlight. At once the crowd began to shout: "KING OF THE WOOD! KING OF THE WOOD!" Over and over again, the shout becoming a chant, and Hring's feet began to stamp to the cadence of the chant, and the stamping led into the first steps of the dance and Hring was off through the streets of the village, the weight of his costume suddenly gone as he felt the leaves and flowers and stalks of grain sprout roots and the roots sink into his flesh.

He held the staves stiffly out at his sides as he danced, bringing each foot high, canting the knee outward so that the sole almost touched the other knee, turning from side to side so that the great cloak of leaves swept wide and the people tussled for possession of the occasional leaf that fell from it.

He stopped once at the brewhouse, and was brought a cup of ale and one of mead. He drank them down and shouted: "The brew will be plenty, the hives will be laden, and none will go thirsty, this I decree as King of the Wood!" He said this in one long cry without taking breath, for the leaves were now breathing for him.

He danced to the field of the tall pole and as the children danced around it, he gave his staves to Yngva and chased the young women whose hair was unbraided. When he snatched them from their mock flight he lifted them in his arms as if they weighed no more than spring lambs. His hand plunged beneath their skirts and when it touched what it sought he shouted: "Bear well and die not!" while the girl squirmed and squealed.

He walked slowly and solemnly toward the horse pens, and he could feel trailing behind him the green, viny tendrils that connected him to every one of his people, and from them to the living things of the field and forest. Beneath his feet he felt the earthworms crawling and the dead things decomposing to bring new life.

At the center pen, two great white stallions waited, fighting their handlers. One horse wore a golden sun disk bound to his brow, the other a silver crescent moon. Four mares in season were rushed into the pen next to the stallions, and as they caught the scent their nostrils flared and their eyes rolled and their penises slid from their sheaths as ready as drawn swords.

"One of you will be God Horse," Hring cried. "Decide!" And with that the stallions were loosed and lunged for the mares. When neither could force a way through the fence they turned on each other in rage and lust and hate. Their necks swung sideways and the massive heads met with a loud crack. The moon horse staggered and the sun horse's head snaked out and bit into his enemy's neck. The moon horse shrilled and jerked loose, spun on its forelegs, and slammed both hind hooves into the sun horse's side. The snap of breaking ribs was loud above the neighing of the mares and the shouts of the crowd and Hring heard Yngva cry out like a woman in ecstasy.

The sun horse went down, and the moon horse leaped, coming down on the sun horse's head with both front hooves. The silver moon flashed high as the victor reared back on his hind legs and pawed the air, neighing its triumph, and Hring raised his head and returned the cry as the crowd cheered, for his spirit lusted and triumphed with the God Horse, just as it lay and bled its life out with the vanquished, for he was King of the Wood.

He led the final, long dance out to the grain fields. The flocks and herds were brought into his path and he touched them with his staves. Then through the orchards, where he blessed the still-green fruit. Last of all, the field. This was where the last sheaf would be left standing after harvest, braided while still rooted into the corn dolly that would hold the spirit of the harvest, and the people would take turns casting their sickles at it until one would finally cut it loose, then take it home and hang it beside the hearth to bring good luck all year long. The rest of the fruits of this field would go to the harvest bonfire as sacrifice.

Only the younger men and the women of childbearing age were with him now, including those not yet wed. He felt the stirring fertility in their loins passing through him and down his legs into the ground, where it spread out through the roots of the grain and into the forest beyond. They all stripped off their clothing as they walked into the fields and lay down between the furrows. This time, they needed no command from the King of the Wood. Any child conceived by an unwed woman through this rite would be legitimate, given the surname of King's-son, for it was King of the Wood's seed being sown here, through the intermediary of his people, bound to him as closely as acorns to a mighty oak.

The King of the Wood stood at the boundary of field and forest, watching his people as they struggled and cried out amid the corn. There was nothing of Hring in him

now, as his toes grew downward and extended into strong
roots and his body lengthened, thick and barky. He dropped
the staves and spread his arms and the fingers grew and
sprouted leaves and then he was looking down on them all
from a great height, still feeling their writhings and spurt-
ings through his roots which touched them all. Far below
he saw the top of Yngva's yellow head. She was naked for
the rite but did not go out into the field, but instead
watched, leaning against his trunk like a dryad, and from
her came the strongest aura of fertility and magic, and he
longed for her, but there was no way he could plunge his
woody stalk into her now, so instead he showered her with
white beads of mistletoe, and she looked up at him and
smiled warmly, embracing his trunk.

He led them wearily back to the village at sunset. There
was yet one public rite to perform. A long fire burned in
the trench dug before the great hall, near the tall oak. A
few steps from the fire, his great leaf cloak was taken from
him and the old woman shouted; "The corn grow high as
his heels!" As the people cheered, he ran toward the fire.
There was still some of the potion's magic in him, and as
he leaped he soared like a bird, jerking his heels to his
buttocks, and as he landed far on the other side the
greatest cheer of all went up and he was surrounded by
people who were tearing his costume from him. The divine
garments were put on a wicker effigy and a noose braided
of new grass was slipped around its neck and it was
hoisted high into the oak, to hang swaying there in the
gentle breeze.

As the people fell to the feast, Hring was ignored until
Yngva took him by the hand and led him naked across the
courtyard before the great hall. His erection was as hard as

the oak he had recently been and the need was on him so fierce that he did not care who saw, but none took notice except to call out ribald good wishes.

It was cool and dark in the hall, and the two passed beneath the horse's heads and through a curtain at the far end where Yngva had her bower. He grasped her as soon as they were inside but she thrust him away with her magical strength. "Not just yet, Red Man," she said and left the room. When she returned, she was as he had seen her that day so long ago at the pool: naked with her hair unbound and falling in shaggy waves to the backs of her knees. Instead of going to him she crossed to the room's single, small window. "Come look," she commanded. He walked up close behind her, until they were almost touching and he could feel her warmth, the smell of her as strong and compelling as that of the mare tethered in the pen outside.

As they watched, the God Horse was led into the pen, its silver crescent glittering above its head. "It will be a moon year," Yngva murmured. Her breathing deepened as the stallion, frantic with its daylong separation from the mare, ran to her and mounted. The mare planted her hooves and shrilled as she was penetrated.

Yngva turned to Hring, her eyes for once not icy but glowing strangely. She walked to the bed but did not get in. Instead, she turned her back to him and dropped to her knees, bending forward across the bed. She looked back at him over her shoulder. "I'll be your mare, Red Man. Come and ride me."

He felt a chill as he woke. He felt the bed beside him for Yngva but she wasn't there, though her scent was thick in the room. He rolled over on the sodden mattress and groaned. He was sorer than he had been after the fights with the outlaws and the berserker. Yngva's lovemaking, like everything else about her except her soft body, had been violent and brutal. He heard noises and went to the window to investigate.

The fire, still lowly burning, cast a bloody light on the proceedings in the horse pens. The people stood silently around the pen, and the God Horse stood in the center. The only other occupant of the pen was Yngva. Still naked, her body slicked with sweat and her hair damp and dark with it, she cradled its splendid head, stroking it and calming its trembling. Its broad tongue licked the sweat from between her breasts. Hring could study her coolly now. He saw a beautiful, powerful, frightening woman, and he no longer wanted her. It had nothing to do with satiety. Whatever spell she had laid on him he had shot back into her voracious body, to be used on some other poor fool.

Yngva stood back from the God Horse, her inner thighs ruddy in the firelight and making wet sounds as she moved. She bent and picked something up from the ground. Her hand darted forward with inhuman speed and the thing in her hand flashed silver for an instant before it slammed into the glorious neck, stayed there for an instant, then was jerked downward and out. The horse, rigid with shock, tried to draw beneath to scream, but couldn't. Then the blood shot out in a powerful jet and Yngva stood under it with her head thrown back as the arterial spurts inundated her from crown to heel.

Hring turned and ran from the room, remembering now the odd words Yngva had spoken to him one night on the trail: *"The King spurts twice for the gods: white for Frey and Red for Odin."* He rushed to his hut to gather his belongings. To his surprise, he found them all neatly bundled, and standing over them was the Skraeling girl, Winter-Grass. She held his clothes out to him and he dressed quickly as she spoke. "You must fly now. I wanted to warn you but with the witch-woman's spell on you it was no use." Hring knew that this was true. When he was dressed, he followed her into the darkness outside. She took him to the edge of the forest, where two horses were tied and saddled.

"Only on a festival day could I slip away with two horses without notice," she said.

"Why are you doing this?" Hring asked. "You owe me nothing."

"You and your friend were kind to me. She was not." She seemed to want to say something, but could not bring herself to. Hring remained silent. At last she said, "She is a witch. She may not couple with men except to make magic. But she has a woman's hungers. Stronger than most, and she must satisfy them some way. Her mother is the same." The girl looked away into the woods and Hring, remembering Yngva's violence, from which he would not recover for days, felt sympathy. A witch-priestess was above the law.

"Come with me," the girl urged. "My family is a good one, my father is powerful. You could become a chief among the Absaroka."

"Always," Hring muttered, "always, I'm offered new futures. Always I'm led like an ox with a ring in its nose. The gods grant the ring doesn't lead me back to this accursed village." He wheeled his horse. "No, girl, I must follow Halvdan. I must get out of these trees and onto the sea. The sea washes a man clean or it kills him cleanly, and I'd prefer either to life on land just now. Farewell, and good fortune.'' He nudged the horse into the forest and her voice came softly after him: ''You'll come when it is time. Farewell, Hring.'' And he heard her horse's hoofbeats fading away to the west.

He wandered east, until he came to a grove. It was one of those that had been forbidden him on his hunting trips, and he was half minded to go around it, but it was the shortest way to the coast and he rode on. The horse shied at the thick, sudden stench of blood. In the moonlight, he saw a clearing, with a central oak surrounded by nine others, and in each of the nine a form was hanging. Nine oaks for the nine days that Odin hung in the tree, before putting the spear into his own side. Nine oaks for the nine days Odin fell to Niflheim. Nine oaks for the nine runes Odin tore out his eye to possess. Nine oaks with nine men hanging in them. But there was a tenth, and Hring rode to see.

In the central oak, another man was hanging. Not by the neck like the others, but by one foot. The other foot was tied behind the knee. His hands were tied behind his back, and blood had run from the cut throat to soak the once-yellow hair and drip to the ground beneath. Hring nudged his reluctant horse forward and dismounted, bent forward to look into the hanged man's face.

''Where is your arrogant smile now, Halvdan?'' he asked the corpse with a heavy heart. ''Did you leave me for this? To be Odin's man to the end?'' He bent and kissed the bloody mouth. "No man can escape his wyrd, brother," he said, and the dead mouth seemed to show a shadow of that mocking smile. Hring mounted and rode east.

Book Two

The Wanderer

Chapter 5

The wind had been slacking off all morning. The big, two-masted knarr was making little way and the current was causing it to drift slowly but inexorably toward a cluster of small islands to the south. Thin columns of smoke rose from promontories and hilltops among the islands.

"They've seen us," said the gray-bearded steersman. He leaned out over the steer board to spit. The man beside him sat on the deck, his face shaded by a broad straw hat. His hands were busy with splicing a rope. When the job was finished, he stood and pushed the hat back to study the clouds building on the horizon. The face so revealed was brick-red, what little of it could be seen through the dense red beard. His nose was peeling, as were his bulky shoulders. Three years in these waters had not inured him to the blistering sun of the Southern Sea.

"Hurricano coming," Hring said. Both looked aloft to

where Halbjorn was sitting astride the yard of the newfangled topsail conferring with Knut Eagle-Eye, captain of the watch. The ship-master slid down a stay to the deck.

"They're coming," he said calmly, "all hands to arms." There was a brief scurrying as sea chests were opened and weapons were taken from their sealskin wraps. This was a familiar routine in these savage waters, so nervous talk was at a minimum. Shields were set into their brackets along the gunwales, an additional defense from stones and arrows in the initial onslaught, handy to grab if it came to boarding.

"Arawak?" Hring asked, fastening the chin strap of his halm.

"Carib," Halbjorn replied.

"Worse luck," said gray-bearded Trygve, the steersman. "Bad enough being slaughtered without being eaten."

"You'll probably not notice," Halbjorn said. "I've heard nobody complain that he was served up at a Carib feast after being killed."

"Then you've been talking to the wrong turds!" shouted young Rapp, and the ship roared with laughter.

"It's good to have a merry crew," observed Halbjorn.

"Will the Caribs reach us first, or the hurricano?" asked Hring.

"It'll be a race, either way," said Halbjorn. "They're a hardy lot to set out after us with this sky."

"Perhaps they're just hungry," Hring said. He thumbed the edge of his sword, knowing already that it was keen and that no speck of rust stained its mirror polish. He sheathed the sword and made sure that his sax was loose in its sheath. He strung his bow and laid out his arrows. A few of the men were donning jackets covered with scales of horn, but Hring had little faith in such protection. His mail shirt would drag him to the bottom if he should fall in. Except for his helm he wore only his sailor's loincloth. He knew that, unless armored, it was unwise to wear a shirt or trousers into a fight. A cut from a sharp blade was likely to be clean, but if bits of cloth or leather were carried into the wound, it would fester.

The canoes were visible now, and closing fast. They were big double-hulled vessels, the twin hulls connected by a platform and hulls and platform were crowded with warriors. The broad paddles flashed in the sun and they could now hear the high, wailing rowing-war chant. The gunwales and prows of the canoes were hung with human skulls and thighbones. The warriors were all naked, their bodies covered with grease and painted green and vermilion. The fronts of their heads were shaven, the rest of the hair gathered into feathered topknots. They raised their seven-foot bows and loosed a ragged volley of arrows, tipped with stone or bone, and the Norsemen crouched behind their shields, beginning to shoot back now. The arrows driven by their powerful yew bows punched through the Caribs' light wicker shields and warriors began to topple from the platforms. Still, they came on.

The two canoes separated and one came around to attack the knarr from the port side, while the other engaged it to starboard. They were casting slingstones now, and short spears. The spears had stone heads, and along the sides were rows of shark's teeth, set in pitch-filled grooves and laced with rawhide thongs, pointing backward. Those teeth could drag a man's guts out when the spear was withdrawn.

Hring loosed arrows until his supply was exhausted, and now the Caribs were boarding. He saw Rapp pitch backward into the hold, spraying blood, a spear through his throat, then he was at the gunwale, slipping his forearm through his shield straps and drawing his sword. The others stood well to his side, for they knew that the red-haired man fought with a wild fury and it was best to give him sword room.

The canoe crunched alongside and all was screaming and flashing weapons and needle-filed teeth shining in painted faces. Hring clove a feathered head and severed a hand that came over the gunwale. Most of the Caribs had the long, slashing iron jungle knives that were traded among the islands; vicious weapons as well as useful tools. He fended a slash from one with his shield, made two short chops to right and left, and had a clear space at the gunwale. Bracing his foot on the shield rack, he jumped over the gunwale and into the canoe. With a wild shout, others of the Norse crew followed and carried the fight to the enemy.

The Caribs, crowded into the canoe, were at a disadvantage, and a few moments' grim execution cleared most of them from the canoe and then Hring was on the connecting platform, striking furiously. In spite of his red rage, he wasn't fighting with a berserker's madness but making calculated, effective blows while keeping himself well covered by his shield. There was a shouting from the ship behind him, but Hring could not spare it a glance. Whatever it was, he knew that to take eyes off the enemy before you was to die.

He was past the platform now and slashing into the tightly packed Caribs in the other hull. Many of them began to jump into the water, preferring a scramble up the sides of the ship to fighting this death-harvesting creature in the hopeless confines of the canoe. Hring was clearing the last of the Caribs from the second hull when, without warning, a wind struck and the craft heeled up wildly. The hurricano! In the fury of the battle he had forgotten it. Hring grasped a flailing rope and drew himself hard up against a gunwale of the canoe. He managed to get his sword sheathed and got free of his shield and lashed himself tight to the side. Then he could spare a glance for the ship. His companions who had followed him aboard the canoe seemed to have made their way back aboard the knarr. Some few Caribs were still trying to scramble up the sides, but most were in the water trying to reach the second canoe, which had disengaged and was paddling desperately for the islands. Then a wall of wind-driven rain obscured his view and the waves grew into mountains.

For two days and nights the hurricano had blown the canoe mercilessly about, and for two days more he had drifted. Hunger was gnawing at him, telling him that, unless he ate soon, he would weaken and die. Hunger and the merciless sun were making him light-headed as well. Sometimes he would hear voices, then look about and see nothing. It might be the vengeful ghosts of the Caribs. There was a dead Carib in one of the hulls, and Hring had been thinking of him all day. A man had to eat something. And, in any case, the Carib had intended to eat *him*.

Wearily he stood and staggered over to the corpse. The smell hit him from several feet away. He had waited too long. Disgustedly, he cast the corpse overboard to remove the temptation. He watched with interest as the sharks converged to tear into the corpse. Lucky sharks, he thought, to eat what I cannot. Sluggishly, a thought came to him. The sharks! Sharks are fish, and a man can eat fish. He drew his sword and waited until one of the smaller sharks came alongside.

As the tail slid past, he grasped the fish where the body narrowed just before the tail. Hauling half its six-foot length across the gunwale, he swept the sword through a giant arc and down against the thrashing body, severing it and spraying him with foul-smelling fluids. The front half of the shark dropped back into the water, to be instantly attacked by the others.

Hring watched the half carcass thrash about for a while. When it was still, he drew his sax and cut back the tough hide, exposing the pink-white flesh beneath. He carved out chunks and ate them from the point of his knife. The flesh was tough and nearly tasteless, but as he swallowed he could feel the elemental strength and life of the shark spreading through him. He wasn't going to die just yet.

He awoke to the sound of chanting. Shaking his head, he sat up. It could be another hallucination. The chanting was coming from a group of fishing canoes, and they were towing him ashore. A breeze had sprung up last night just before he had gone to sleep. It must have blown him inshore, and these early fishermen had found him as they went to their fishing grounds.

Were they taking him to the mainland or an island? The men in the boats wore cotton clothing. Not Caribs or Arawaks, then. He called out in the trade Nahuatl spoken along the coast. Some of the men looked back at him, but said nothing. He could spy a village ahead. He tried not to feel elation. In all probability, he had traded one manner of death for another. That village was probably part of the Azteca Empire, and Azteca ordinarily killed outlanders who blundered into their territory. Only licensed traders were allowed at certain ports.

Even in this danger, Hring could not help feeling a stirring of excitement. Like all Norsemen, he had heard of the mighty Azteca Empire: of its unimaginable wealth, its tremendous possessions in lands and peoples, of its incredibly bloody religious practices. Unlike most, Hring had actually visited the port of Tuxpan on Halbjorn's annual voyage there. Even confined to the waterfront area, he could see temples farther inland that staggered his mind: pyramids larger than all the other buildings he had ever seen put together. The merchants they had dealt with had dressed in clothing more spectacular than any worn by the princes of Europe.

When the Carib canoe was hauled ashore, Hring belted on sword and sax, donned his helm, and leaped over the side, to confront these people on his feet, armed and in control. The sand pitched beneath his feet and he fell. He pushed himself upright again, but the ground continued to heave, and he staggered sideways several steps before falling again. Earthquake? Nobody else seemed to notice it. Hring bit back a curse. He had been in the tossing canoe for so long that he had lost the use of his legs. It might be hours before he could stand steadily.

The natives conferred among themselves. The language didn't seem to be Nahuatl. There were so many along the Azteca coast. A tall man came forward, wearing a long white cotton robe and a headdress of green quetzal feathers. His earlobes were stretched over jade plugs, and he had a small gold plug in his lower lip, with a small gold bell attached to it. This was undoubtedly the village headman. He walked to where Hring sat chewing his ignominy.

"You talk Nahuatl?" the headman asked.

"A little," Hring said. He struggled to remember words. He pointed to himself. "Sailor from North. Licensed trader. Fight Carib"—he waved his arm seaward—"many day east. Big wind come. Hurricano." The litter of storm wrack about the village told him that this place hadn't escaped the storm, either. "You Azteca?"

"Maya," the chief said, waving toward the village. Hring had heard the name. The storm had taken him far south. The Maya were one of the many subject peoples. "You come chief house," the headman continued. "Eat. Runner bring Azteca warrior, Azteca priest." Hring felt a quaking in his bowels. An Azteca priest would have him across an altar stone in a second, his heart ripped, still beating, from his living body. There was no help for it, though. He was too weak even to stand.

Hring was helped to his feet, and, with an arm around a man to each side, he staggered to the chief's thatched house. Seated on a woven palm-fiber mat, he was brought a steaming bowl of maize gruel cooked with chunks of fish, tomatoes, and fiery peppers. He shoveled it down greedily, eating with his fingers and washing the food down with drafts from a jar of whipped chokoatl and cane syrup. His body, starved for sugar and fluids, reacted to the drink as if to strong wine. He put the vessels down, belched loudly, as local custom seemed to dictate, and felt much better about the world. Now he could almost face that Azteca priest. He was given a bath, his malodorous loincloth was exchanged for a clean cotton kilt, and he was given a hut to sleep in. He needed several tries to get securely into the hammock, much to the amusement of the Maya detailed to assist him. His weapons were not taken from him. No guard was put over him. To what end? Where could he run? What could he gain by fighting? A fine net was spread around him against mosquitoes, and a smoldering fire was brought in in a clay bowl, to repel those and other insects. Swaying gently in the unfamiliar hammock, with the smell of incense-laden smoke in his nostrils, Hring drifted off to sleep.

He woke to a clamor. Starting up and reaching for his sword, he overturned the hammock and was dumped on the floor. Cursing his skinned elbows, he scrambled to his feet and swept aside the netting. Buckling on his sword, he strode out the doorway to see about the excitement. He was gratified to note that today the land was but gently heaving, like a deck in a sheltered harbor.

There was a wailing of flutes and a pounding of hooves and drums. Two matched black horses thundered into the village square, each ridden by a man who beat a steady tattoo on small drums slung from his saddle. The drumsticks were human thighbones richly ornamented with silver, and the drums were made from the bowls of human skulls, and Hring didn't want to guess what kind of skin was stretched over them. The men wore black feather cloaks and headdresses of black feathers and their faces were painted black. Both wore necklaces of tiny silver skulls.

They were followed by a double file of horsemen bearing shields covered with feathers in jagged patterns, wearing long swords and carrying in their hands spears ornamented with gold. Each of these men wore gilded scale armor and a helmet wrought in the shape of a frowning eagle's head, his face looking out through the gaping beak. Their faces were painted green or red.

When the square was encircled by horsemen facing

inward, another man rode in. Hring had been dazzled by the splendor of the Azteca horsemen, but this rider made them seem shabby. The horse wore a bard of yellow feathers covering it from crown to fetlock, a spray of crimson feathers cresting the golden serpent mask that covered its face. The rider wore a cloak so splendid that Hring could only blink in stupefied amazement. He now knew that the cloak he had seen on the wall in Al-Sindar and had thought so beautiful had been a poor thing, fit only for foreign trade. From the shoulders, which were scarlet, it shaded downward to crimson, to orange, to gold, to yellow, to saffron, then to aquamarine, green, blue, and finally to violet. The furlike fineness of the feathers and their metallic sheen told Hring that this cloak was made from the feathers of hummingbirds. The man's face was hidden behind the golden eagle helmet, crowned with a complex golden crest which supported a plume of green quetzal feathers.

The rider touched a catch at the side of his helmet and the beak sprang open to reveal a face painted in red and green stripes. He pointed at the village headman with a golden fan and the headman began crawling toward him on hands and knees, stopping frequently to beat his head against the ground. All the other villagers were lying on their faces, covering their heads with their arms.

The rider said a few words to the headman which Hring could not catch, and the headman replied in a low voice. The green and red face turned toward Hring. The broad jade plug in the lower lip dragged the lip down, revealing the lower teeth and giving him a fierce expression. "You come," he called, gesturing to his side with the fan. The gesture swept the cloak aside, revealing that the man was clad from neck to toes in a suit of tiny metal scales, silver scales alternating with gold. In the center of each silver scale was set a blue stone, sapphire or turquoise. In the center of each gold scale was a red stone, ruby, coral, or garnet. This man had to be the Emperor of the Azteca, or at least a subject king or great prince. Why had such a mighty one come to investigate one shipwrecked mariner?

He looked at Hring with disdain and snorted. "Northern barbarian! Not allowed here." There were several more phrases Hring could not understand, then: "You talk to gods." The rider pointed toward the low pyramid of stone-faced mud that was the village's temple. Hring reached for his sword. He'd hack a few feathers from this overdressed savage before they stretched *him* across the stone!

"Wait." The calm word was spoken from a litter which had just entered the square. Hring had not heard it arrive, because his attention had been occupied elsewhere and the litter was not horsedrawn, but carried on the shoulders of men. The litter was the size of a small house, thatch-roofed and borne on two long poles, each pole carried by at least twenty men. To Hring's surprise, the glittering horseman dismounted, strode to the litter, and bowed down until his forehead touched the dust of the square.

The hanging at the front of the litter opened and a man emerged. Immediately, two young men stepped before him, swinging clay pots on chains that emitted fragrant smoke, so that the figure was wreathed in it. He was taller than most of the natives Hring had seen, his age difficult to guess because his face was painted black on the upper half, white on the lower, and his hair was coated with some black, sticky substance that made it stand out in stiff, jagged spikes. He wore a long, simple white cotton robe and straw sandals. The plugs in his earlobes and lower lip were of carved jet. The only dash of color about him was a bouquet of flowers in one hand, which he sniffed at from time to time.

This strange figure drew close to Hring, reached out and pushed the heavy fringe of red hair back from his forehead. He gazed at Hring's brow for a long moment, then said: "This one belongs to the gods." He said more, but Hring didn't understand. Then: "You need learn tongue. I teach." With that he turned away and walked to where the villagers lay in abject prostration. The priest pointed to one and his assistants grasped the man by the arms and raised him to his feet. Numbly, without protest, he let them lead him up the steps of the low pyramid. The priest followed and turned toward the square when he reached the top. As four assistants laid the man on his back on the altar stone, the priest took a knife from another assistant. The knife had a broad blade of flint and this he raised toward the sun overhead as he chanted a song of which Hring could understand only a few, scattered words: "Gods . . . Hear us . . . heart. . . ." The priest brought the knife down with both hands to bite into the chest next to the breastbone, then he ripped across to the armpit. Two of the assistants reached into the wound and spread the ribs apart while the others held the jerking victim down. The priest reached into the cavity and drew out the heart, writhing and beating. The knife flashed once more and the organ was free and the priest held it overhead as blood sprayed from the severed tubes that waved to the heart's futile beatings.

The priest descended the steps, wiping the blood from his hands onto his hair. Now Hring understood his odd coiffure. The bloody robe was taken and the priest donned a clean one. Hring was shaken, but he'd seen worse. Besides, it might have been him on the altar. It might still be.

The priest beckoned for him to follow, and Hring climbed into the litter with him. The poles were raised to the bearers' shoulders, and they left the village.

Chapter 6

The road was a wonder to Hring. Wide enough for two of the huge litters to pass one another, it was surfaced with cut stone, gently humped in the middle to drain water, and it ran straight as an arrow, connecting one town after another. And the towns! There was one in each mountain-flanked valley, each with a stone-paved market and stone pyramidal temple. Sometimes, they passed steep-sided pyramids standing upon colossal stone platforms, and these, the priest told Hring, were old structures, now abandoned, built by the Maya, once a great people, but now subject to the Azteca.

The priest, whose name was Two-Earthquake, taught Hring the Azteca tongue with great skill and efficiency. He explained that, as a young man, he had taught in a school which had taught nothing but the proper use of the Nahuatl tongue, and this was a great wonder to Hring. Their language was a strictly structured one, of which the Azteca were very proud, and no member of a subject people could hope to earn advancement at court, whether as courtier, priest, or poet, unless his command of the language was perfect.

Hring learned many other things. The land was thickly populated, but the great masses toiled in the maize fields, clad in the linen kilt or loincloth, and few shared in the splendor of the Azteca.

He learned that the Azteca were not the true people of the country, but a small conquering aristocracy who had controlled this loose "empire" for less than two centuries. They had come to power by enlisting as warriors first to one and then to another of the many nation-states encircling the high central valley called Mexico. Soon they had dominated all and the Azteca, once despised as barbaric nomads, were offering the hearts of their enemies on their altars.

They did not even call themselves Azteca, a word which the Norse had first learned from the coastal tribes, but Tenocha, and were somewhat resentful of the other name. There were many other peoples in this land far more ancient than the Tenocha, the people from whom the newcomers had derived their culture. Two-Earthquake himself, for instance, was of the people called Toltec, and when he spoke of the Tenocha, he could not keep a certain tone of contempt from appearing.

Before the coming of the Tenocha, human sacrifice had been rare, but none could deny its effectiveness in obtaining the favor of the gods. Had not they raised the Tenocha above all others? Hring listened much and said little. Dieter and Halbjorn had both taught him that this was the best way for a man to make his way in the world. For the moment he was alive, against all odds. He had escaped the dangers of outlawry, the horrors of Ash Grove, the assaults of the Caribs and the hurricano, summary execution or sacrifice by the Azteca. He seemed to be a man blessed with luck. But it was an uneasy kind of luck. Two-Earthquake, another bloody priest, had seen the mark traced by Yngva on Hring's brow, a mark Hring himself could not see, and it meant something to him. It was the seal of the witch-priestess that had saved him, and he knew that he was not yet free of her.

The procession climbed from the mountainous jungles of the southern lowlands, with their insects and monkeys and raucous, brightly hued birds, up into the high central plateau, where the land turned flat, the towns bigger and ever closer together as they neared the center of the empire. From the top of one of the high pyramids, a man could stand and see the tops of five or six more. The markets were brilliant with dyed cotton stuffs, the feathers of tropical birds, and the flowers that these people loved so dearly, and the steps of the pyramids were incarnadined with the blood of the daily sacrifices.

At each new province, the guard of horsemen was changed. The man Hring had thought a king was merely a minor noble, of the Order of Eagle Knights, responsible for the coastal province in which Hring had landed. Truly the wealth of this empire was great beyond the imagination of a Norseman, and Hring now realized that he came from one of the world's poor backwaters.

In one way, though, he knew that this place was no better than Thorsheim: men here still bought the favor of their gods with the blood of victims. Here, as everywhere, the workers in the fields toiled to support the splendor of a few. He felt no particular sympathy for the peasants. After all, he had himself been a lord once.

"Holy Two-Earthquake," Hring asked one day, "where do all the speakers come from? So many are sacrificed each day!" The Tenocha called their victims "speakers" because they believed that they could speak directly to the gods, and carry the messages of the living.

"The gods choose the speakers in a number of ways," the priest said. "Many are captured in war. The Tenocha wage unceasing warfare on all borders for this purpose. Some are levied as tribute from the subject peoples. Some may be chosen by lot. Many volunteer, because they want to see the gods and rejoin their kinsmen who have gone into the next world." Hring reflected that this was also a fine way of depriving the subject peoples of men of fighting age. "In each major temple," the priest continued, "three speakers go beyond each day—at dawn, at noon, and at sunset. But there are many festivals of the different gods at intervals, and in these the sacrifices vary. For some, young girls are sacrificed, for some, only warriors, for others, children." Hring knew that Two-Earthquake was not an evil or vicious man. These people simply did not believe that the victims actually died. They merely entered a new life that was, in most respects, better than this one. This was why so many submitted peacefully to the bloody rites of the pyramids.

"In Tenochtitlán," Two-Earthquake said, "the great temple of Huitzilopochtli is almost complete. It will be dedicated in a great ceremony when the stars are right." Huitzilopochtli, the "left-handed hummingbird," was the Tenocha god of war. "This is the greatest of the gods. Others belong to the Toltec, the Zapotec, the Mixtec, the Maya, many others. Huitzilopochtli is god of the Tenocha alone. Each morning he rises, fights the night, the stars, the moon, brings in the day. He fights the evil gods unceasingly to protect his people. Since he fights so hard for them, he must have food for life and strength.

"Some gods will eat the corn and fruits and drink that are burned upon their altars, bût Huitzilopochtli must have the blood of warriors, the very liquid of life. The King"—here he used a word that meant "Great Speaker," signifying that the King was actually the chief voice in the Tenocha council—"has been waging war in the South for two years to gather speakers for this ceremony."

"How many will there be?" Hring asked. Two-Earthquake named a figure that Hring couldn't understand. The priest elucidated with simpler numbers, using a stick with sliding beads to make clear his meaning. Hring could not believe that he understood and asked Two-Earthquake to repeat it but there was no mistake. Twenty thousand. Twenty thousand hearts to be ripped from living breasts and laid steaming and spurting on the altars of the god. Twenty thousand bodies to be rolled down the steep flights of steps, flayed, dismembered, and eaten in communion with Huitzilopochtli. Hring sat back in the litter, shocked to numbness. What manner of people had he fallen among?

Over the weeks of the journey, Hring became almost inured to the new splendors he was exposed to every day, as he had become inured to the smoke of incense that was burned constantly in the litter and accompanied Two-Earthquake wherever he walked. The Tenocha were great believers in the purifying properties of the fragrant smoke, and the priests above all had to lead lives of utmost purity. It served the additional purpose of driving away the flies that were attracted in swarms to the blood-stiffened hair of the priest, hair that must never be washed.

All too soon, they reached Tenochtitlán.

Nothing that had gone before prepared Hring for his first

glimpse of the capital city. It lay before them like a cloak of intricate featherwork spread across the valley just beyond the last range of mountains, cupped within its girdle of peaks and smoking volcanoes like a jeweled amulet in the goblet of a giant.

The whole center of the valley was a lake, or series of interconnected lakes, and the city was built around and even upon the water, much of it on islands constructed, Two-Earthquake explained, by hand, at an unimaginable cost of labor. The polished white stone of the temples and palaces, the tiled roofs, the great gardens, gleamed with an unsurpassable magnificence. Hring could count at least twenty great pyramids, and many smaller ones.

On a great island in the middle of the water stood the citadel of Tenochtitlán itself. In the center of the island was a pyramid so immense that Hring took it at first to be a natural hill. This was the new temple of Huitzilopochtli, soon to be inaugurated with a mass slaughter. Three long causeways led from the mainland or other islands into the citadel, each causeway with a small fortress at both ends. The gold and silver trappings of the temples, the weapons and armor of the warriors, made a continual glitter that set the whole vast city asparkle with gemlike points of colored light.

The fields round about were worked by subject laborers under the watchful eyes of Tenocha guards. The Tenocha, once citizen-soldiers who left the fields to take up the spear at the call to sacred war, labored no longer. Every adult male Tenocha was now a full-time warrior who fought behind a shield which bore the symbol of his clan. If he distinguished himself greatly in battle, he might be enrolled in one of the elite military orders, the Eagles or the Jaguars. Once foot soldiers, these knights had fought armored and mounted for the last three centuries or more.

The procession wended its way lazily down the mountainside and into the valley, and everywhere it passed, work stopped in the fields and the people knelt and bowed to the ground. Even processions of mounted warriors left the road to make room. Two-Earthquake had told Hring that he was not a terribly important man in the priestly hierarchy. The respect in which the Tenocha held their priesthood made that accorded by Christians to their clergy seem at best polite deference.

In the villages on the mainland surrounding the lake, all was swarm and bustle. The Tenocha could be easily distinguished from the subject peoples by the weapons they carried and by their always painted faces. The face paint varied widely according to clan, caste, occupation, military duty, or religious dictate. What was most surprising was the comparative lack of noise. There were barking dogs and neighing horses, but people conversed in low voices and there was no shouting. Music of flute and drum could be heard now and again, and the occasional distant bray of a conch signaling some religious ceremony in one of the temples. On the whole, though, the entire city seemed to generate less noise than a small Treeland fish market.

They halted before an immense palace and the litter was lowered gently to the ground. Hring climbed out and stood to one side as an elaborate carpet was spread for Two-Earthquake to walk on. People came from neighboring houses to pay their respects, and a subdued murmur went up when they caught sight of Hring, for a foreigner was a rare sight in Tenochtitlán. Like most of those who went about the city, they wore wreaths and carried bouquets of flowers, and these they cast before the feet of Two-Earth-quake.

The priest signaled Hring to stand beside him, and soon two figures appeared at the top of the stairway. One was a man, attired and painted identically to Two-Earthquake. The other was a woman, about nineteen years old, as near as Hring could judge from the firmness of her breasts and flat, unlined belly. She wore a short kilt of green feathers and bracelets and necklaces of jade. Her face was painted pale green and her hair dyed purple. Unlike the Tenocha men, the women wore no lip plug.

"This is Nine-Death, high priest of Xipe Totec," Two-Earthquake muttered. "Next to him stands his sister, Lady-of-the-Golden-Bells, priestess of Coatlicue, the earth mother, and of Metztli, the moon goddess." Hring felt a shudder at the priest's ominous name, though by now he realized that Tenocha men's names were merely the titles of the days upon which they were born in the complicated ritual calendar. There would be thirteen days named Death. Women's names could be more fanciful. Golden-Bells was one of the names of the moon goddess.

The two descended the stair and Two-Earthquake bent to touch the bottom step, then raised his fingertips to his lips. Hring followed suit. The priests exchanged compli-cated ritual greetings in a tongue Hring could barely understand. This was the archaic form of Nahuatl spoken by the Toltec, still the language of religion. When the greetings were over, the three went up the steps to the palace, and Hring followed.

At the top of the stairway was a broad platform sur-rounded by a railing of stone worked in a geometrical fretwork. Most of the platform was occupied by a carefully kept garden riotous with multihued blooms. Dotted here and there about the landscaping were stone lanterns of fanciful design in which incense burned constantly, sending up plumes of fragrant smoke of many colors.

The palace proper was a low, tile-roofed building of one story, with large doors and windows which gave the interior a comfortably spacious airiness. In a wide room, Hring was seated on a thick straw mat and servants laid out food while the priests conversed. Hring studied the walls, which were decorated with colorful paintings. The stylization of Tenocha art was such that Hring had a difficult time deciphering them, but Two-Earthquake had explained to him much of the iconography, which was at first so confusing. The subject matter of the wall paintings seemed mainly to be the doings of the Tenocha gods, most of whom were depicted in the acts of giving birth, fighting, and eating one another.

Golden-Bells herself served Hring a platter of fruit and dishes of maize porridge, followed by a spicy stew of green peppers, monkey, and dog. Hring shoveled it down greedily and belched loudly. Only when he had finished would the woman speak.

"Honored guest," she said, "the priests will be conferring for some time concerning what's to be done with you. In the meantime, may I show you our city? It is the greatest and most beautiful in the world, as well as the holiest."

"I'd like that very much," Hring said. He rose and followed her from the palace. She led him down the steps and into the swarming streets. To his surprise, while he drew many curious stares, Golden-Bells received no particular awe.

"Do priestesses not receive the kind of respect shown to priests, then?" he asked her.

"Of course they do," she answered. "But I'm not wearing my holy regalia. Unless I am on holy business, I am only a Tenocha lady of the sun clan." They walked through the Dog Market, where villagers brought in the fat, hairless and incredibly ugly dogs that they raised for food. Golden-Bells pointed out nearby a small, beautifully proportioned temple painted green. "This is the temple of the Lady-of-the-Jade-Skirts, goddess of rain and sister of Tlaloc, the rain god." Hring was about to ask how they decided which to pray to when they wanted rain, but decided not to. The very rudiments of Tenocha theology would be a lifetime study for a foreigner.

There were sounds of cheering from nearby. Golden-Bells led him up a broad stair and onto a low platform. In the center was a rectangular pit with sloping tiers of seats descending to a paved court perhaps fifty yards long. In the court, two teams of ten Tenocha were playing a ball game. Golden-Bells guided Hring to a section of seats which, to judge by the richness of its inhabitants' trappings, was reserved for the higher nobles. She greeted friends and was told how the score stood.

"The object of the game," she explained, "is for one team to score thirteen goals against the other. This they may do by driving it against the wall of the other team's end of the court." This Hring could follow easily. It was quite similar to a ball game played between Saxon villages in Treeland. The priestess pointed to two stone hoops which protruded vertically from the midst of each of the court's long walls. "If the ball is driven through the hoop, the team which does that wins the game, no matter how the score stands. If you see the ball go through the hoop, be ready to run, for the clothing and jewelry of the spectators is forfeit to the winners if they can't get away fast enough.'' She explained that the game commemorated some long-ago battle between gods and demons, that the teams represented different gods, and that the betting in the stands could be frantic, with wealthy nobles betting gold, jewels, cornfields, and slaves.

"And what of the losing team?'' Hring asked.

"Their captain is sacrificed to the winner's god,'' she said. Hring studied the play with interest. The ball was of hard rubber and could injure a man if it struck hard enough. The players could not touch the ball with hands or feet, only with knees, elbows, hips, or buttocks. To this end, they wore pads on those portions of their anatomies. The hole in the hoop was only slightly larger than the ball itself.

Eventually, with an especially adroit blow of the elbow, a player drove the ball through one of the hoops and a great cheer went up, followed by a mad scramble as the winning team pulled themselves up the sloping wall of the court, heading for the richly dressed nobles. Amid much laughter and shoving, Golden-Bells and Hring tried to push their way free, but a particularly swift athlete reached Golden-Bells and ripped loose her green-feathered skirt with one hand while he pulled her jade necklace over her head with the other. As he waved his rich trophies above his head and sang praises of his own prowess, Hring and the priestess pushed out onto the plaza, still laughing amid the jeers of the spectators who had been more lucky.

They continued their tour of the city, Golden-Bells seeming not at all nonplussed because she was now naked except for her remaining jewelry and sandals. Hring noted that even her scant pubic hair was dyed purple. She took him to the Market of Featherworkers, where she bought a new skirt, then to the Market of Goldsmiths, where Hring gaped at the profusion of the precious metal, worked with wondrous skill and almost demented imagination into the semblance of everything on earth and many more things from the heavens and hells. Golden-Bells settled on a necklace of tiny alternating skulls and human hearts, so accurate in detail that an anatomist could not have found fault with them.

Wending their way back to the palace, they took a boat which was poled along the many canals of Tenochtitlán, and the priestess pointed out the old Great Temple, soon to be surpassed by the new one. The old temple was surrounded by racks of skulls from former victims sacrificed there, and the plaza around it was nearly buried under pyramidal piles of more skulls, until Hring was numbed by the joyful morbidity of these people.

At the palace, they found that a priestly conclave had been called to discuss the thorny theological problem of what to do with Hring. By now, Hring was convinced that all paths in the Tenocha Empire led eventually to the top of one of those pyramids, but he had at least the uncomfortable assurance that his wyrd was somehow controlled by the mark that Yngva had traced upon his brow, for good or ill.

Golden-Bells took him to a small room where slaves undressed them and brought in crocks filled with red-hot stones. Water was cast upon the stones, and soon they were sweltering amid the inevitably perfumed billows of steam. Slave women washed Golden-Bells, removing the paint from her body and the dye from her hair, and for the first time Hring saw what she really looked like. He had been right about her age. She was a woman of no more than twenty years, with fine, aristocratic features and glossy black hair, her body very finely proportioned and, like most Skraeling women Hring had seen, legs rather short for her height. Her skin was palest gold except for three blue lines tattooed from the center and ends of her lower lip to her chin. The large earplugs which, like all Tenocha, she wore, had stretched her earlobes so wide that Hring could almost have put his fist through them.

"What is the nature of the debate concerning me?" Hring asked, trying to act as if the prospect of having his heart ripped out was of no more concern to him than it seemed to be to most Tenocha.

"There is a question of both civil and religious law to be settled," she said as slaves scrubbed her back. "Foreigners who arrive anywhere except at the treaty ports are routinely sacrificed at the nearest temple as gifts to the gods. But it seems that you are consecrated in a manner not entirely clear to us. The gods of your people may be our own in different guise, and it might offend them should you be sacrificed before your time. On the other hand, your gods may be their enemies, and we might offend them by not sacrificing you immediately. It is most complicated." They were interrupted by a minor priest who arrived to ask the day and hour of Hring's birth. Hring gave it to the best of his knowledge, and when the priest had left asked Golden-Bells the significance of this.

"The astrologers have been consulted," she explained. "I know that they have many books about your foreign customs, and your calendar is a very simple one. They should have no trouble finding your proper signs. You need not worry. Our holiest and most learned men are working on it, and I'm sure a proper solution will be reached soon."

"That sets my mind at ease," Hring said glumly.

"I must go and prepare myself for my evening cere-

mony,'' Golden-Bells said. ''Would you like to attend? It
is one where men are permitted.''

''I should be honored and overjoyed,'' Hring said, though
yet another Tenocha ceremony was the last thing in the
world he wanted to see. What he wanted to see was a swift
horse and an open road, or a good ship and the sea,
anything but more priests and priestesses and appease-
ments of ravenous gods.

After a light supper of fruit and roast maize, Hring was
conducted by a servant to a small temple which opened off
a wing of the palace. It was really no more than a roofed
terrace, with no features except an altar stone and, behind
it, a huge moon disk, tall as a man and thick as Hring's
hand with fingers spread, of solid silver. There was quiet
music from flutes in the incense-laden air as the open
space gradually filled with attendants, mostly women. They
all wore wide, fanlike headdresses of feathers of many colors,
and long feather cloaks. Hring was led to a corner where
he could observe without being in the way.

Golden-Bells appeared, and his breath caught at the
sight of her. She was completely naked, her body painted
solid black, then dusted with thousands of tiny silver
flecks. Her lips, nails, and nipples were painted silver, as
were her eyelids. A large silver bead was imbedded in her
navel. Her only attire was a silver moon disk bound to her
brow. Her hair was so saturated with silver dust that no
black could be seen.

''Bring the speaker,'' she said. The crowd parted
wordlessly and a young woman stepped forward. She was
also naked, painted yellow, her hair laden with gold dust,
her nails and nipples gilded, a golden orb in her navel. A
sun disk was tied to her brow. Golden-Bells walked to her
and took her hands, telling her in the archaic Toltec the

messages to be taken to the gods. She led the calm young
woman to the altar and pushed her gently back upon it by
the shoulders. Four male priests held down her arms and
legs. The priestess gazed at the western horizon, visible
through the open end of the temple. The last tiny arc of the
sun disappeared, staining the sky red. "The sun dies," she
said, in words Hring could understand. "The night is
victorious. The moon reigns." She took the stone knife
and raised it high.

Hring lowered his eyes and stared at the floor. He did
not want to look, but he still heard the meat-chopping
impact, the wet ripping as the blade was drawn across,
the sucking noise of the heart being ripped free, the sound
that was like an overheated ale keg when the tap was
turned too quickly. As the audience dispersed, Hring hur-
riedly left. Why did the victims never scream?

Something, a sound outside, woke Hring. His hand
closed around the hilt of his sword, which lay beside his
pallet. The Tenocha did not sleep in hammocks, a fact for
which he was duly grateful. The room was spacious and
airy, the whole of one wall being open to the terrace
outside, separated from it only by a gauzy hanging which
billowed in the sultry breeze.

The sound came again. It was a rattling in the next
room. The hanging separating the rooms was swept aside
and a dimly illumined figure entered. Hring relaxed his
grip on the sword. It was a woman, carrying a small clay
lantern pot in which a wick floated in scented oil. He
could not discern her identity in the murk, but he could
guess. He leaned forward in tense anticipation. A woman
was not likely to have any subtle reason for coming to a

man's room at so late an hour, and he had been womanless for longer than he cared to think.

"Seven-Wind?" the woman asked.

Hring flopped back on his pallet, his disappointment bitter. "You have found the wrong room, lady. I am Hring, the foreigner."

"Of course, you couldn't know," said Golden Bells, for it was she, "the astrologers have determined that you were born on Seven Wind, so that shall be your name among us." That was better. And the name could have been worse. At least he hadn't been dubbed Three-Monkey or Five-Rabbit or Twelve-King-Buzzard.

"It occurred to me, Seven-Wind, that your fiery hair and skin show the special favor of the sun god. Such a blessing should not be lost and I would count it an honor if you would introduce them into my clan through me." It was one of the odder propositions of Hring's experience, but no less attractive for all that. There were dangerous objections to be cleared up first, though.

"Um, lady, I am most honored, but—I trust you are not married?" The Tenocha had punishments for adultery that were ferocious even by their own standards.

"Oh, no. I may not marry while I am consecrated to the goddesses. I cleared this with the advice of my brother, the high priest and head of our clan."

"That is a comfort," said Hring, reaching for her. She held him off with a hand at his chest and reached for a vial which hung from her girdle. She poured some scented oil into her palm and began to rub in into his chest. The flowery aroma reached his nostrils and Hring began to long for an honest stink again. Then he remembered the stench of the Tenocha temples and was satisfied to put up with incense and perfume.

She rubbed him all over with oil. He kissed her on the lips, to which she did not respond. "Is that a loving gesture?" she asked. "Among my people, yes," Hring said. "How odd. I shall have to consider it." She continued her ministrations.

With a sudden inspiration, he took the vial, poured out some oil, and began to imitate Golden-Bells' actions. Her progressively deeper breathing told him that he was at last catching on. He took her by the waist and tried to roll her beneath him, but she protested.

"Do your people not know how to make love?" she asked.

"After our fashion, yes," Hring said, fuming with impatience and frustrated lust.

"Let me teach you how this is done among civilized people." She moved him into the middle of the pallet and made him squat on his heels. She stood, straddled his knees, then sat in the juncture of his belly and thighs. She moved with the limberness of a lubricious eel, but his legs soon began to cramp. This was the most uncomfortable position in which he had ever attempted this.

"I see," she said at last. "You are not made quite like us. Your legs are too long. Well, we shall devise something." They did.

Hring was breakfasting on fruit and the inevitable maize cakes when Two-Earthquake brought him news of his fate. After sharing breakfast and trading polite small talk, the priest came to the point.

"A splendid compromise has been reached, my friend," he said.

"And the nature of this compromise?" Hring asked.

"We have decided to let the gods choose your fate.

There is a special ceremony, one rarely performed, in honor of Huitzilopochtli and his mother, Coatlicue the earth mother. It takes place only when we have captured an enemy captain who has fought with outstanding bravery and is worthy of such honor.

"At the summit of the temple of Coatlicue is a low stone pedestal. The honored one is tethered to this pedestal by a rope that is long enough to allow him considerable freedom of movement. He then engages in armed combat with five warriors in sequence. Two of them are Eagle Knights, two are Jaguar Knights."

"And the fifth?" Hring asked.

"He may be of any order or clan, but he is left-handed."

"I see. A single combat of five battles, but I am handicapped by being tethered?"

"There are further disadvantages to being the honored one," Two-Earthquake admitted.

"So I had feared," sighed Hring. "You might as well tell me the rest."

"The others will be fully armed with shield and macuahuitl, the ancient flint-edged sword. They will wear the old-style padded armor. Your macuahuitl will have edges of cotton instead of flint. You will have three casting javelins, but these are symbolic, mere sticks of wood."

"You are describing," Hring said, "a fight which I cannot possibly win."

"Oh, it is possible, if the gods will it," the priest hastened to reassure him. "No more than a century ago, a Tlaxcalan chief was captured and given the honor of the combat pedestal, and he conquered all five warriors sent against him. He was made a general over the Eagle Knights, and led Tenocha armies to glory before demanding the honor of being sacrificed."

"Well, if this Tlaxcalan did it, then so may I, and no man can escape his wyrd. When does this great event take place?"

"On the day judged most auspicious by the astrologers, Three Alligator. That will be some thirty days hence."

Hring's first order of business was to get himself in condition for the ritual. The weeks of sitting in the litter with Two-Earthquake on their journey to Tenochtitlán had left him weak in the legs and wind. Besides, for some years now he had been leading the life of a seaman, not that of a land-based warrior.

At Two-Earthquake's suggestion and guided by Golden-Bells, he betook himself to the military training ground at the mainland end of one of the causeways leading from Tenochtitlán. This was a huge rectangle surrounded by galleried buildings housing barracks, arsenals, store-houses, and stables. Hring could see men practicing with bow, javelin, spear, and sword under the supervision of instructors.

An officer in padded training armor, his face painted green, left a knot of similarly attired men and walked to where Hring and Golden-Bells were watching young men practice with swords. He bowed respectfully and Golden-Bells made introductions. "Seven-Wind, this is One-Reed, commander of the Order of Jaguar Knights, at present director of training of the military school."

"I am most honored, Seven-Wind," the officer said, "and please accept my warmest congratulations for the honor you have been accorded." Hring accepted the compliment with the proper phrases and explained what he needed. One-Reed gave instructions to a boy hovering nearby and the boy ran to the far end of the enclosure. He returned minutes later with a huge man, the first southern Skraeling Hring had seen who was bigger than himself.

"This," One-Reed said, "is Smoking-Crest, the greatest living master of the macuahuitl." Smoking-Crest, both from his name and from his appearance, Hring knew to be of one of the subject peoples. He was barefoot and wore a loincloth of ocelot skin. His long hair was gathered into a topknot worked with colored beads. His face was unpainted, but instead was tattooed with vertical stripes. He was much more primitive-looking than any Tonocha.

One-Reed returned to his duties and Golden-Bells returned to the city, promising to meet Hring at the evening meal, with an unspoken gesture that promised a later and more intimate meeting. Hring turned to Smoking-Crest as the boy runner struggled up to them and dropped a bag from which several wooden handles protruded.

"These are macuahuitl," rumbled Smoking-Crest, bending to the bag. "Finest weapon in the world. The Tenocha were fools to give it up for those." He pointed to a group of young warriors who were slashing at stuffed dummies with long swords. These swords were nearly a yard in length, single-edged, and broadening toward the tip. They were lineal descendants of the iron jungle knives the Norse traders had dealt in from the time they first learned of the market with the southern Skraelings.

"They think the swords are better because they are iron, and only the Tenocha may own iron." He gave a contemptuous snort. The big man spoke Nahuatl with an accent that Hring had difficulty following, but his words were simple and that made the task easier. "But in Oaxaca we still use it, and we spilled the guts of many Tenocha before they overcame us by numbers." He hauled a pair of the weapons from the bag and handed one to Hring.

It was a flat paddle, thicker in the middle than at the edges, widening toward the tip and square-ended, perhaps twenty-five inches long in the "blade" section. The edges were grooved and into the grooves were set square blades of obsidian embedded in pitch. Hring thumbed the edge. It felt sharp, but not as sharp as a well-honed sword of steel.

"This is the one-handed macuahuitl," said the Oaxacan. "It is used with the shield." He spun the weapon through a series of blurring spins that bespoke a powerful wrist. He pulled another from the bag. This weapon was half again as long as the first, with a much longer handle. "This is the two-handed macuahuitl. In Oaxaca we call it the Horse-Slayer, because, three hundred years ago, when the Northerners first came against us with the new animals, the hero Obsidian-Serpent killed the first horse seen in Oaxaca. He beheaded it with one blow of his two-handed macuahuitl."

"The feats of the dead heroes," Hring observed, "are often difficult for the living to repeat." He was skeptical of the crude-seeming weapon's capabilities.

"I have done it myself," Smoking-Crest said, "many times."

Hring was silent as Smoking-Crest led him to where the men were slashing at the dummies. These were made in the form of men with outstretched arms, built of tightly wrapped bundles of damp straw. On one arm of each was a shield of wood faced with hide, and the body was cased in quilted-cotton armor. The slashings and sawings of the students had cut the dummies here and there to a depth of a few inches, but it was too early in the day for them to be in tatters.

Smoking-Crest pointed to one. "Try it with a sword."

Hring took a sword offered by one of the students and gave it a few practice swings. It was something like a Norwegian long sax, the flaring tip giving great shearing force to the last third of the blade. He tested the edge. It was fresh-honed and fit for shaving.

He took a stance before the dummy, and the students and their instructor dropped their exercises to watch this novelty. His left arm horizontal before him for balance, as if he were carrying his shield, Hring slashed downward at an arm with all his strength. The arm was cut nearly through, and sagged. The tough fibers of the tight-woven straw had more resistance than flesh and bone, and seemed to drag at the sword's edge.

"Again, this time the body," Smoking-Crest said. Hring swung the common downswing blow, to meet the dummy's left shoulder. The sharp blade sank in a full six inches. There was polite applause from the students at the shrewdness of the blow and Hring stood back proudly.

"Excellent!" said the instructor of swordsmanship. "On a man, the arm would have been severed, the shoulder blow would have been to the heart. You see," he said to his students, "that is how the sword should be used when you must kill."

"Not bad," said Smoking-Crest, "for sword work." The Oaxacan stepped up to the dummy, swinging his macuahuitl lazily. Then the weapon flashed in three cuts so swift and precisely timed that they seemed to be one. Both arms of the dummy fell to the ground and the head toppled free. While Hring tried to swallow the lump that had suddenly appeared in his throat, Smoking-Crest picked up his two-handed macuahuitl and swung it in a blurring, chest-high, horizontal arc that didn't even slow down when it struck the dummy but passed right on through, shearing through padding and straw as if it were so much smoke. The terrible weapon stopped at the end of the almost-complete circle that giant Oaxacan had swung it in, and as the last bits of straw and cotton fluff pattered to the ground, Hring knew that he had found the one man who might get him down alive from the pyramid.

Chapter 7

His days were set in a pattern, now. A slave woke Hring
an hour before sunrise and he set off at a run through the
deserted streets of Tenochtitlán. He would finish the run
with a dash up the steps of one of the many pyramids. It
was best to do this early in the morning, before the steps
became slick with blood. At first, he could only make it
halfway up the stair of a small pyramid dedicated to
Mixcoatl, the Cloud Serpent, Tenocha god of the Milky
Way. He intended, by the day of the fight, to be able to
run to the top of the gigantic Pyramid of Huitzilopochtli.

After a light breakfast, he repaired to the training ground,
where Smoking-Crest drilled him intensively in the use of
the macuahuitl; more specifically, in how to avoid it.
Hring had to unlearn all that he had ever known of fighting.
The square stance of the Norse swordsman was no help
against an enemy as evasive as Smoking-Crest. A Norseman
stood his ground and moved his feet as little as possible. If

he had to advance or give ground, he did it in a straight line, always keeping his shield leg forward.

The Oaxacan seemed to fight as much with his feet as with his weapons. Hring would swing a head blow with the edgeless, practice macuahuitl, and suddenly his foe would not be there, but behind him, kicking against the back of his knee, bringing him to the ground and grasping his hair in the Tenocha prisoner-taking gesture. Against this fluid style his old way of fighting left him helpless. It took many of these sessions for Hring to learn the rudiments of complex footwork.

Then there was the shield. Unlike the heavy Norse shield, the native equivalent was a light construction of tough wood or woven cane faced with hide. It was not used to block a blow, but to parry it to one side. Time and again, Hring would instinctively try to block one of Smoking-Crest's terrific blows, only to be knocked sprawling.

"Remember," the Oaxacan reminded him, "your macuahuitl will have no obsidian edges. It will be just like these practice weapons. Use it as you would in stick fighting. With the sharp weapon you can attack the soft parts of the body, where the flesh can be cut deep; the belly, the thigh, the buttocks, or the throat. With a stick, you attack bone, where the skin is stretched thin, and you can break bone or cause much pain. Attack the knee, the shin, the elbow, the wrist, the skull. A quick thrust into the throat below the edge of the helmet can kill. They will wear loin pads, so an attack to the groin is useless."

When Hring had picked up the basics of this new style, Smoking-Crest tethered him to a post by a nine-foot rope to stimulate the one he would be tied with on the day of the combat. At first, Hring continually entangled his feet and tripped himself until he was in despair of ever learning to cope with it.

"Learn to fight even with this handicap," Smoking-Crest urged. "Even this may be turned to your advantage. The platform is very small for fighting. The sides of the pyramid are very steep. They can fall off. You cannot. This allows you to fight closer to the edge than they dare to. Go close to the edge when you need a breathing space. They will not attack you vigorously."

On another occasion, the Oaxacan lectured Hring on Tenocha fighting psychology: "Go for a kill as quickly as you can. In this you have an advantage over them. You have always fought to kill. They fight to take prisoners for sacrifice. These warriors need extra time to make up their minds to strike a killing blow. This you can use against them. It is not their intention to kill you in the combat, but to defeat and disarm you, then put you on the stone." It was a lesson not wasted upon Hring

At Hring's request, One-Reed searched Tenochtitlán, then several surrounding towns, for a left-handed warrior to practice with. He found none. Hring had heard before that left-handedness was extremely rare among Skraelings. Among the Tenocha, it was equated with sorcerous power, and this was why the god Huitzilopochtli was "the left-handed hummingbird," a name that could also be translated as "hummingbird wizard." One-Reed apologized and told Hring that a left-handed warrior-priest was being brought in from a distant northern city by horse relays for the day of the fight.

Hring was not greatly discouraged. Left-handedness was relatively common among the Norse and Hring had trained against many left-handed men.

As he trained and wandered about the city, people would

approach him shyly and ask to be allowed to touch him
and share in his luck. The tether fight was a great privilege,
and only took place in Tenochtitlán perhaps once in a
decade. All those to be sacrificed were considered fortunate and treated with honor, but one privileged to fight
atop the Pyramid of Coatlicue was honored above all.

Hring was feasted nightly by various military and priestly
organizations, and would have had his pick of highborn
young maidens had Golden-Bells not kept him occupied
nightly. On one memorable occasion, he attended a banquet of the priests of Mayahuel, goddess of pulque. She
had four hundred breasts, to nourish her children, the Four
Hundred Gods of Drunkenness. Drunkenness was punish-
able by death among the Tenocha, save on those occasions
when it was a mandatory religious observance. Hring's run
the next morning was slow and shaky.

As the day of the fight drew near, Hring examined his
situation. He had been avoiding this, trying to keep his
mind clear of all except the coming trial. There was cer-
tainly little point in worrying beyond the day of the combat,
since he was unlikely to survive it.

Still, he had a Norse nobleman's self-confidence, and
now that he had mastered this new way of fighting, he
allowed himself to believe that he might come through the
trial alive. And what then? From the time of the hurricano,
when he had given himself up for lost, events had moved
too fast for him to take hold of them. The overwhelmingly
lavish Tenocha civilization with its stupefying ritual slaughter had nearly robbed him of his powers of judgment and
will to resist.

But if he should win? Golden-Bells had told him that,
should he win, all honor would be his, even, she hinted,
adoption into a high Tenocha clan and marriage to a lady

of the highest. Did he want that? A lordship among the Tenocha meant material wealth greater than the dreams of any prince of Christendom. That was attractive. Golden-Bells was a beautiful woman who would no doubt be a devoted wife. But could he live with a woman who ripped the living hearts from helpless victims morning and evening? No, what he wanted above all was to be free of this place and these people. He was sick of blood and death. He was sick of people who went in such fear of their gods that they poured out the best blood of the land in torrents to appease them. He was sick above all of people who meekly went to their deaths. But they were not all like that. He thought of Smoking-Crest, the resentful Oaxacan and, he hoped, his friend. A thought began to take shape.

On the morning of the fight, Hring was given a feather headdress and a cloak of flowers, his whole body painted in vertical stripes of red and white. He walked in procession through the streets of Tenochtitlán, which had been bedecked for the occasion with entire continuous blankets of flowers. Before him walked young priests swinging censers. Beside him was One-Reed, dressed as a bear. He was to be Hring's second, who would hand him his casting spears when he needed them. Hring would have preferred Smoking-Crest for this office, but the Oaxacan was not Tenocha and therefore unworthy.

Next came the two Eagle Knights, followed by the two Jaguar Knights, chosen by lot from among all those stationed at this time in Tenochtitlán. Last came the left-handed warrior-priest. He was dressed in the stylized serpent costume of the Order of Rattlesnake Warriors, a prominent military fraternity in the northern part of the empire. These warriors were showered with nearly as many flowers and as much praise as Hring himself.

He strode very slowly up the steps of the pyramid, so as not to reach the top winded. At the top, as his cloak and headdress were taken from him and he was tethered to the stone, Hring studied the colossal statue of the goddess Coatlicue. Coatlicue, lady of the Skirt of Serpents, Mother of Gods, was hideous and grotesque even among Tenocha deities. Her hands and feet were clawed, for she was the devourer of the corpses of men. True to her name, her skirt was of braided serpents and belted with a serpent. Her breasts, which had nourished both gods and men, hung flaccid, partially covered by a necklace whose central ornament was a human skull, the rest made of alternating severed human hands and hearts. Her own head had been severed, and the two fountains of blood which came from her neck took the form of two great serpents whose heads met in profile and formed a fantastic fanged and fork-tongued face. This was the epitome of all the Tenocha loved and feared and they called her "Our Grandmother."

Hring turned from the statue in disgust and vowed that, if he had any say in the matter, he wouldn't die on the altar of *this* obscenity. Hring was given a heavily padded loincloth to protect his groin and a sleeveless, lightly padded jacket. There was a covered litter on one corner of the platform, in the shade of one of the two tiny temples that crested the pyramid. As One-Reed gave Hring his shield and cotton-edged macuahuitl he explained.

"The Great Speaker is home from the South. The flowery war is over and he has brought the prisoners for the dedication of the Great Temple." A flowery war was one fought for no other purpose than to take prisoners for sacrifice. "If you win, the Great Festival will have begun so auspiciously that there is nothing he will not give you. Nothing!''

Hring swung his macuahuitl a few times as the great drums were beaten on the platform just below the crest of the pyramid and conches blasted and flutes shrilled and priests shouted and intoned in the archaic Toltec dialect. From the top of the pyramid, Hring could see the whole Valley of Mexico, his view blocked only in the direction of the even taller Pyramid of Huitzilopochtli. The plaza below was packed with people, and the sides of all the nearby pyramids were crowded with spectators. Hring vowed to give them a show that would make their trouble worthwhile. The noise faded and his first opponent stepped forward.

Hring transferred his macuahuitl to his shield hand and reached back for one of his ''javelins.'' It was only a stick of wood, about fourteen inches long and tapering from the middle to both ends. It was, though, of a stout, heavy hardwood, and Hring had been raised on boy's stick fighting.

His opponent was one of the Eagle Knights. He didn't wear the elaborate gilded metal helmet and scale armor of his order, but the padded armor of centuries before. He wore long padded trousers and a long-sleeved jacket of padded cotton. His helmet was of gilded wood, and his green-painted face looked out through the gaping eagle beak, which did not close like the visors of the modern helmets. It was more of a headdress than a helmet, and was crested with fine eagle feathers. This might have been one of the men Hring had laughed and feasted with this last month, but that mattered not at all. Now he was a Tenocha warrior out to gain sacrifice for his gods, and as fierce as any.

Hring gripped his stick at its midpoint and watched the man come closer. Suddenly the Eagle gave a wild war cry and raised his macuahuitl high. As it descended, Hring stepped in and raised his shield obliquely to parry the blow, simultaneously kicking his opponent's shield aside. He brought the stick up and forward viciously, and the pointed end punched through the eye and into the brain behind it. The Eagle Knight stood dead on his feet until Hring pushed him off the platform to tumble down the steep pyramid to the plaza two hundred feet below. There was silence for a moment. Nobody had seen what had happened, most were not even aware that the fight had begun. They had seen the Eagle walk toward Hring, then they had seen him fall. A great cheer went up anyway. They all assumed that some god had intervened. Perhaps the Eagle had not been worthy.

The next man came forward. One-Reed handed Hring his second stick, saying: "That was splendid! Do it again." The new man had learned from the other's overconfidence, though. This was the second Eagle, his face painted red, and he kept his shield high. He bent low and aimed short blows, trying to force Hring back against the pedestal. Hring gave ground. Above all, he must not let the weapon cripple him. The tiny facets of the obsidian edges cut not like a knife but like a smith's hacksaw, so that, when swung shrewdly, it would shear through flesh and tendon and bone more efficiently than any sword of steel.

When his back touched stone, Hring sprang up and back to stand upon the waist-high pedestal to which he was tethered. This came in the midst of a hard blow from the Eagle, and his weapon's obsidian edge shattered against the stone. As the Eagle spun his macuahuitl to bring the other edge into play, Hring cracked his stick against the

Eagle's wrist, causing him to drop the weapon. As the Eagle grimaced with pain and tried to pull back, Hring dropped his own weapons, grasped his rope in both hands, and whipped a loop around the Eagle's neck. He hoisted the man off the platform and held him, dangling and kicking, until he was still. Then Hring dropped from the pedestal, carried the Eagle to the edge, and cast him over. This time, the cheering was deafening.

One-Reed hastily brought him his weapons and now the first Jaguar Knight was advancing. Three to go. Hring knew that he had to eliminate the next two quickly, else exhaustion would overtake him before the duel with the left-hander. This man wore a suit of padded jaguar skin, and came in warily. Hring faked a few attacks, and the man covered quickly with his shield at each feint. Too cautious. That would be his undoing. Hring flung his stick straight at the man's face and he jerked his shield high to block it, only to have Hring's foot sink deep into his solar plexus. Even through the padding, the blow took the wind out of him, and as the Jaguar doubled forward, the narrow edge of Hring's macuahuitl crashed down on the back of his neck below the wooden helmet. The bones parted with a loud crack and Hring tumbled the corpse to follow the other two. The cheering was continous now; it hadn't stopped since the second Knight had died.

The second Jaguar came forward now, his face visible through the open, fanged cat mask. His upper face was painted green, its lower half black. He attacked wildly, swinging his macuahuitl swiftly, like the berserker back at Mjolnir Sound. Hring played him as he had the berserker, giving ground and backing toward the edge of the platform. As the Jaguar checked his attack slightly to avoid getting too close to the edge, Hring leaped forward and to one side, going past the Jaguar in a rolling tumble. The Jaguar tried an awkward, backhanded blow at the rolling target. The obsidian flakes slashed Hring's thigh, but the blow threw the man farther off balance, and when Hring gave his rope a sudden jerk it snapped around the spotted ankles and sent the knight tumbling and screaming to be shattered on the plaza below.

Now the screaming from the crowd below was truly hysterical. Even One-Reed, in his bearish outfit, was dancing and whooping, singing the praises of his champion. Hring stood, panting and trembling, trying to calm his breathing and the thudding of his heart, which was now pounding in time to the drumbeats below. To those who watched, he might have seemed to have made little effort, but there is no stress as great as a mortal fight, and each blow had taken as much toll as ten minutes of a brisk practice bout. He was sweating buckets and was monstrously thirsty. Besides, the slash on his thigh was burning and bleeding. He didn't want to look at it and he knew that it could make his footing slippery.

The noise abated fractionally, Hring's breathing slowed a little, and the Snake Man came forward. He was a man of some northern tribe, tall and lean in contrast to the stocky Tenocha. His face was painted in a scale pattern and he wore no helmet, only a short cloak of rattlesnake skins in addition to his padded loincloth. He swung his macuahuitl lazily in his left hand, like one well accustomed to its use. Like Smoking-Crest. This was not a swordsman using an unfamiliar weapon like the others. As he strode forward, the anklets of serpent rattles at his feet clashed and hissed.

An odd, light-headed thought spun through Hring's mind: What had Halvdan's poems called the rattlesnake and its warning? "Loki's Laugh," that was it. Then the man was on him. The macuahuitl flashed swiftly, at head and side and thigh, and Hring managed to get his shield between himself and the weapon at each blow, but pieces of the shield flew away at each impact. Hring retreated quickly to the edge of the platform to gain breathing time and reconsider his strategy. True to Smoking-Crest's prediction, the man slowed and circled instead of attacking.

Hring stood, breathing in great gasps. The plaza was quiet, now, and the drums had fallen silent. This was going to be no quick victory. Hring had one stick left and he took it from behind his shield. He advanced a little away from the edge and the Snake Man closed in. Hring feinted high with his paddle-like club and the Snake Man raised his shield and sprang back slightly. He then came forward again without hesitation and Hring tossed the remaining stick beneath the man's advancing foot. The Snake Man stepped on the stick and it rolled beneath him. He was swift, and regained his balance almost instantly, but the second's break in timing had been enough. He had raised his shield a few inches to catch his balance and in that instant Hring's macuahuitl was beneath it in a crack at the ribs. The shield snapped down and now the club was over it and cracking against the man's jaw. Hring had time for no more, as the Snake Man charged to end the fight before his hurts told against him, and Hring retreated to the limit of his tether and the deadly macuahuitl swung in a great vertical arc to split Hring in two, but the Snake Man had not quite regained his timing and Hring bent low under the blow and seized the man by the waist, straightening and casting him over his back, over the edge of the platform. As the man went over, Hring felt the sharp obsidian bite agonizingly into his back. He turned, unable to believe that the fight was over, heard the deafening roar and saw the crowd surging up the sides of the pyramid.

Hring turned at a touch on his shoulder. It was one of the priests who had been watching the fight from one of the little temples atop the pyramid. The priest bowed low and said: ''Sir, the Great Speaker bids you join him in his litter.''

Walking stiffly, beginning to feel the wounds in thigh and back, as he knew he would be feeling them far worse and for some time to come, he approached the litter. An attendant opened the litter and a figure seated inside graciously signed for him to come in and sit.

Hring's eyes gradually became accustomed to the dimness inside and he felt the palanquin being lifted to the shoulders of bearers, then beginning the slow descent of the steep stair down the face of the pyramid. The skillful bearers kept the litter almost level. The man beside Hring waited thoughtfully for his breathing to calm. He seemed unperturbed by the blood, sweat, and body paint that were staining the inside of his lavish conveyance, but then, what Tenocha could be bothered by a little blood?

''That was the most magnificent feat I have ever seen,'' the man said at last. ''The gods could not have sent a clearer message that they are pleased by our sacrifices.'' Hring studied him. To his surprise, Izcoatl II, Great Speaker of the Tenocha, was a very young man, little older than himself. Unlike other Tenocha, he wore no paint, only the three tattoo lines from lip to chin. His lip plug was small but of fine jade, as were his earplugs. He wore only a plain white cotton loincloth and his hair was gathered in a topknot. Unlike the other Tenocha Hring had seen, the Great Speaker had a beard, although it was sparse, carefully combed, and trimmed to a long point. Beards meant magical force to the Tenocha.

"You must accompany me to the palace," Izcoatl said. "If the people could reach you now, they would tear you to pieces and devour your smallest fragment to share in your sanctity. This would be a great sin, for the gods have decreed that you are to live. They must have some great future in store for you." Izcoatl was the Great Speaker's reigning name. His given name was Two-Jaguar and, like other Tenocha, he had a secret, "true" name, known only to himself, his parents, and the priests and astrologers who presided at his birth. This name must always be kept secret from evil spirits that might use it against him.

"I thank you," said Hring, feeling slightly faint and very nauseated.

"It is I who am honored," Izcoatl said. "There will be physicians at the palace to attend your hurts. The gods will be pleased with the blood you've shed and not be jealous of your glory. It's best for heroes and Great Speakers to bleed once in a while." Izcoatl reached out and felt Hring's bristly red beard.

"Such a fine beard," he said. "It must have great force. Many of the gods are bearded, but they have not been so generous with us." He stroked his own thin growth. "Do you think that, by this sign, they wish to teach us humility?"

"I have no doubt of it, Great Speaker," said Hring, who was not interested in beards—his own, Izcoatl's, or anybody else's. What he was interested in was some rest, something to drink, and above all something to relieve the terrible pains that were beginning to make their way past his quickly fading battle numbness.

"I am glad you think so," said Izcoatl, not seeming to notice that he was sitting in a slowly widening puddle of blood. "A man cannot consider too deeply the ways in which the gods communicate with us. You I can perceive as a man of rare gifts, both physical and spiritual." He reached out through the litter's curtains and made a gesture. Instantly, a foaming jar was thrust inside. Izcoatl took it and handed it to Hring.

"I think you can drink this now without being made sick. It is chokoatl mixed with sugar and pulque. A man who has lost much blood recovers more quickly if he takes sugar." The Tenocha were experts on the subject of bleeding. Hring took the jar and drank greedily. The thick, sickly-sweet liquid did little for his raging thirst, but it did quiet his stomach to a marked degree, and the pulque had a gratifying effect.

"When you are recovered from your hurts we must talk about how to honor you properly. Unless you insist upon being sacrificed right away?" He looked at Hring with some eagerness.

"Not just yet, Great Speaker," Hring said. "As you have so astutely pointed out, the gods must have other plans for me."

"Quite right. In any case, this feat of yours today will be one of the glories of my reign, to be remembered for centuries. You may have whatever you ask of me." But Hring was slumped against the side of the litter, unconscious.

"We took this from your back," the priest said. He held an oblong piece of obsidian before Hring's eyes. It was one of the blades from the Snake Man's macuahuitl. "There is another," the priest continued, "imbedded in your back. The cutting required to remove it would do more damage than leaving it. The flesh will heal over it if you live. One day it may work its way out. Stones are content in the earth, but restless in the body.''

Hring's wounds had been cleaned, the lips of the cuts clamped together by holding big, fierce ants to them and letting them pinch the flesh in their mandibles, then breaking the bodies off. It was an unnerving procedure, but one that worked well. He was given the benefit of much incense and the eye of a fox was tied to the muscle of his upper arm to guard against infection.

The room was crowded with well-wishers. Golden-Bells was there, and Two-Earthquake, Nine-Death, and One-Reed. There were flocks of others, each trading on whatever slight acquaintance he could to be near this heroic concentration of sanctity. Hring lay naked on his belly, feeling as heroic as a long-dead fish.

"Seven-Wind," Two-Earthquake was saying, "you must take this obsidian to a jeweler and have it made into an amulet to protect you always from the weapons of your enemies." All made gestures of assent at the sage advice.

"Ask the Great Speaker for the command of the Eagle Knights," One-Reed urged him. "He will grant your request and you will make us invincible." There was grumbling from a few Jaguar Knights in the crowd, but all fell silent when one of the Great Speaker's stewards arrived.

"Great Seven-Wind," he said to Hring, "the Great Speaker wishes to know whether you will feel well enough to attend a Holy Banquet this evening."

Hring felt like nothing of the sort, but he knew that a man must strike while the iron is hot. "I shall be happy to attend," he said.

"The Great Speaker has instructed me to invite all of you," he addressed the crowd packing the room, "Seven-Wind's friends, to attend also." There were murmurs of pleasure. Not only proximity to the illustrious Seven-Wind, but attendance at a Holy Banquet given by the Great Speaker himself. The gods were indeed propitious.

When time came for the banquet, runners came with a small litter to take Hring to the banqueting hall. He sat stiffly in the seat slung between two poles as the bearers wound their way through the labyrinthine palace. He grew weary of studying wall paintings and statues.

By the time his litter arrived in the banqueting hall, the other guests were all seated on the floor in a great rectangle, facing inward. Servants scurried about, filling cups with mildly alcoholic or narcotic beverages, proffering trays of salty or spicy tidbits. Hring was carefully set down at one end of the rectangle, between Golden-Bells and Nine-Death. The space opposite him was empty.

Hring had little appetite, but the smells that came from an adjoining room piqued his interest. It smelled like pork. Cattle and pigs and sheep were still rare creatures in the Valley of Mexico. The natives had never taken to such flesh, preferring their fowl and dogs and game. Apparently, the feast was to feature exotic fare.

All bowed as the Great Speaker arrived and took his place opposite Hring. He said some lengthy prayers in the dialect Hring still could not understand, then the first courses were brought in. Hring asked Golden-Bells about the wall decorations, which were of a type unfamiliar to him, glittering with brilliant intensity instead of displaying the colorful but flat quality of the usual wall paintings.

"These are mosaics," Golden-Bells explained. "They are built up of tiny bits of glass and precious stone instead of paint. Some Moors on the coast have been teaching the art to our craftsmen. Aren't they beautiful?" Hring murmured agreement. "That one over there depicts

Mictecacihuatl, Lady of the Underworld, devouring the dead, and that other one is Tezcatlipoca, the Smoking Mirror. His image is made up of obsidian." Hring pretended interest as the meat was brought in. The others were served thin-sliced flakes of the pork, but Hring was given a platter of game birds. Disappointed, he asked Golden-Bells; "Why am I not served some of that?" He had been craving pork and beef and mutton for weeks.

To his astonishment, she gripped his wounded thigh painfully and hissed: "You must not speak such sacrilege!" Her face had gone pale.

Nine-Death touched his shoulder and said, quietly so that nobody else could hear: "Great Seven-Wind, you do not know our ways well enough yet. These are your sons we are eating, in communion with the gods."

Thoroughly mystified, Hring saw a bone lying on one of the platters, its flesh now gone. It wasn't a pig's bone. His stomach gave a great lurch as he realized what he had asked to be given. He had known of the Tenocha's anthropophagous habits, but he had not yet seen them in practice.

"But," he muttered, regaining control of himself, "my sons? I don't understand. I have no sons that I know of."

"You took these men prisoner this morning. They are your sons and therefore it is forbidden you to eat them. They have been sacrificed in your stead."

"I took no prisoners," Hring said. "I slew them."

"It is the same thing," said Nine-Death patiently. "There are many ways to make sacrifice. Cutting out the heart is only one. Taking a prisoner is among us a vital principle, with many interpretations."

"Yes," said Golden-Bells, also speaking in a low voice, "for instance, when the litter of Huitzilopochtli is borne across the sky, it is carried by warriors who have taken prisoners in battle, and by women who have died in childbirth.''

"Women dead in childbirth?" Hring was sure that he was missing some vital point.

"Don't you see?" she said. "They have died taking men prisoner also. Their unborn children.''

Hring's brain was reeling from revulsion, confusion, and the shock of his wounds and blood loss. He could never live here. These people were at one moment amiable and familiar and at another as alien as people from some other world. He could never hope to understand them. Never.

He stood on the verandah of the palace in which Golden-Bells and Nine-Death lived. Below, he saw Nine-Death going through the ritual of Xipe Totec, to encourage the incoming year. A young girl had been offered on the altar for sacrifice. After her heart had been cut out her corpse had been flayed and now Nine-Death was dancing, dressed in her skin. Thus was symbolized the earth putting on the raiment of the new year. The priest's eyes looked out through the girl's gaping lids, his white-painted mouth showed through her open lips. Her skinned hands dangled from his wrists like obscene gloves.

Hring shrugged his shoulders, accustoming them to the weight of his new Eagle Knight armor. He carried his helmet under his arm and wore his old sword at his side. Golden-Bells was still pleading.

"Why do you do this, Seven-Wind? You could be a general of great armies. You could live here in Tenochtitlán, in splendor. You could have me to wife, and as many concubines as you wish. There is no honor that would be withheld from you. Why give it all up for an obscure command far in the North, where you may never be heard from again. That is where malcontents and those out of favor are sent to be forgotten.''

"Golden-Bells, I am not Tenocha. I am something altogether more primitive: a Norseman. My gods are not yours. My blood is not yours. Trying to live your way of life would send me mad, shortly. In the North, I will be able to live the only life I was raised for: that of a warrior. The demands on my—flexibility will not be so great.'' He left her weeping silently.

He rode past the training ground at dusk. "Wait here,'' he told the men who rode with him. He dismounted and walked about until he found Smoking-Crest. The Oaxacan eyed his new Eagle Knight uniform warily, and there was little friendliness in him. "I saw the fight,'' he said. "It was a good one. You learn well.''

"I would not have lived long without your teaching,'' Hring said.

"So you are Tenocha now,'' said Smoking-Crest.

"Never,'' Hring said. From where they stood, they could see the top of the Great Pyramid of Huitzilopochtli. The dedication had commenced. On the crest, two teams of priests, relieved by frequent relays, were sacrificing men from two lines that led down the stairs and far out into the city below. The sacrificing had been going on nonstop for two days and would continue for several more. The entire city reeked of blood. By the end of the festival, the entire contents of the hearts and veins of twenty thousand men would have poured in torrents down the sides of the temple.

"Many Oaxacans there,'' muttered Smoking-Crest.

"Smoking-Crest,'' said Hring, "I shall come back here, and when I do it will be with an army at my back. I know not where I will find it, but when a land has wealth like this one, men can be found who will want to take it. Will your people rise against the Tenocha when I come?''

The Oaxacan looked at him long before answering. ''I can raise Oaxaca. There will be others. The Mixtec, the Zapotec, maybe the Maya and the coastal people. The Yaqui of the North will fight. Not the Toltec, they have thrown in their lot with the Tenocha for too long. This is brave talk, but an army of words will not defeat the Tenocha.''

''It will be no phantom army that I bring,'' Hring said. ''It will be a bloody day when I take Tenochtitlán, but when it's done, men will not march meekly to their death at the top of that pile of stone.'' He jabbed a finger at Huitzilopochtli's new house as if that gesture alone could smash it asunder. ''And priests will not dance in the fresh-flayed skins of girls. Listen for news of my arrival, Smoking-Crest. When I come, get you to Oaxaca and raise your people. There will be Tenocha to slay and plunder for all.''

Smoking-Crest said nothing more, but watched Hring with steady eyes as he remounted and took the north highway. Atop the Great Pyramid, more hearts were ripped forth to spray their blood for the god.

Chapter 8

This season, it was the Dineh. The fierce, wily mountain tribesmen came down to raid in the fall, when their neighbors' harvests were in. The scout came riding back down the canyon to report to his commander, his surefooted, wiry pony picking its way delicately among the litter of fallen stone and cactus on the canyon floor. He drew up beside the officer, who doffed his Eagle headdress to hear better. His red beard made a sharp contrast among the swarthy Snake Warriors of his command.

"The Apache went single file up that canyon," the scout said, using his own tribe's name for the Dineh. "Maybe a hundred of them. They followed the path to the top of the canyon, then scattered."

Hring raised in his stirrups and stretched, pressing his palms against his saddle pommel and trying to crack the kinks out of his spine. He did not look the glittering Eagle Knight he had appeared when he left Tenochtitlán. His fine scale suit was rolled up in his saddlebag, along with his golden helmet and feather cape. These were foolish trappings to wear when hunting Dineh. Hring's uniform was of light cotton, painted with a feather pattern and dyed tan to blend well with his surroundings. His headdress was woven of straw and painted, with its upper beak jutting out over his eyes as a shade against the merciless sun of the Northern Desert.

"Ambush?" he asked.

"I think so," the scout said. "There are three good places along the canyon. Good cover, big rocks along the rim to roll down." This was the kind of warfare the Dineh specialized in: using the land itself against their enemies, never exposing themselves unless necessary.

"Let's spring their trap," said Spotted-Lizard, Hring's second. Spotted-Lizard was a Yaqui, and hated the Dineh with a black passion that stretched back for centuries and made the enmity between Christian and pagan back East seem warm comradeship by comparison.

"Let's not be hasty," Hring said. "We're deep in their territory now, and far from ours." They had been chasing the Dineh up the valley of the Northern River for days. This was still officially part of the Azteca Empire, but most of the natives would dispute that. They were far north of any Tenocha fort, and had been chasing this band for days. It was led by a chief named Natay and had been making a great nuisance of itself. Hring squinted at the black clouds building above the mountains a few miles to the northwest.

"We'll make our move now," said Hring, addressing his command, "else we'll never catch them this year." The sixty or so Yaqui horsemen growled happy assent. They all carried bows and lances, and many had macuahuitl thonged to their pommels. "Spotted-Lizard"—Hring pointed at his second—"you take the Sidewinder Troop and ride the north ridge of the canyon. I'll take the Diamondbacks. When we find their ambush, force them down the sides of the canyon and finish them off with arrows. Don't follow them down the canyon wall, because the wash will be neck-deep in water in a couple of hours, if I'm any judge." He pointed toward the ominous clouds.

With his half of the command, Hring picked his way slowly up the sides of the bluff to the rimrock that crested the canyon. He took his men well back from the canyon and began to patrol along its length. They were halfway to the end when the scout pointed out where the Dineh lay in wait. Hring might not have spotted them unaided. The Dineh lay along the edge of the canyon, camouflaged beneath gray blankets, still as the stones, their attention centered on the bottom of the draw, where they expected to see the Tenocha force momentarily. With hand signals, Hring instructed his force to spread out in line. He knew that Spotted-Lizard was doing the same on the other side. At a trot, the force began to cover the quarter mile that separated them from the Dineh.

By the time they had closed half the distance, it was futile to try to keep quiet as Dineh heads began turning. Shouting war cries, they broke into a charge and closed in. The Dineh burst from beneath their blankets and snatched up their bows. The air was instantly thick with arrows. Hring managed two quick shots, then he dropped his bow and snatched the lance from its socket beneath his stirrup leather. He got it in line just in time to catch a Dineh warrior beneath the jaw, then he had to release the lance and draw his sword.

The Dineh, taken by surprise and with no practicable

line of retreat, fought wildly. Two attacked Hring, trying to seize his bridle and topple him from his horse. He disposed of them with two short, economical chops and looked to see how his command was doing. The Dineh, now demoralized, were beginning to scramble down the sides of the canyon, trying to make a run for it. Hring saw some of his men following.

"Stop!" he yelled. "Back to your horses and use your bows" There was no stopping the Yaquis. They were out for Dineh blood and no Tenocha orders were going to stop them. Within minutes, every man of Hring's troop was dismounted and chasing the Dineh, slipping and scrambling in the loose scree of the sides, swinging ax and macuahuitl at the shaggy black scalps a few steps below. Hring could see the same thing happening on the other side of the canyon, where Spotted-Lizard's troop were disobeying his instructions also, with Spotted-Lizard among them, no doubt.

Hring grabbed up a Dineh bow and a handful of arrows and began firing downhill, missing his first few shots as he got the feel of the unfamiliar weapon, then beginning to strike on target. He was taking aim at his fourth Dineh when he heard the rumble from upcanyon. He cupped his hands around his mouth and shouted.

"Flash flood! Get back up here!" over and over again. His men were too blood-maddened to hear him or the approaching flood. The screaming and slaughtering went on unabated until Hring saw the wall of foamy mud appear upcanyon, tossing a litter of cactus, creosote branches, and last year's dry brush before it. Most of the men struggling amid the mess of blood on the canyon floor never noticed the water until it snatched them up and dashed them against the boulders of the canyon sides, spinning them toward the mouth of the canyon with impersonal contempt. Within five seconds, the floor of the canyon was under twenty feet of water.

Hring watched for perhaps fifteen minutes, until the water was reduced to a trickle. There was no sign of life in the canyon below, only a few bodies wedged among the rocks. His entire command, men he had led for the last three years, had been wiped out in an instant by a force of nature and their own reckless ferocity.

On the rimrock, Hring filled his pipe, took smoldering punk from the fire gourd on his saddle, and sat down to consider his position.

Upon reflection, he decided that his three years had been well spent. He now was intimately familiar with the northern defense line of the Tenocha Empire. He knew the dispositions of all the tribes along the hazy northern border, and their sympathies. They also knew him.

Now there was nothing to keep him here. He had once been offered a life among the mountains to the north. It was time to follow that offer. He knocked the ashes out of his pipe and got to his feet.

Remounting his own horse, Hring rounded up all the others he could catch and practicably lead without attracting too much attention. He stripped off his Tenocha headdress and uniform and left them lying on the ground. Clad in leather tunic, clout, and leggings, his sword girt to his side, Hring rode north.

The trapper's trading post lay in a tiny valley flanked by mountains well above the food line on the breaks of the Manslayer River. He had tried to find Tosti's Holding, only to be told that it had been burned to the ground four years before in a Pawnee raid. Tosti had moved farther west, to be the first trader to get his pick of the new season's pelts. This made him the more exposed to Skraeling raids, but Tosti was not the man to be unnerved by life's vicissitudes.

Hring had only his mount and one packhorse now. The others had been traded away for the things he needed or stolen by Skraelings. He had a great yew bow now, and had given up wearing his sword in favor of a sax and hatchet, such as the trappers favored. He was learning the ways of the mountains and plains, as once he had learned the sea, and later the desert. He had lived among friendly tribes of plains nomads along his way. Most of the plains Skraelings were at peace with the Norsemen, finding them no threat and prizing their trade in metals and other things the nomads could not make for themselves: beads for decorations and high-quality paints and powerful bows.

The gate of the stockade was raised when Hring hailed the gatekeeper, and he rode inside. The post itself was a long, low structure with log sides and a roof of turf. There was a pen for horses and Hring unsaddled and curried his mount and packhorse before turning them into the pen. Only then did he go inside.

A big, gaunt, gray-bearded man met him at the door. "I'm Tosti," he said, "and welcome to my steading. Come in and have a cup." Inside, twenty or so men, Norsemen for the most part, sat drinking ale and talking. They looked up to study the newcomer, and as his eyes adjusted to the dimness, Hring searched their faces. He saw none he knew.

"I'm Hring Kristjanson, once of Treeland, then of Thorsheim, then of Halbjorn of Laxdale's knarr. Just now, I look to earn my ale as a trapper. Ragnar Hringsson told me to inquire of him at Tosti's old steading. Has any here seen him?''

''No one's seen Ragnar from near two years,'' Tosti said, puffing pensively on his pipe. ''He may be dead. Or he may just be wandering. Ragnar's a man of odd whims.'' He introduced Hring to the men present. Most of them, it turned out, were making up parties to winter and trap in the mountains.

Hring spent several days at Tosti's Holding, listening to the advice of the veteran trappers and laying in such supplies as he needed. He paid for most of his supplies with the last of his Tenocha gold, and took the rest on credit against the season's take. He saved back one package, however, for which he had plans, and let no man see it.

When the first winds of winter began to chill the air, Hring set out for the high country with two brothers named Knut and Ketil. They were young men much like himself, exiled from the Christian lands for excessive indulgence in vengeance. They had roasted their father's murderers over a slow fire and had to flee while their kinsmen dug up wergild to placate the families of the slain and the authorities. They had only a year left of their outlawry, but they loved the mountains and didn't care if they never saw Treeland again.

Hring spent that winter in congenial near-solitude, trapping one upland valley while the brothers trapped another, only getting together infrequently at their cabin when blizzards came.

They descended into the lowlands when spring came with a good store of pelts. Hring felt almost purged of the blood and death he had been soaked in since the slaying of his half brother years back. The mountain life suited him. Still, at the back of his mind, there was the resolution born when he watched the prisoners marched up the pyramids of Tenochtitlán. He knew that he would never be truly at peace until that matter was settled. No rush, though. Not while springtime was in the mountains, and the air was fresh and free, and the land's bounty was to be had without spilling someone else's blood to buy the favor of some god or other.

There were still times, though, when he would dream that he was once again King of the Wood. Towering high over the forest, his roots connected to everything that lived in the greenwood, embodying the god force they all worshiped and took their life from. He would wake from such dreams wishing he could go back to sleep and dream some more. Other times he would dream that he was playing God Horse again, lunging into Yngva's mare haunches, and as he jetted his seed she would look back over her shoulder at him with her pitiless smile. These dreams he woke from covered in chill sweat, knowing no relief from the unburdening of his loins.

They were two days from Tosti's Holding when Hring's horse went lame. It was nothing serious, but they had lost some mounts to the big cats this winter, and Hring wanted to spare the beast. It needed at least a week of rest, and Hring sent the brothers ahead to get a good price for their furs, for the boatmen would be arriving soon, and the first in with pelts would get the best price. Hring would follow.

He was fishing the stream next to his camp. His attention was on the float that was beginning to bob in the water, waiting for a sure bite. There was the snort of a horse behind him. Hring did not look around. He gave no sign of alarm, but he knew from the sound that the horse was not his. His eyes slid sideways and fixed the position of his bow and hatchet a few paces away. He already knew where his horse was tethered. Only when he had fixed in his mind where all his gear was, how he could get to it and away with greatest dispatch, did he slowly stand and turn around.

Twenty of them, at least. No sense fighting, then. They sat their horses in a semicircle around him. Absaroka, the Crow People. The Absaroka were not implacable enemies of the Norse trappers like the Pawnee and Comanche, nor were they friendly, like the Cheyenne and Mandan. They were unpredictable, their young men split up into many warrior fraternities, some of which were at war with Norsemen or other Skraeling tribes, some not. Hring made the hand sign for friend.

They made no return sign. Hring studied them. They were fine, handsome young men, with long, black hair that in some cases spilled over the backs of their ponies. They wore breech-clouts, and some wore leggings, but little else. Hring had heard other trappers say that the Absaroka were the handsomest of all the plains tribes, and now he believed them. They were also notorious horse thieves, and other tribes thought their skill with horses magical.

One of the men, apparently the leader, rapped out some words in a language that had a lot of strangling and spitting sounds. He pointed to Hring's horse, signing for him to mount. Finding this preferable to instant death, Hring complied. He wasn't sure what they had in mind for him, and he suspected that they didn't know either. These were probably young, impulsive braves who might kill him or lay on a feast for him according to whim. More than likely, they were taking him back to their encampment to get the advice of their elders.

As they rode, they shot game from horseback, and they rode out to perform tricks and feats of horsemanship to show off or just from youthful high spirits. Hring had to smile at this and admire both their horsemanship, which was indeed matchless, and their fine sense of style. Upon reflection, he could not conceive of a happier people, or a people so well adjusted to their surroundings, even if they were a bit bloody-minded at times.

He looked forward to arriving at their destination with a mixture of interest and trepidation. Life had made him somewhat of a fatalist and he almost believed that he must die as the witch-woman willed it. At least, according to the tales of other trappers, the Absaroka did not indulge in torture, as did many of the other Skraelings, most notably the Dineh. They did, though, practice that singular Skraeling ritual of self-torture, whereby young men absorbed power and induced visions by undergoing colorful ordeals and mutilations. He saw that many of the braves around him had hideous scars on their pectorals, caused by having slits carved in the muscles of the chest, then thrusting pegs beneath the flaps of skin so provided, then attaching rawhide cords to the pegs and hoisting the brave to the roof of the lodge and leaving him to dangle until the flesh tore through.

The Norsemen discussed this phenomenon frequently, and speculated whether a man who had endured this ritual was indeed a more powerful warrior, or just a proven fool.

The camp was a straggling line of big, conical tents pitched in the deep grass along a small river. To Hring's nose, used to the clean, high-mountain air, it was not fragrant. No habitation of man was. The leader of the braves signed for him to dismount and Hring did so, to be surrounded by curious people and inspected closely by children. He was guided to a tent of somewhat larger proportions than the others, where a gray-haired man sat smoking.

The old man gestured to a heap of skins beside him. He looked up at Hring. "Sit. You want eat? Smoke?" Hring made a hand signal in assent and sat. A fat woman brought him a bowl of dog stew and a filled pipe. Nobody said anything until he had finished eating and was puffing contentedly.

"You wait," the old man said at length. "We bring one, she speak you tongue good." Hring nodded and continued to smoke. Soon a woman appeared, wearing a lavishly beaded skin dress. She stared at Hring with growing astonishment. Her hair was pale. Somehow, Hring was not surprised. There was no coincidence, only wyrd.

"I greet you, Winter-Grass," he said. "And I rejoice that you found your way so many long leagues back to your people."

"It is you! Hring! I never thought to see you again."

"Nor I you. It was a long journey that brought you here, and you so young. You must tell me of it."

"In good time. Now a decision must be made concerning you."

"What manner of decision? Why was I taken prisoner?"

"Two Absaroka were killed some days ago. The killer was a Norseman."

"Those men who took me were the first Absaroka I've seen. I have killed no one here."

"Nobody believes you to be the actual killer. But if the real killer is not found, there are some who wish to kill any Norseman in vengeance." She said this with great sadness. Hring nodded in understanding. This was quite within the Norse code of lawful vengeance. If your kinsman's slayer has fled, and his kin refuse to pay wergild, then it is proper to kill any member of his clan in revenge.

A number of the Absaroka of both sexes had gathered to witness the proceedings, and Winter-Grass spoke to them with great animation and many gesticulations. Her tale seemed to be a long one, and Hring puffed smoke contentedly while she talked on. These people would think him a man of little worth if he showed anxiety while his life was being debated. Winter-Grass finished her tale and turned to him. "I have just told them that you helped me escape from my captivity."

"As I recall it," Hring said, "it was more the other way around."

"Yes. But they don't know that. I made it a good story, and now you are a benefactor of the tribe. I also told them what a great warrior you are. Now some may favor adopting you into the tribe. At least it may keep them debating until the killer is caught." With that, Hring had to be content.

"That's a fine dress you wear," Hring said. "You seem to be a woman of some standing."

"Among us, a woman's standing is determined by that of her menfolk."

"Your husband is a great man, then?"

"I have no husband yet. My brother is a war chief with many horses and coups. This is my uncle"—she nodded toward the gray-haired man, who sat smoking and staring into space—"Talks-to-Spirits. He is priest and counselor." Hring would have been apprehensive at the mention of a priest, but he knew that the word had a different meaning among the plains people. The man would be a sort of doctor and teacher of the young.

As he considered Winter-Grass, he found a certain gratification in knowing that she was not married. She had grown into a beautiful woman since he had last seen her. The thin lines of girlhood had given way to a long-legged, doelike gracefulness that spoke well for the advantages of mixing Norse and Skraeling blood. In spite of his predicament, Hring was stirred by her presence. It had been a long winter in the mountains. Besides, this at last was a woman whose life had been thrown together with his who was not some kind of priestess.

"Did you find your sea captain, then?" Winter-Grass asked.

"I did. It was a good life, sailing among the southern isles, trading and fighting now and again. Halbjorn and the rest are probably all dead, now. The Caribs and a hurricano struck us both at once. I was cast ashore on the Azteca coast. Some strange things happened there, but in time I escaped and made my way here." His pipe had gone cold and a woman brought him a fresh one.

"So few words for so much adventure!" Winter-Grass said with a laugh. "This tale will make for many evenings' entertainment. You will talk and I will translate. Everybody will come and listen."

"Will I have so much time then?"

"You may," she said, suddenly serious again. "If you make your story interesting enough, the people will not want to kill you until it is told. And by then, the real killer may have been found, or another Norseman, or something exciting may happen and they will have forgotten why they brought you in."

"Does your tale of my helping you escape weigh in my favor?"

"A little. They are glad to have me back, but a woman's

life counts for little here, and saving a life is not a feat highly thought of. It is sometimes considered to be"—she searched for a word—"bad form, or at least a thing of possible ill consequence for both saver and saved."

"Strange," Hring mused. He turned over in his mind several possible methods of escape. He rejected those that involved Winter-Grass's cooperation. It was little reward to someone to whom he owed much already. In any case, escape might not be necessary. All the mountain trappers and traders said that, to survive long on the great plains, it was necessary to have good relations with some of the ranging tribes. And who was more numerous or powerful than the Absaroka? The chance of becoming brother to such a people might be worth the risk of staying among them.

The bison cow raised her huge, shaggy head for a moment and the three hunters froze. The cow stood at the edge of the herd, cropping the tall grass. She snorted once and lowered her head again. The hunters sat their horses a hundred yards away. They made no attempt at hiding. The near-blind beasts were perfectly oblivious of them.

"Can you reach her from here?" Winter-Grass asked.

"Easily," Hring said. He stripped the case from his long yew bow. The third rider watched with interest. This was Stone-Hammer, Winter-Grass's brother. He was chief of the Fox warriors and a man of great prestige. Winter-Grass rode with bow and lance, for among the Absaroka it was common for women of adventurous spirit to hunt like the men. There were women warriors also, famed among the tribes.

Hring selected an arrow, fitted it to the string, and took aim. At this range, he scarcely had to allow for trajectory.

The bow had a pull of over a hundred pounds, more than twice that of the Absaroka bows. There was a snap of the released string, and the arrow sped to the cow's side, just behind the foreleg. She raised her head and looked about indignantly. The hunters watched patiently, waiting for her to collapse and die. The other bison took no notice.

"My brother wants to know how you can shoot so far. We have to ride down on the beasts and shoot from a few feet."

"That's because of the way you shoot," Hring said. "Your archers draw the bow by pinching the arrow between the thumb and forefinger. You are limited by the strength of your grip. We draw on the string, using three fingers and a shooting glove. This is much more powerful, and it is the strength of the arms, the shoulders, and back that counts. Also, we draw to the ear, instead of to the chest. This gives a longer draw." The warrior nodded as his sister translated. He said something.

"My brother says this is probably very wise, but ours is a better way to prove courage and skill. With us, the hunt is training for war."

"He may be right," Hring said. "It depends on how badly you want to eat."

By this time, the cow had collapsed to her foreknees and bloody foam streamed from her nostrils. The three rode forward at leisure, and the small herd pulled away from the dying cow. Stone-Hammer drove his lance into her heart, bringing a quick death. The hunters dismounted and the two men wrestled the carcass onto its side. Winter-Grass stripped off her fine doeskin shirt and stood in breechclout and moccasins while she opened up the cow's side and drew out the steaming liver. This she placed on the ground, atop a flap of fresh hide. She reached back into the carcass and pulled out the gallbladder. She then cut strips from the liver and sprinkled them with gall. The three then sat and ate the raw liver. By the time they were finished, a team of women and children from the village had caught up with them and were butchering the cow.

Every part of the beast would be used. Hring had learned that the plains rovers valued the liver above all else, then the tongue, brains, kidneys, the fat hump, and the hump ribs. Least valued of all was the lean meat, which was used mainly to make jerky, which was stored for winter or traded to other tribes. Some of the jerky would be pounded to shreds, mixed with dried fruit, and rendered hump fat, and stuffed into sections of gut for winter pemmican. Pemmican tasted awful but would keep a man alive and healthy through a long, lean winter.

That evening, a council was held, all important personages of the tribe sitting to decide Hring's fate. The debate was lengthy and vociferous, with much shouting and advising from the sidelines, for this was a form of entertainment which all enjoyed.

Stone-Hammer and Winter-Grass extolled Hring's virtues while the kinsmen of the slain men clamored for his blood. His great skill with the bow was lauded, along with his fine stature and magnificent red beard. His innocence of murder was also mentioned but was quickly dismissed as irrelevant. Eventually, a consensus was reached, and Winter-Grass turned to Hring.

"They have decided not to kill you," she said, beaming, "if my brother will adopt you into our clan. He has agreed to this. If, of course, it is agreeable to you."

"I shall count it an honor," Hring said.

There followed a complicated ceremony, which to Hring's relief did not include stringing him by his pectorals, although some blood was shed and he had to crawl through an arch formed by the spraddled legs of all the women of the clan. As he did this, the women groaned as though giving birth. When he reached the end of this prolonged birth canal, a medicine man breathed into his mouth and gave him his ceremonial name. He then had to pretend to be an infant for several hours, taking milk from the breasts of young mothers before graduating to solid food. This process was immensely enjoyed by the women, who vied with one another in devising indignities to inflict upon this warrior turned infant.

When all was finished, Hring was ceremoniously given his own weapons back. He was now a full-fledged warrior of the Absaroka.

Chapter 9

Hring sat outside his lodge, puffing his pipe. Life with the Absaroka agreed with him well, so far. They hunted and roamed and one day was much like another. The bison were beyond number, the antelope plentiful, the plains and sky as unbounded as the sea. There were only a few small clouds on Hring's horizon.

He still nursed his plan to return to Tenochtitlán and bring down its temples. But where were the men to be found? The tribes of the plain were brave and fierce, but totally without military organization. They were splendid light cavalry, but more would be needed to bring down such a people as the Tenocha. Besides, they had no greed for the gold and gems of the South.

The Norse had greed in plenty, but they were too few in number to pull off more than a raid in force. A truly massive Viking attack of the old style would result in fine plunder, but the Tenocha would quickly reorganize their forces after the first shock and drive the Norsemen back to the coast. No, a seaborne Norse attack could maintain itself for only two or three weeks before having to withdraw. He considered the possibility of a two-pronged attack, with the plainsmen striking from the North and the Norse landing simultaneously on the eastern coast. A good plan, but how to organize such disparate and individualistic peoples as the plainsmen and the Norsemen. In any case, such a force would only be able to disrupt the Tenocha Empire for a year or two at most, and result in much mutual slaughter while in the end accomplishing nothing. Bitterly, he thought that he must put away his dreams of conquest as the grandiose plans of inexperienced youth.

His other problem was far more pressing. The time had come, as he had known it would, when he arose in the night to seek out Winter-Grass's sleeping place. He discovered her fumbling her way among the lodges, looking for him. Laughing quietly, they fled hand in hand to his lodge and sank down on a pile of bison hides and trade blankets. At last, Hring could savor the rich contentment of the love of a woman with no blood on her hands, no sorcery in her heart. Winter-Grass was as natural as the elemental world she lived in, but far gentler. She slipped away before the sun rose, and after that came to him every night. In public she behaved toward him exactly as before, and this he took to be a sign of her natural modesty.

One night, she told him that she was taking precautions not to get with child.

"Why bother?" he asked, lying back in great contentment, an arm under her pale-brown tresses. "I'll just steal enough horses to make your uncle happy and we'll be wed. It's time we did. What do you say, eh?" He grinned, but that faded as he saw her face turn most serious.

"You do not know what you are saying, Hring. What we do here together is forbidden."

"Eh? I'd not thought your people were so severe in matters of fornication. All the more reason for us to be wed, then."

"You don't understand," she said. "This is not fornication. It is"—she searched her Norse vocabulary for a seldom-used word—"incest!"

"What are you talking about? We have no blood relation. Among my people, foster brothers and sisters often marry."

"It is not thus with us, Hring. When you were adopted into the clan, you were forbidden relations with every woman of the clan, including me. If we are found out, we will be tied on scaffolds and shot with arrows until we are dead."

Hring sank back on his bed. At length he said, "It is not in my wyrd to be fortunate with women."

All this went through his mind as he sat before his lodge. His attention was drawn by a commotion at the edge of the camp. A small party of Norsemen were entering on horseback. They were leading by halters two Norsemen who struggled along on foot. Hring recognized the Norse leader and leaped to his feet.

"Ragnar Hringsson!" he shouted, running up to the trapper.

Ragnar looked him over with puzzlement. "I think I know you, but where did we meet?"

"Dieter's train, six years ago in Bluemensgard."

"Young Hring!" He broke into a broad smile and took Hring's hand. "You've grown a man's beard since I saw you last. Decided to take my advice and come West, eh?"

"That I did, though not directly. This is not a safe place

for you, Ragnar. I've been adopted into the tribe, but there's bad blood between the Norse and the Absaroka."

"I mean to settle that presently," said Ragnar. "I have the killers here." He jerked a thumb at the two on halters. "They had too much drink one night and grew boastful. I'm not one to take up other's feuds, but just now it's important that there be no enmity on the plains."

"How is that?" Hring asked, puzzled. Enmity and blood feud were the norms of existence in every land Hring had ever seen.

"There will be a great meeting in one moon's time at Tosti's Post. All Norsemen and all the plains chiefs are to be there. It is of the greatest importance to all."

"Has this something to do with your whereabouts the last years?" Hring asked.

"I've been North," Ragnar said, "and there's trouble brewing there, trouble such as none of us has ever dreamed of."

Tosti's Holding was packed within the palisade, and the lodges of a dozen tribes spilled out over the surrounding plain. Ragnar was a man much respected by the tribes, and his summons was taken seriously. Besides, the summer hunt was over, and it was not yet time for winter trapping. As good a time as any to get together and trade, drink, and gamble on neutral ground.

Hring was glad to be among Norsemen again, and away for a while from the dangerous situation in the Absaroka camp. He would miss Winter-Grass, but that was better than being the cause of her death. Here there was strong ale, and a skald with the latest news from the East, no more than five or six months old. Sweyn of the Scyldings was sounding out his nobles, testing their will for a new war between Thorsheim and Treeland, but he was having no luck. Sitting next to Hring in the knot of men listening to the skald was Ragnar.

"This fellow's not half the skald that your friend in Dieter's train was. What was his name? Halvdan, that was it. What became of him?"

"Dead," Hring said, suddenly shot with pain at the memory.

"So, well," Ragnar said, "it comes to all of us, soon or late. Anyway, he was Odin's man, and such are not known for long life. He's in Valhalla now, singing for the heroes and taking rings from the High Seat."

"He didn't die with his sword in his hand," Hring said bitterly. Ragnar was silent for a while. At length, he spoke.

"Such a man as he dies only one of two ways. If he died on the tree, it is the same for him as death in battle."

"I see," said Hring, strangely comforted. Then Ragnar was getting to his feet to address the assembled throng. All had to fall silent, for Ragnar's mild voice did not carry well.

"All of you know me," he said, "and you all know that I have not been among you for some time. I've been North, and what I found there makes me fear for all of us. The Norsemen here know who the Mongols are." A surprised murmur swept the assembly. What could Ragnar be getting at? The Mongols belonged to another world. They quieted down so he could continue.

"For the Skraelings here, I'll explain. These Mongols are also a plains people who live on horseback. Generations ago a great leader rose among them whom they call the Great Khan. He forged the tribes into a single people, an army which swept all before it. They took the land of

Asia, which is greater than all the lands we know put together, their peoples as numerous as the stars of the sky. One by one, then in groups, the kingdoms of the East fell under their horses' hooves: the two kingdoms of China, Samarkand and the lands of the desert, the tremendous lands of India, of Arabia and Palestine and Egypt. Last of all fell Constantinople, and when that city fell, my own grandsire was among the Varangian Guard who died defending the throne. The cities we Norse reared along the Volga and others in the land of the Rus, Kiev and Novgorod, all were conquered. They stopped at the Danube, sparing western Christendom and Muslim Iberia because they seemed too poor to be worth the effort.'' He paused as his last words were translated for those who knew no Norse. His audience was mystified. These were the words of old stories to the Norse, and the names and places meant nothing at all to the Skraelings.

"For years now," he continued, "they have been at peace. Their last great campaign was against the island nation called Nippon a generation ago. Four great seaborn invasions failed, because of storms and battles fought to a standstill, for the warriors of Nippon are as fierce and skilled as the Mongols, and were fighting on their own land. The fifth campaign succeeded, and to allow the Nipponese to save their honor, the Great Khan of that time allowed them to send fighting men to reinforce his armies instead of paying tribute.

"Today, the Great Khan fears for his empire. His armies are without a land to conquer, and so they have fallen to fighting among themselves. To save his land, he has had to find a place to send his excess of idle warriors. He heard of the western lands of the New World, from Norse traders and from Asian seafarers who have been trading for furs among the tribes of the western coast. He knows that this is steppe country, like the native lands of the Mongols, rich in grass for their herds.

"And so he has built a great armada to transport an army. They are here. I have been living among them for the last two years, as they build up their strength for a sweep to the South."

The meeting broke into a buzz of conversation. Ragnar continued when all was quiet. He wanted to send a delegation to the Mongol army, made up of Norsemen and chiefs from all the plains tribes to come to some kind of understanding with the Mongols and avoid a terrible slaughter, for once the Mongols took up war against a people, they usually pursued it until that people no longer existed. On the other hand, they were generally most generous and evenhanded with those who would acknowledge their overlordship and pay a token tribute, usually in the form of young men to fight as irregulars in their army, which consisted solely of cavalry.

Many of the plains chiefs lost interest when they learned that the Mongol army was now encamped three months' journey to the north, awaiting the arrival of the last shipment of horses from Asia. They could not imagine anything so distant to be a threat.

"How can I convince them?" Ragnar fumed among his fellow Norsemen. "These Mongols are warriors beyond our imagining. They can cover twice that distance in a single summer's campaigning."

"I think you are drawing the long bow, Ragnar," said Tosti. "Surely these horsemen are not as fearsome as all that. We're all warriors here. We've fought the tribes, and some of us have been a-viking among the southern isles. Hring over there has even fought in the Azteca army. Why are these Mongols so much to fear?'' Many nodded at these words.

"Because they don't fight as a tribe, or as an army, but as a nation on horseback. They campaign at a dead gallop and nothing slows them down. When they shoot, their arrows fall in clouds, and they mass and maneuver like pieces on a chessboard. Their bows are made of horn and wood and sinew and our yew bows are children's toys by comparison. Don't you see, these are the people who ground Miklagaard to powder; do you think we can fight them?

"Unless an understanding is reached, the plains tribes will try war on them. They won't be able to help themselves when they see the mass of horses the Mongols bring. There will be raids, then battles, then extermination.'' He looked around at the somber faces. "We Norse free traders and trappers have made a fine life for ourselves out here, the finest in the world. I don't want to lose it. Who will come with me?'' One by one, men stood to volunteer. Hring was among them.

They set out as the sun rose, fifty Norsemen and about the same number of Skraelings, representatives of the most important plains tribes. It was doubtful, though, that many of the Skraelings would see the journey out to its end. Many would turn back when the snows set in, others because they would feel insulted by members of rival tribes in the expedition.

Hring rode up to Ragnar. "Do you speak the Mongol tongue, Ragnar?''

"Passably. At least as well as most of their army speak it. Not many of them are true Mongols. They come from many nations, but the Mongol is their common language.''

"I've a ready tongue," Hring said. "In the last years I've learned Nahuatl and Absaroka. We're in for a long journey. Will you teach me Mongol?"

"Gladly. It will help pass the time, and we'll need as many negotiators as we can get. I wish some of these others had your keenness. I think most of them came along just for the adventure."

"I have a plan, Ragnar," Hring said, choosing his words carefully. "I won't tell you what it is yet, you know that's bad luck, but if it works as I have planned, we will not only save the plains for ourselves but pull off the greatest feat since Hrolf took Paris."

"Brave words!" said Ragnar, laughing and slapping his saddle. "You're a rare one, Hring, I knew it when I first saw you in Bluemensgard. It's as if you were marked by the gods for great things."

"Not by my own choice," Hring said, rubbing his brow.

Chapter 10

The camp was well sheltered, cupped within high bluffs which surrounded it on three sides. They had been sheltering for three days from a bitter northeast wind that bore little snow with it, but blew what it had with enough force to strip the hide off a man. The men sat huddled around several tiny fires that were wholly inadequate to the task of keeping them warm in such weather, but they were all hard men, and made no complaint. There were not so many, now, as had set out.

Many of the Skraelings had lost their enthusiasm, or had fallen out with each other or with the Norsemen, and now there were only a score left. There had also been attrition among the Norsemen. Gunnar had had to turn back after being bitten by the serpent whose dry chuckle was known as Loki's Laugh, and a companion was required to accompany him. Three brothers named Bjornson had discovered that the band contained a pair of brothers named Hanson, and between the two families lay an ancient blood feud, which they proceeded to carry out by a holmgang on a small river island. Hazel wands were found for staking out the ground and the five had at each other in matched pairs until only one Bjornson and one Hanson were left alive, neither in any condition to continue the journey. A man related to neither stayed behind to nurse them back to health, at which time both swore they would finish the fight.

Ragnar shook his head over such wastefulness, but he knew well that no matter on earth took precedence over vengeance and blood feud. Such quarrels as arose on the trail he could settle as leader, but how could he put right a dispute between men's grandfathers? At all counts, feud and misadventure had reduced the Norse ranks to no more than thirty, and several of these had frostbitten fingers and toes.

Four men sat about a twig fire rubbing their hands and holding them up to the feeble heat. They were Ragnar and Hring. Feng the horse doctor, and Knut, the skald who had been singing at Tosti's Holding.

"So you are the Hring who fought the berserker at Mjolnir Sound?" Knut was saying. "How is it that we've been traveling together for months and I've not heard this? The story was all over Thorsheim, though no one dared sing of it before King Sweyn. That must have been a fight to see!"

"It was a fight," Hring shrugged. "No doubt it grew in the telling. Now, you should have seen Ragnar here when Dieter's train was ambushed in Bluemensgard. That was a real—" Hring fell silent as Ragnar raised his hand, his nose high and sniffing the breeze.

"Is Sigurd on watch yet?" Ragnar asked quietly.

"I saw him go out to relieve Gunther a little while past," Feng said.

"Good. Sigurd's a steady man and will do nothing ill considered."

"Trouble?" Hring said, loosening his sax in its scabbard.

"Not if we comport ourselves mildly." He raised his voice and addressed the company: "All of you listen! We have visitors, but they'll do us no harm if you keep your hands away from your weapons." He then called out some words in a tongue which Hring now knew to be Mongol and to mean "Come in peace."

A few moments later, a party of mounted men came into the weak firelight, moving as silently as the Dineh of the South. Before them walked the Norseman Sigurd.

"They were ten paces from me before I saw them, Ragnar," Sigurd said. "Ten of them had their bows at full draw. They'd have skewered me if I took a deep breath."

"You did well, Sigurd. A shout from you might have killed us all." He waited as one of the horsemen came forward. Hring watched the newcomers with wary interest. They were small men, mounted on shaggy ponies. Many held strong bows in their hands and some wore helmets and bits of armor and most had curved sabers slung across their backs. The prevalent dress was a long, thickly padded coat and a furry hat which closely muffled their faces, making their features difficult to discern. The man who rode forward was more richly dressed than the others. He wore a long coat of light, silvered mail over his padded garment, and he wore a spired and fluted helmet with mail neck guard. His saber had a jeweled handle and was on a decorated waist belt. Behind him rode a man with a banner.

"I am Kutan the Kipchak, hundred leader in the tuman

of Lord Ashikaga. Who are you and what is your destination?''

''I am Ragnar and this is Hring. We represent the Norse free traders and trappers, and with us are representatives of the plains to the south. We come on an embassy to your Khan to avoid bloodshed between our peoples.''

The Kipchak laughed shrilly. ''I have always heard that you yellow-hairs are fond of bloodshed.''

''Within reason,'' Ragnar said. ''Among ourselves, and with enemies carefully chosen. Raiding and feuding are our heritage, but this business of war to the death between nations is a sorry thing, and no one does well out of it.''

''We've done quite well with it,'' the Kipchak said.

''How many Kipchaks are there now, since they fought the Mongols?''

''The weak die,'' Kutan said, ''as heaven wishes. But, I take your point. Yes, you are doing the wise thing. Khan Bogotai will be pleased to see you. The Kha-Khan has forbidden us to molest people who make him obeisance and pay their tribute. We will abide here tonight and travel to my lord's camp at first light. This patrol is due to return at any rate; we may as well travel together.''

''How far is the camp?'' Ragnar asked.

''Ten days for us. Twenty traveling at your rate.''

''Twenty days' ride!'' Hring said. ''You call that a patrol?''

''Ah, you speak the tongue too.'' He dismounted and a man began to unsaddle his horse. ''Young redbeard, I have been on patrols in the Caucasus that separated us from the main body of our troops for six months. In Egypt, I took part in a reconnaissance that lasted two years and took us to Gibraltar before we turned back. This was not a campaign, mind you, that was the next year. Do not confuse the kind of brawling you call warfare with what we practice." He sat down cross-legged at the fire and a man brought him a bowl of congealed white paste which he forked into his mouth with two fingers. The Norsemen sat also, and Hring passed Kutan a skin of sour wine. The Kipchak took a drink and screwed up his face in disgust. He shouted and one of his men brought a hide bottle. Kutan washed out his mouth with its contents and passed it to Hring. "Here. This is kumiss, a man's drink. No wonder you people are so pale, drinking that sour stuff."

Hring threw back his head and took a long swallow. He choked and his face grew purple. It was the vilest, most nauseating liquid that had ever passed his teeth.

"What is that stuff?" he asked in Norse, when he was again master of his throat.

"Fermented milk of mares," Ragnar said blandly. "Quite palatable when it's properly made. Of course, men in a mobile camp have neither the leisure nor the facilities to make it as it should be made."

As the two parties rode side by side, the Norse and Skraeling party nervous and wary, the Mongols unconcerned, Hring's respect for the small but powerful horsemen grew. They rode tirelessly, able to live for days on their wretched gruel and kumiss, rations that would have left a Norseman on his back and gasping with starvation. They never seemed to go to sleep on guard duty, something unique in Hring's experience. Once he saw a Mongol bowman bring down an antelope from a range he would not have believed possible. Once Kutan allowed Hring to try drawing his own bow of laminated horn and sinew. With three fingers on the string, Hring strained to bring the bow to full draw, but the string cut so cruelly into his fingers that he had to leave off before his string hand touched his ear.

"We do not draw with the fingers," Kutan said. "We use the thumb ring and lock the thumb with the forefinger." None of the Mongols' thumb rings would fit Hring's big hand, so he wrapped a piece of stiff rawhide around his thumb and tried again. With the ring bearing the pinch of the bowstring, he was able to make a full draw, but it was a strain. He judged the pull at about two hundred pounds. He shook his head as he handed the bow back. Mongol archery surpassed the Norse by the same margin that the Norse surpassed the Skraeling.

"The Lord Ashikaga," Ragnar asked one afternoon as he and Hring rode along with Kutan. "His name does not sound Mongol. Where does he hail from?"

"My lord is Nipponese," Kutan answered. "Khan Bogotai favors warriors from those islands. They are adequate bowmen, not as good with horses as we men of the steppe, but for close fighting there is nothing like them under heaven. Their swords and lances are so fine that demons must make them. Their warriors are called bushi and my lord is the greatest among them. His sword splits lightning in twain and his horse's hoofs shake the earth."

"If this is what your tuman commander is like," said Hring, "then what of Khan Bogotai?"

"Him I don't even like to talk about," said the Kipchak.

The Mongol camp was an immense sprawl of odd, domed tents snaking along a river bottom. Everywhere there were horses and men riding them. Above some of the tents towered banners and standards. As Kutan's patrol was spotted, a party of horsemen rode from the camp to meet them.

Hring saw quickly that these were men of a different breed from the Mongols. Instead of the drab, padded overcoats worn by the steppe men, they wore quilted garments of silk tailored closely to their bodies. Over this they wore odd-looking armor of innumerable small splints laced tightly together with silk cord. On some, there was so much lacing that the metal could scarcely be seen at all. Their helms were low and round, knobbed all over with rivets, and with wide-spreading neck guards of rows of the laced splints. Big, square plates hung from their shoulders and all were heavily armed. Each had a longbow cased behind his shoulder, and each wore a long curved sword with a handle long enough for two hands, as well as a short dagger. Besides these, most carried spears, and many of these had long cutting blades curved at the tip. The first impression, though, was not of the alien quality of their dress, but of its color. The silks were dyed in many colors and patterns, the metal splints of the armor were all lacquered in contrasting hues, the silk cords lacing the armor worked into startling patterns. The sword scabbards and bow cases were likewise lacquered. In their way, Hring found these men to be as colorful as Tenocha cavalry.

"Will these be your bushi, then?" he asked Kutan.

"That they are. Be careful of your manners with them. They are most touchy about their honor, and see insults where no man of another nation can." Then the new horsemen were among them and Kutan was chattering with their leader, speaking Mongol too fast for Hring to follow.

They were led down into the camp, where Hring studied with interest the round felt tents. He could see no pegs or tie ropes. And no man seemed to walk. Sometimes a man would emerge from his tent, leap on a horse tethered there, ride to a tent twenty feet away, dismount, and go inside.

They rode through the camp for more than two hours before reaching a compound surrounded by a high curtain erected as a windbreak. Above this towered the highest standard yet; a pole with crosspieces from which dangled six white horsetails.

The leader of the bushi turned to Hring and Ragnar.

"You two dismount and come inside. The rest of your men will be taken to a campsite." He chopped out the words in short, guttural, growling barks that were difficult to understand. Ragnar gave instructions to Feng and he and Hring handed their reins to a handler squatting outside the windbreak.

Inside, they were disappointed to find only another domed tent, just like all the others. Beside it, though, stood a man different from all the others they had seen. He was taller than the other Asians, and he was handing a hawk to an attendant. He paid them no attention. His quilted silk garments were black, and the close-fitting armor he wore was lacquered black. He wore a half mask covering his brow and cheeks, and this was black, too. His helm was without the wide neck guard the others wore, and instead had a veil of small hexagonal plates connected by mail. His sword was longer than most, its scabbard, guard, and handle all lacquered black. Some small silver ornaments in the sword handle were the only touches of color about the man. A bushi began helping him out of his armor and for the first time he took notice of the newcomers.

"Who are these, Kutan?"

"An embassy from the South, Khan." Kutan, who had been on his knees with his forehead on the ground, looked up and saw that Hring and Ragnar were still standing. "Bow, you ignorant barbarians! This is a mighty khan!" The two Norsemen took no notice. Two bushi lounging nearby were on their feet with swords out so quickly that it seemed like some conjurer's trick. Ashikaga barked an order and they resheathed.

"No need," he said. "This is an embassy, and I am but a humble soldier. I suggest, though, that you yellowhairs comport yourselves differently should you meet Khan Bogotai." The bushi took Ashikaga's helm and mask. His face was thin, unlike the round countenances of the steppe men, and he had long mustaches. His hair was long and gathered on top into a knot which the bushi unbound so that the shiny black hair dropped into a long tail between his shoulder blades. He stripped off his cuirass with its hanging skirt of square plates and now he was wearing only his skin guards and a pair of armored sleeves atop his padded silk arming suit. The sleeves were of mail worked in odd patterns and covered only the outside of the arms.

An attendant brought cups of fizzy white liquid and gave them to the Norsemen. Hring braced himself and drank bravely. To his relief, it was not kumiss, but some kind of wine.

Ashikaga signaled for them to follow him into his tent. Hring and Ragnar sat next to the central fire while the Khan listened to Kutan's detailed account of his patrol. Servants brought food: strips of grilled meat, bowls of hot, spicy soup and cakes of cold rice with a dark, salty sauce to dip them in.

"I'm Bakhu," said a servant who offered a platter. "I've been assigned to serve you. But don't think because of that that I'm a servant. I'm a warrior. There was no ship space for proper servants so us low-rankers got pressed into service. I'm a horseman of the Merkits. Don't be afraid of those white cakes. They're rice. That's a grain the Chinese and Nipponese raise. It's not bad once you get used to it.''

"I've had it in Bluemensgard," Hring said. "That is far to the southeast of here, on the coast. The people there are Moors and they raise rice, but it doesn't stick together like this.''

"Dip it in the shoyu," Bakhu said. "Otherwise, it has no taste. I know about the Moors. They're Muslims. We have lots of Muslims in the army. Buddhists too, and a few Christians. What are you?''

"We worship Thor," said Ragnar, "and Odin, and other gods of our folk. We don't bow down and crawl, though. We ask our gods for help and guidance but they are not our masters.''

"That's a good way to be," Bakhu said, sitting down cross-legged and helping himself to one of the platters he had brought. "Now, we Merkits worship the Everlasting Sky, except for a few who have become Muslim or Christian, and the Sky is not a demanding master, except that he sometimes sends lightning to kill you. But I have noticed that his lightning kills indiscriminately, without regard to religion or behavior, so it makes little sense to exert oneself in devotion.''

"There is wisdom in that," Ragnar said.

Ashikaga finished hearing Kutan's report and signaled the Norsemen to sit nearer to him.

"Now tell me," he began, "just who you are and whom you represent.''

Ragnar started, explaining the nature and extent of Norse trade and exploration among the mountains and plains of the West, of the nature of the plains tribes and their relations with the Norsemen and each other.

"This feuding and bickering among the little tribes must

stop," Ashikaga said. "They may not know it yet, but they are now living within the Khanate of the White Horde, subjects of the Kha-Khan, as are all under heaven. From now on, the only enemies they are permitted will be the enemies of the Kha-Khan."

"That may not be a simple matter to accomplish, Lord," Hring said.

"It will be most simple," Ashikaga said. "They will obey or they will be annihilated." The words were spoken mildly, but Hring had no doubt in his mind that the Nipponese Khan meant every syllable. He knew, likewise, that there was nothing in the world that he could do to stop this from happening. These Mongols were a force of nature, like some great river, as powerful, destructive, and unstoppable. While Ragnar tried to argue Ashikaga around to a peaceable dealing with the Norse and Skraeling inhabitants of mountain and plain, Hring pondered the plan he had been turning over in his mind since first hearing of the new invasion. A river might not be stopped, but it could be diverted.

"Great Khan," Hring said when Ragnar had run out of wind, "there is something I would like to show you."

"What might that be?"

"Gifts for your leader, the Khan Bogotai."

"Young man," said Ashikaga, smiling thinly, "the Khan Bogotai has had little training as a courtier, but he is of the highest royal blood, of the Altun, the family of Temujin himself. He will not scorn gifts from an embassy, but he is accustomed to receiving far more than you mountain traders could possibly have brought on this hasty mission. I suggest you wait until a more auspicious time, when you are better prepared. The pick of the furs from next year's trapping might be adequate. The Chinese especially prize fine furs, and the Khan's more highly placed royal kin are practically Chinese these days."

"What I have brought," Hring said, picking his limited Mongol words carefully, "is more valuable than furs. I think you and your Khan will appreciate both their value and their"—he searched his vocabulary for a word meaning "implications" but found none—"what they signify."

"You intrigue me," Ashikaga said. "By all means, bring in your gifts." Hring instructed Bakhu to bring in the bundles loaded on his packhorse. The Merkit returned, waddling under the unaccustomed weight of the load.

"What have you got in here?" he demanded. "If it's gold you're a fool to be out trapping in the mountains. This weight in gold coins would buy a small Chinese city."

"Peace, Merkit," Ashikaga said. "If you can't hold your tongue, I'll send you to wait on my bushi."

"First," Hring said, "let me ask you; what do you know of the empire of the people called the Azteca, or Tenocha?"

"Our sources have said that such a kingdom or empire lies far to the south. A few Chinese traders who have made their way that far south say that it is very rich. We've heard similar tales from some Iberian Moors." He shrugged. "Such tales are common. The farther from the unknown land, the richer the kingdom."

"That is very true," Bakhu broke in. "I was once sent on an expedition to a kingdom on the coast of southeast Africa. There was supposed to be a fabulous kingdom there, with roofs plated in gold. All we found was a big city of mud. The women were ugly and smelled foul."

"Merkit," Ashikaga growled, "what did I tell you?" Bakhu looked abashed. "Besides," the Khan said, "you are lying. That was in your father's time."

"Well, my father told me about it," Bakhu muttered, and the Norsemen struggled to keep their countenances properly solemn, as befitted ambassadors.

"Your tales are vague," Hring said, "because the Tenocha do not allow foreigners within their empire except under very special circumstances. The traders see only a few coastal ports, and they are poor things compared with the cities of the interior. These are rich beyond your imagining."

"My friend," Ashikaga said, "I have seen Kamakura, and Peking, and Constantinople. If you had seen them, you would not put such boundaries on my imagination."

Carefully Hring untied and drew the wrappings back from the first bundle. From it he took his great helmet of the Order of Eagle Knights, covered with gold and worked with precious stones. Next he unrolled his suit of golden scales. The weak winter sunlight streamed through the smoke hole in the roof and was shattered by the precious metal into thousands of yellow spots that bespattered the walls of the tent.

Bakhu sucked in a deep breath. Ashikaga was silent, but his eyes rounded slightly. "Is there more?" he asked without expression. Hring opened another bundle and spread out his magnificent cloak of hummingbird feathers. In the silence, Ragnar spoke up.

"It has been noted, Hring, that you never seemed greatly concerned whether you got a good price for your furs."

"Merkit," Ashikaga said, "send my courtesies to the Great Khan and say that I urgently invite him to my ger on a matter most secret and important. And, Merkit"—Ashikaga turned a look as hard as stone upon Bakhu—"if any smallest word of what you've seen leaks into the camp, I'll have every inch of skin off your carcass while you cook over a slow fire.''

"As the Khan wishes," said Bakhu, bowing to the ground. For once chastened, he darted from the tent with a look compounded oddly of fear and exultation.

"We'll say no more of this until the Great Khan arrives. When he does, do not be as proud as you were with me. I am a patient and tolerant man. Bogotai is not. You will bow when he enters. All the way to the ground, and if that is not low enough to suit him, I suggest that you eat earth until the angle of your necks is satisfactory." The Norsemen said nothing, but sat and sipped their wine, nibbling at an occasional rice cake or strip of grilled meat. Ashikaga left the tent and went out to confer with his bushi. There was a flurry of activity and Hring could see through the doorway that a cordon of Nipponese warriors was forming around the tent, with bows in their hands and arrows on string.

"You are doing well," Ragnar said. "There is no wisdom in showing excessive humility to these people." He chuckled shortly. "I thought I would foul my breeches when you showed that golden byrnie. No wonder you kept those packs hidden! There aren't three Norsemen in the mountains who wouldn't kill you for what's in them, and I'm not sure that I'm one of the three." He nodded approvingly. "Your plan's a good one, if it's what I have in my mind. Thor's balls! What chief with an army would fight a pack of starveling savages or yellow-haired traders for some grazing land for sheep when there's wealth like this for the taking?" Hring nodded and loaded his pipe. Before it was burning well, there was a commotion outside and the Bushi drew their bows, then relaxed them when they saw who had arrived.

From the midst of a group of horsemen which had come riding through the windbreak, one dismounted. Ashikaga drew close to the man, dropped to his knees, and bowed until his forehead touched the ground. The other said something and the Nipponese rose and followed his master into the tent. As they came inside, Hring and Ragnar rose to their feet. The two Asians waited for a moment, staring at them.

"Bow," Ashikaga said levelly.

"We greet the Great Khan Bogotai," Ragnar said.

"Bow!" Ashikaga barked.

"It is not our custom, lord," said Hring. Ashikaga's sword was out swifter than the tongue of an adder. Bogotai said nothing, but walked forward until he was examining the two Norsemen from a few inches away. Hring was expressionless under his gaze, but his bowels quaked, for he knew that he was in the presence of one of the world's great killers.

The Khan Bogotai was shorter than Ashikaga, but much bulkier in the chest and shoulders. He wore the padded coat of the steppes, but his was made of fine red silk. From a richly jeweled belt hung a dagger which was his only visible weapon. Its hilt was of solid jade. Bogotai's face was of the type Hring had come to expect of the Mongols: round, flat, with a short, upturned nose and tilted eyes, the skin the color of tanned leather from a lifetime in the sun and wind. Unlike his followers, his hair was not coarse and black, but fine and brown with reddish highlights. His eyes were a disturbing pale green. It was not his appearance which made him so fearsome, though. Rather it was an aura, bred of generations of conquerors for whom the destruction of cities and their inhabitants was a matter of less importance than buying a new horse. The man smelled of death and havoc.

"I could have you and all your followers put to death with torments that your worst nightmares could not prepare you for." Begotai's voice was low and hoarse.

"That may be, lord," Ragnar said, "but it would not change our custom." Bogotai stared a few moments longer, then burst into a laugh that would have sounded raucous coming from a hyena.

"By the Everlasting Sky!" he shouted. "They did not lie who said that these lands breed some men! Come, Ashikaga, let's allow them to live a little longer and show me these wonders they have brought." Repressing a sigh of relief, Hring drew a blanket back to display the golden armor and feather cloak.

Bogotai sat and picked up the helmet. He examined it carefully. Next he took the armor, then he fingered the fabulous cloak. All the while, the green eyes glittered with a light that was almost beatific. He looked at Ashikaga and smiled. At last he put the things away and sat back with a deep sigh. Ashikaga brought his Khan a jug of kumiss and Bogotai drank.

"How did you get these?" he said at last. "You must have murdered the Emperor for them!"

"I was, for a while, a high officer of the Eagle warriors," Hring said. "This is the uniform of such an officer. There are thousands like it in the Empire."

Bogotai smiled almost gently. "Tell me about it," he said. "Tell me everything."

It had grown dark outside by the time Hring finished his recitation. A bronze brazier of burning charcoal was brought into the tent, and warm furs for those inside. Bogotai rocked back and forth slightly, with the look of a man whose greatest wish has been realized.

"Ashikaga," Bogotai said softly, "all of my life, I have cursed the fate that had me born so late." His eyes glowed eerily in the red light from the brazier. "All the great conquests were over. China fell to the Ancestor. Samarkand, Isfahan, Baghdad, to succeeding generations, India to his great-grandsons, finally, Egypt in my grandfather's day. Since then, nothing worth a khan's trouble. You and I have spent our lives on petty campaigns, putting down rebellions of petty chieftains, regaining provinces that broke away a generation or two ago." Ashikaga grunted assent.

"When I was given this command by the Kha-Khan, to take a new land that was vast but empty, to conquer to his greater glory a new pasture for sheep and goats, I confess that the unthinkable thought of rebellion crossed my mind. But I am a khan of the Mongols, and one of the Altun, and I obeyed.

"Now, at last, I am to be rewarded. There is another great and wealthy empire to conquer for the Kha-Khan." He bent a blood-freezing glare upon the Norsemen. "As Mongols, it offends us to see so many little kinglets. There is one sun in heaven, and one Kha-Khan on earth."

Hring was surprised to hear the Great Speaker of the Tenocha referred to as a kinglet, but he let it pass. Bogotai lurched to his feet and waved a hand toward the two Norsemen.

"Give these men a ger, and presents befitting ambassadors. Their embassy has pleased me greatly. This is a great day for us and we shall owe them much before this is over. If, that is," he qualified, with a glare at Hring, "this young man's information proves accurate." He swept from the tent, and his going was a relief as great as the removal of the burning iron to a man under torture.

"By the goddess of the sun," Ashikaga swore, when the hoofbeats of Bogotai's horse had faded, "but you are the most foolish and fortunate men under heaven! The Great Khan kills men as others kill fleas, and you refuse to bow to him! For such insolence from an embassy, he has been known to destroy the nations that sent them!"

"It is not—" Ragnar began.

"I know!" Ashikaga barked. "It is not your custom! Well, let me advise you, your customs are luxuries for which you may soon pay with your lives. Bogotai has never been known for his forbearance. This day you have brought him the only thing that could ever have made him forget his wrath. By all the big and little gods, a real nation to take at last!" Ashikaga grinned and clapped his hands in a most unusual display of glee.

"Now," he said, solemn again, "go you to where your men are camped. The weather is good tonight, you can sleep in the open. In the morning I will find gers for you all, and you will receive your presents." He remained sitting, staring into the brazier, as Bakhu came in and led the two Norsemen away.

It was a short ride to where the Norsemen and Skraelings were camped, with their beasts picketed nearby. They had been given plentiful firewood and food and most sat near the warming fires in great contentment. Some had already developed a taste, or at least a tolerance, for kumiss. Feng caught sight of the two as they walked from where they had tied their horses.

"Hoy there, Ragnar, Hring! How did you make out with the yellow buggers?"

"I think," Ragnar said, sitting and stuffing leaf in his pipe, "that they are open-minded enough to see things in the light of reason."

Chapter 11

Hring watched with absorption as his new ger, as the domed tents were called, was raised. A team of men unfolded a collapsing lattice of wood and bent it into a circle, then they laid in the roof poles which radiated from a central structure which formed the smoke hole. Walls and roof of felt were drawn over the framework and the ger was inhabitable. The whole process had taken no more than three quarters of an hour.

Hring walked inside and looked around. "No fastening to the ground," he noted. "This thing will blow over in the first strong wind."

"They stay fast to the earth no matter how the wind blows," said Ragnar. "The stronger the wind, the tighter they grip the ground. It's something to do with the shape, they told me, in the camp where I stayed the last few winters."

"Where was that?" Hring asked.

"With a tribe called Petchenegs, picketed a few days' ride west of here, under a subchief." He chuckled. "Gods, when I first saw their camp, I thought I'd stumbled on the main horde. The whole camp wouldn't have crowded one of the horse pens they have here."

A file of Mongols entered the ger and began piling the presents on the earth floor: swords, bows and full quivers, leather armor, saddles, skins of wine and kumiss, furs for bedding, hangings to divide the ger at need into sections, clothing both rich and warm, cups, plates, and pots, cakes of dried and powdered milk, sacks of dried fruit, bales of rice, and, last of all, two fine hawks on perches. Bakhu proudly directed the placement and storing of these items.

"We'll need twenty horses to move all this!" Hring said.

"You have each received twenty-five horses," Bakhu said.

"These Mongols value us more than I'd thought," Hring said. He knew that the horde was still short of the horses they needed for full campaigning strength. They believed in mobility, and each lowest trooper needed five mounts at a minimum. Ten was better. A Mongol army on the march did not look like an army; it looked like a gigantic herd of horses with mounted men riding on the outskirts.

A man on horseback galloped to the ger and pulled his horse up in a cloud of dust and grit. He flung himself down and strode into the tent.

"Lords, the Khan Bogotai wishes you to attend a conference in his enclosure this evening at sundown."

"We'll be there," Ragnar said. To Hring, he said: "The Khan seems to be wasting no time."

"He never wastes time," said Bakhu, ready as ever

with information. "He now has a great campaign to plan, instead of a simple migration of peoples. From now on, all will be conferences, drills, planning sessions, inspections, and the like. It is all most tiring, but necessary to a properly run conquest. The Great Khan Bogotai allows no slackness on a campaign, which cannot be said of some leaders these days, who have fallen away from the traditions of our ancestors and take jewelry and women and such with them when they go to war."

"It is true," Hring said, "these Mongols are organized as tightly as Jomsvikings."

"Are those a steppe people?" Bakhu asked. Hring threw a sheepskin at him.

There were many officers of high rank present, wearing the garb of various nations. No more than a third were plainly Mongols. Of whatever nation, though, they all shared one thing in common: they all looked tough enough to eat horseshoes and spit nails. Hring surveyed them. Under Bakhu's guidance, he was learning to pick out the small details of attire which distinguished the various peoples: Mongols, Merkits, Kipchaks, and Tatars from the central steppe, Manchu and Chinese in their nail-studded silk coats, Koreans from the peninsula north of Nippon. From farther west were Alans, Bulgars, and Petchenegs. There were Avars there who were not Asiatic: tall, handsome hawk-faced men in long coats and towering fur hats. There were the Nipponese in their colorful garb. All walked with the rolling gait of men who lived their lives on horseback. All had the bulky shoulders of master bowmen.

The men sat in a circle around the periphery of Bogotai's huge ger. In the center of the carpeted floor rested Hring's gifts. Many of the men were grinning, and there was abundant evidence of high spirits, not all of it attributable to the sacks of wine and kumiss that were being passed from hand to hand.

"My men have examined your gifts, Norseman," Bogotai said, from where he sat on a slightly raised dais with a golden backrest. "I've told them something of your story. Now they wish to question you. All you see here are tuman commanders or higher. Answer them as you would answer me."

The questioning began without preamble.

"How do these Tenocha fight?" from an Alan.

"Mostly on foot; tribal levies from among the subject peoples are the bulk of the army. There is a core of heavy cavalry led by the knights of the various orders. They use lances and long, slashing swords. Most of the tribesmen who aren't Tenocha aren't allowed iron weapons. They fight with bow and sling, javelin and hatchet. Some use macuahuitl, which are like clubs or paddles edged with flint or obsidian." He saw many contemptuous smiles. "They are more effective than you might think."

"Horse archers?" snapped a Mongol.

"Very few. Their archery is primitive. Some of the coastal people use very powerful crossbows, for hunting jaguar in the southern highlands, but they are not permitted to make war. You must remember, the Tenocha are not accustomed to killing in war. They try to take prisoners that they can sacrifice to their gods."

There was much merriment at these words.

"How are their cities fortified?" asked a Chinese.

"There are no city walls," Hring said. "Just a few small forts along the northern border, against the raiding Dineh."

"No walls?" said a Bulgar, incredulous. "Cities as rich as you describe have no walls to defend them?"

"They have never fought as we of the Old World do, with armies marching to seize cities and plunder. When the Tenocha wish to make war on another state, they agree on a battlefield and fight until one side or the other prevails. Then, the losing side pays tribute in men and women and treasure. A small Tenocha garrison is quartered in the conquered territory to remind the losers who is master now and to collect taxes. Otherwise, life remains much as always in the subject state. They keep their language, their customs and gods.

"But the city of Tenochtitlán will be no easy prize to take. It is on a man-made island in the center of a great lake. It can be reached only by three narrow causeways, easily defended against men on horseback."

Bogotai looked toward an elderly Chinese. "Liu Chi, you are a siege engineer. How might we take such a city?"

"No use to try tunneling such a lake," Liu Chi said. "If we cannot force the causeways, we may have to organize work gangs from the natives to fill the lake with earth and Stone."

Hring stared at the Chinese. These were not men who shrank from large tasks. "Lord, may I make a suggestion?"

"Speak."

"Should the Tenocha be struck from the north by an enemy they never suspected even the existence of, the effect would be devastating. It might be far more so if they should at the same time be engaged against an enemy landing on their east coast."

"Continue," Bogotai said.

"Khan, your people are not alone in feeling that the days

of great raiding and conquest are past. Once my people were the terror of Europe. The longships raided in England, Spain, France, even North Africa and Italy. To the east, trading and settling expeditions pressed down the Dnieper and Volga and founded the nation of the Rus.''

"I have heard some of this," Bogotai commented.

"Since we settled the coast of the new land, men form Viking expeditions of the old type, but these are only shadows of the great raids of four and five hundred years ago. They raid among the southern isles. The tribes there are not wealthy and they fight hard. Sometimes they take coastal towns that do not enjoy sufficient protection from the Tenocha. Never do more than two or three ships at a time go on these outings, and they are forced to trade when resistance seems too fierce.

"If I sent word that the loot of the Azteca Empire was there for the taking, hundreds of ships would descend upon the eastern coast, ravaging and disrupting, forcing the Great Speaker to send the bulk of his army there to repel the invasion. Also, the tribes and nations of that coast are the most numerous peoples of the empire, and they hate the Tenocha. Most would readily rebel and side with the Norsemen.''

"We have never needed help in winning a war!" snorted a Mongol.

"Still," Bogotai said, "it is not the Kha-Khan's policy to refuse an offer of alliance, freely given. How long would you need to organize this invasion, Norseman?''

"My companion Ragnar could head back toward Thorsheim immediately. He travels fast through any weather, and he can be in Thorsheim by spring. If he spends the spring and summer traveling through Thorsheim and raising men, he can lead the sea force early in the next spring.

The winter can be spent building ships and laying in arms and supplies.

"Also, the word will travel north quickly. The urge to raid is no less strong in Treeland than in Thorsheim."

"Is this Treeland not a Christian land?" queried Bogotai.

"For an enterprise of this size, the two lands would make common cause, as they did nearly two centuries ago, when the King of Norway sent a war fleet to assert his suzerainty over the new lands."

"Prospect of rich takings will often unite old enemies," said a Turk sardonically.

"United until it is time to share out the plunder, anyhow," said Ashikaga.

"That may be," said Hring. "It is true that the Norsemen will not form a force as united as your army. I believe that Ragnar will be able to keep command of the greater part of the raiding force. King Sweyn of Thorsheim will try to seize control, but he enjoys little loyalty from his liege men."

"What do yellowhairs know of loyalty anyway?" said Ashikaga, but Bogotai frowned at him and said: "Go on."

"Some petty chieftains will try to lead independent forces. Some will raid ahead, hoping to get to the rich loot before the rest. This will actually help us, because the Tenocha will think they are only fighting a gradually increasing series of pirate raids. Their forces will concentrate in the East. They may even strip the northern border of men to meet his threat."

"And what would you be doing while your friend raises the Norsemen?" Bogotai asked.

"I will travel among the tribes of the plains. They will make splendid light cavalry. Their knowledge of the land is great. They can be your skirmishers and scouts, raiding

along the fringes of your advance while you reserve your
Asian cavalry for the important objectives." Hring sat
back and took a long drink of wine. He had done what he
could, now the rest was up to Bogotai. If the plains peoples
cooperated with the invasion, the Mongols would not perse-
cute them. With the aid of the Norsemen in the conquest,
they might be more benevolent when they cast eyes toward
Thorsheim and Treeland. Perhaps the Norsemen would get
off with a token tribute.

The conference continued well into the night, punctu-
ated with much shouting as men grew drunk. Bogotai
cut off the supply of drink to restore order. Hring dozed
off.

He awoke when someone shook his shoulder. He blinked
and a face swam into his vision in the dim, smoky light.
It was Ashikaga.

"The Khan approves of your plan, redbeard," the
Nipponese said. "You and your friend are to begin your
tasks immediately. From now on, you are both ambassadors of the Kha-Khan. This gives you certain privileges
and protections. If you need a mount, any Mongol you
meet is required to dismount and surrender you his horse.
You may requisition food, supplies, shelter, even an escort
at demand. You are answerable only to the Khan Bogotai."

"I am apt to run into few Mongols where I am going,"
Hring grumbled. "It is the same with Ragnar."

"That is true. Still, the protection of the Khan is not to
be despised."

"How will he protect me in lands which he does not
control?" Hring asked.

"The Khan's protection extends beyond the grave,"
Ashikaga assured him.

"How may that be?" Hring said.

"Should you or your friend be killed while on the Khan's embassy, the nation responsible shall be obliterated." He looked solemnly at Hring. "We have done this before, many times."

Book Three

King of the Wood

Chapter 12

The snow was melting. The mountain streams were bursting their banks in the struggle to drain away the runoff from the winter's heavy snows. Some early trees were beginning to bud. Before the moon turned again, the bears would be foraging the mountain slopes once more.

Hring dismounted and pushed apart some dry brown stalks of last year's grass. Beneath them, tiny green shoots of new grass were pushing up, no higher than the second joint of a man's finger.

"Two moons," Hring said, "then the grass will be high enough for campaigning."

"Three," said Bakhu. "Maybe two and one half. The Khan will want to nurse the horses along." There was no arguing with a steppe man where grass was concerned. "Back on the wide steppe, we used to campaign in winter." The Merkit stood in his stirrups and stretched. "It was better that way, because the rivers froze to the bottom and you didn't need to waste time searching for a ford. Back in Asia, the Kha-Khan's herds are limitless, though, and we could always take horses where we raided. Here, though, it's different. Here, we have to campaign like—like''—he searched for a word to express his contempt for such effete warmaking—"like *Russians!*"

Hring laughed. He and Bakhu had been wandering among the tribes for more than a year. There had been many tribes that had sent no men on Hring and Ragnar's embassy to the Khan and these had to be persuaded with gifts and much talk. The young men were always hot for war, but their elders were more cautious, either fearing to lose many men or else holding out for richer presents.

In the end, he had swayed all that were in the Mongol route of march. Even the fierce Comanche had acquiesced. They were the fiercest and farthest-ranging raiders of all, and would be valuable allies. Some of their lightning raids had taken them as far south as the land of the Maya, striking and running home before the slow-moving Tenocha cavalry could engage them.

Hring had avoided the Absaroka village where Winter-Grass lived. He longed for her, but to return would be death for them both, sooner or later.

"The trouble with these Skraelings," Hring observed to Bakhu, who had dismounted and was gathering wood for a fire, "is that they are a tribal people. They think only in terms of their tribe. Take the Comanche. A Comanche does not think of himself and the Sioux and Cheyenne and the others as Skraelings, and you and your people as Mongols and me and mine as Norsemen. He thinks of himself as Comanche, and everybody else in the world as un-Comanche. If you are not Comanche, it doesn't matter what you are, because you cannot be more different than

you are already. That is why they can never unite." He
paused and thought awhile. "Probably good for us that
they're that way."

"We Merkits used to be like that," Bakhu said. "The
Supreme Khan Temujin taught us different, and the lesson
was costly."

"That's probably what these plains tribes need," Hring
said. "A brown-skinned Temujin with feathers. Pray he
never comes."

"When do we return to Bogotai's camp?" Bakhu asked.
"I've been away from my own people too long. I'm not
like you mountain trappers who spend your lives hidden
away like Buddhist monks. If I'd wanted to be a hermit,
I'd have stayed home and shaved my head and taken the
yellow robe and begging bowl."

"Tomorrow," Hring said.

The army that Hring saw when he and Bakhu arrived in
Mongol occupied territory surpassed belief. For many days,
they rode through immense camps that lined both sides of
the rivers they paralleled. He heard a myriad of languages
spoken, though all could speak Mongol with some degree
of proficiency. A commander told Hring that more than
five tumans, some fifty thousand men, had arrived since
he had set out on his mission. Clearly, the Kha-Khan was
enthusiastic about the prospects of loot from the campaign
against the Tenocha, as well as its opportunities for drain-
ing off his unwanted and disruptive excess manpower.

Hring knew that theoretically the Great Speaker of the
Tenocha could field as many men or more, but that mon-
arch never had and probably never would. And every man
of the Mongol army was a horseman, and an archer to
boot. The Tenocha had kept the horse as the exclusive

possession of the Tenocha aristocracy, except for a few border forces that needed to chase nomads, and this exclusivity would be their downfall, Hring fervently hoped. The Kha-Khan had been lavish with his horse herds when he knew that the return would be rich. Hring's mind reeled when he thought of the distances over which Bogotai had had to carry on his communications with his liege lord. Hring's own wide wanderings during that period were trivial by comparison.

He found Bogotai in his enclosure, now much expanded. There were many new commanders present, as well as some of those who had been present when Hring had first presented his proposal. Ashikaga was there, surrounded by a knot of his colorfully clad commanders. They raised a shout when Hring arrived. The Norseman and the Merkit dismounted. Bakhu ran to a group of his tribesmen and began talking with many gesticulations, while Bogotai gestured to Hring with a folded fan. Hring entered the Khan's ger, followed by several subordinate commanders.

Bogotai heard Hring's report of his mission among the plains tribes without expression, only tapping his thigh with the fan from time to time.

"This is a good service," Bogotai said at length. "Is there word from your coastal friends?"

Hring had been waiting for this. He reached into his pouch and withdrew a packet of oiled skin which crackled when he unfolded it. This had arrived at Tosti's Holding only days before Hring had checked by on his return to Bogotai's camp. Someplace Ragnar had found a defrocked Roman priest who wrote the letters that Hring could decipher, with difficulty.

"My lord, this the word which I have received from the Khan Ragnar." He looked about to see whether there should be any objection to this honorific, but it went ignored. So much the better. With some ceremony, Hring unfolded the thick layers of parchment.

"You read?" Bogotai said. "I didn't realize that."

"Only the Roman runes, my lord," Hring said. "I was high-born, and sent to school under our priests until my sixteenth year."

"Most of my nobles are better-born than you," Bogotai snorted, "and they can't read the death sentences the Kha-Khan sends them. Of course," he added, "the Chinese characters are difficult. Now, what does Khan Ragnar say?" Hring scored a silent, internal triumph.

"These are his words: 'To my comrade Hring, once a prince of Treeland, greeting:

" 'Our plans of raising a navy to attack the Southerners have been successful beyond our highest hopes. I have a firm commitment of five hundred ships for next year's viking.' " A mutter went around the council. This was a respectable undertaking even by Mongol standards. Hring continued. " 'I have expectations of at least that many more, as an irregular force, and Thor only knows how many pirates and such to tag along.

" 'I have a welcome surprise for you. Halbjorn of Laxdale is alive and rejoices to hear that you were also, a year ago.' " Hring explained to Bogotai that Halbjorn was his old shipmaster. " 'Halbjorn [Ragnar continued] has consented to be the admiral of our fleet. I am a landsman and can find no better man for the exploit. I also made contact with Dieter' "—here Hring explained that trader's significance—" 'and he has agreed to take word of our exploit North. I think we can look to see many of your Christian kin a-viking with us. King Sweyn is quite out of countenance and wishes to hang me, but I now have protection. He will come to see reason, soon. There are more stout lads waiting here for a worthy exploit than you would credit. I look forward to leading them as a great chief. Our plan is like something from an old song. There has been no word from the Lady Yngva. Until we meet again next summer. Ragnar.' '' Hring had to make clear the reference to Yngva. The Mongols were somewhat surprised to learn that a woman could have a powerful influence on what they considered men's matters, or at least they pretended that this was the case.

"Can we count on your comrade's assurances?" Ashikaga asked.

"Absolutely," Hring said.

The army moved south. At first, it seemed to move slowly, no more than the walking pace of a horse. But that pace never slackened, indeed it grew faster, as men and mounts grew accustomed to it. Eventually, every day, the entire force was racking along, slowing at intervals to unsaddle and remount. The miles were eaten up with relentless force.

The Mongols would not break into the lightning swiftness which had won them a world until first contact was made with the enemy. After that, they would move at a man- and horse-killing pace, breaking up into multiple forces to raid separately, re-forming to take major objectives, traversing landscapes in rigidly structured and disciplined operations that would leave the enemy confused as to the very number of armies they were facing.

As they crossed the plains, they were joined by the allied tribes: Absaroka, Cheyenne, Pawnee, Arapaho, even the relatively peaceful Flatheads. Farther south, the

Comanche and Kiowa, the Caddo rode in to join the horsetail banners. To Hring's surprise, there were even volunteers from the wily, fierce mountain peoples: the Dineh, the Yaqui, and the Navajo. All these were deadly enemies, but they were willing to put their differences aside, if only temporarily, to take part in such an adventure and take plunder they might never otherwise see in a lifetime. The mountain tribes were not horsemen of the quality shown by the plainsmen, but they were cunning and ferocious fighters whose brutal tenacity could awe even a hardened Mongol.

By the time the last of the allied tribes had joined the army, they were already deep inside territory claimed by the Tenocha. Claiming was not the same as occupying, and the only military presence was a handful of tiny mud forts garrisoned by local tribesmen who surrendered as soon as they saw the fantastic army overrunning their land. The very few Tenocha officers present who tried to resist were usually killed by their own subject soldiers.

As they began to near the major objectives, Hring was sent forward to join the advance force of Mongols and Comanche, the spearheaders who would break the path for the main army. With Hring rode his personal command: some three thousand mounted Norsemen and another five thousand Absaroka, making Hring the commander of a light tuman. The Norsemen had joined as the army swung past Tosti's Holding. Hring had never suspected that there were so many Norsemen in the West, but word had been traveling, and every unattached warrior who found himself too far from the coast to join the Viking force at hosting time had headed west to join the horse army.

Nearly all of the Norsemen had arrived with shield and

sword, ax, helm, and mail—trappings that hadn't been seen on the plains since the Norsemen had first arrived in the West more than two centuries before. Bogotai had been skeptical when he saw the Norsemen.

"How do those fight?" he asked Hring. "Their bows are too long to shoot from a horse. Their lances are for sticking pigs. Those shields are stupid things to ride with. Are these really the fierce Norsemen we've heard about?"

"My people don't fight from horseback, Khan," Hring replied. "We dismount and fight shield to shield."

Bogotai laughed uproariously at this. "You mean I'm taking a pack of suicides who want only to die in battle? These men will be useless!"

"Remember, Khan, that not all the fighting will be on the open plain. There will be cities to take. You cannot take cities with arrows alone. And there will be the causeways of Tenochtitlán to force. For these things you will need men who can fight on foot. That is where the Norsemen and the Dineh and others will earn their share of the loot."

"You are right," Bogotai admitted. "I should hate to waste good Mongols in fighting like that."

The first city was not a large one, but its pyramid was visible for many miles across the arid plain. According to prearranged plan, Hring and the spearhead force simply rode past it, enjoying the gaping stares of the natives who poured from the town to see this incredible visitation. Hring's men then dismounted and blocked the road of retreat, the horsemen sweeping out to subdue any small villages nearby. When the main Mongol army arrived, it caught the townsmen boggling and trying to comprehend what was happening. The army divided into two columns and surrounded the town in a twinkling, shrieking like demons and smelling much worse. The few townspeople who had the presence of mind to run were herded back to the town by Hring's shield wall.

Hring found Bogotai sitting on his horse, exulting. "This is fantastic!" he said. "Not a man lost! Every last warrior was stripped from the town weeks ago to meet the threat on the coast. Look at them!" The people of the town were standing in a daze, almost completely apathetic as their town was ransacked for valuables. Already, files of men were bringing out heaps of gold and silver, jewelry and furs, featherwork and fabrics, dumping them into a glittering heap at the hooves of Bogotai's horse. The Khan's eyes glowed with satisfaction.

"Norseman," he continued, "you may tell these sheep that they are now servants of the Kha-Khan. They will not be molested as long as they keep the peace and pay their taxes. They may keep their gods if they wish, but there will be no more cutting hearts from the Khan's subjects on those pyramids." Hring shouted these words to the throng, who looked back blankly.

"Hulagu!" the Khan shouted. "See to the separation of the Kha-Khan's tenth from this loot, then cut out my share. I want that jade cup"—he pointed to a magnificent piece in the pile of loot—"and I want one of those feather cloaks." He spread his arms and gazed upward. "My Lord the Sky! I thank you for giving me a land as rich as China to loot." Calming somewhat, he turned once more to Hring. "From here we make a swing to the west, then sweep eastward. We'll trap their whole army against the sea and annihilate them."

"I warn you, my Khan," Hring said, "these are not the true Tenocha, but a subject people who have been forbidden to bear arms for generations. When we reach the Valley of Mexico, the story will be different. Then they will be defending their homeland and their temples."

"It shall be as Heaven wills," said Bogotai with a shrug.

Heaven, it seemed, willed a fairly easy campaign in the western provinces. These had been conquered early and long pacified. Tenocha garrisons had been few to begin with and all had been stripped of defenders when the Vikings struck the eastern coast. Bogotai had considered making a clean sweep all the way to the west coast before starting his eastward sweep. But the range of coastal mountains he would have to cross twice would be difficult even for seasoned Mongol troopers to negotiate. He elected instead to smash the Tenocha main force and settle the rest of the empire piecemeal.

When they turned east, there was still no indication that the Great Speaker and his commanders even had an inkling that the Mongol invasion was taking place. Apparently they were still pinned down by the Vikings, who by this time must have landed in full force. Hring almost regretted being with the Mongol force. His blood cried out to see a genuine fleet of dragon ships landing at a foreign shore, lean and black, their sides lined with the painted shields and their decks aglitter with armed men. Those who were fighting on the bloody beaches of the Azteca coast would be envied for generations to come, and take their place in the sagas along with Hasteinn, and Hrolf, and Ragnar Lodbrok.

Those would be true battles, worth singing of, he thought.

There would be warriors standing toe to toe and looking into each other's eyes from under helm or through eagle mask, sword and ax against golden scale and jaguar pelt, slashing jungle knife and macuahuitl against mail.

It was a bitter thing to miss such a fight, and have to settle instead for this impersonal Mongol business of horses and arrows. But all such thoughts left Hring's mind when the great host cleared the final hills and descended into the Valley of Mexico.

Chapter 13

The roads leading into Tenochtitlán were crowded. Those leading in from the east were choked. Word had at last arrived of the Mongol invasion. Columns of weary warriors stretched for miles, their finery smudged, their feathers tattered. The long columns of the knightly orders rode with heads high, proud and confident in their gods even in this dark hour.

Atop the pyramids, the priests would be excising hearts at a frantic rate, seeking to placate the gods, who for some mysterious reason seemed to be punishing their worshipers. Only great amounts of blood could regain the favor of the gods.

Ashikaga sucked in a hissing breath. "It's even more splendid than you described!" Hring sat next to the Nipponese Khan, resting his horse.

"The campaign's been near bloodless so far," Hring said. "Now we start to pay."

"About time," Ashikaga replied. There was a clatter of hooves and Bogotai rode up, surrounded by his staff. The Khan's grin stretched to the side veils of his helmet when he surveyed the city.

"Now," he exclaimed, "there's a city worth taking, at last!"

"My lord," Ashikaga said, "if we attack now, we can cut the roads and split their forces. Those we catch out on the plain will be easy meat, and the city will be under-manned."

"No," Bogotai said, "we'll camp here for now, within sight. Let them fill the city. We could take it today, but then many would get away, and they'd fortify other cities, and we would have to take them one at a time. Let the Tenocha make their capital ready for a siege, along with any allies that care to join them. Then we'll know who our enemies are."

"My Khan," Hring spoke up, "the food supplies in that city are immense. They could withstand a long siege, even crammed with men."

Bogotai looked over the city and shrugged. "It won't be a long siege. It won't even be a long battle." He said this with such sublime confidence that Hring did not care to dispute with him.

"If you are itching for action, Norseman," Bogotai said, "you may take your men and ride in search of your kinsmen, who must now be harrying those warriors from behind. Find out how many they are and their state of discipline, if any. Tell them to halt if they are in pursuit and to camp"—he made a quick sweep of the valley with his gaze and pointed to a range of hills on the far side of the city—"over there, in those hills. Tell them to light campfires where the Tenocha can see them."

"With the Khan's indulgence," Hring answered, "these Norsemen are not subjects but allies, and are very aware of the fact. They may not follow my instructions. Vikings with the smell of blood and loot in their nostrils do not slow down readily."

"You will, of course, use the most diplomatic language," Bogotai said with great patience. "You may also tell them that, should they follow my instructions, the loot will be much greater than otherwise, and they will lose far fewer men. Emphasize to them that they are the Kha-Khan's valued and esteemed allies, in whom he reposes great trust. You may also tell them, very gently, that if they do anything to hinder my siege, I will kill every last one of them as soon as I've settled with the Tenocha." He gave Hring one of his gentle smiles that would kill a charging bison dead in its tracks, as if it were struck by lightning.

"As the Khan wishes," Hring said.

"Meanwhile, I'll send forces out to take the rest of the cities here in the valley. There are a number of them, and some look very rich. It will give the men something to do, sharpen them up for the main battle. Hring, your Norsemen may have the cities on the far side of the lake to loot if they wish, but there is to be no unnecessary burning, or killing of the Kha-Khan's subjects. Kill only warriors who show resistance."

"I shall tell them, Khan," Hring said, wondering how much use his orders would be to a pack of howling, blood-mad berserkers.

He rode through the long twilight across the maize fields, keeping well away from the roads, which were still choked with armies and refugees. Once the half tuman blundered into a camp of Tenocha warriors, and rode right through it without casualties. The warriors were too exhausted to fight, and too astonished at this great force of horsemen who appeared from nowhere and were swallowed up by the deepening night.

Hring's standard bearers signaled with their lanterns of different colors to keep the force together and maneuver them in the dark. They rode cautiously. Mongols would ride like this at night, at a dead gallop, trusting to the signals of the advance body. But then, those were Mongols. Hring's men were still new to this type of campaigning. By the end of night, they seemed to be past the greater part of the retreating Tenocha forces. Hring ordered the men to dismount and rest until full daylight.

They found the Vikings sacking a town whose inhabitants had fled in panic. Hring instructed his men to stay put while he rode ahead. A man at the edge of town looked up from his task of loading a donkey with plunder and caught sight of Hring, and of the force of horsemen behind him. The Norse looter snatched a hunting horn from his waist and winded it. The sound brought a great mass of men boiling out of the town to form a shield wall. Hring nodded with satisfaction. Clearly, this strenuous and lengthy campaign had taught the Vikings some of the discipline of the old days of the Jomsvikings.

As Hring ambled his horse slowly forward, two men detached themselves from the shield wall and stepped forward. "Ho, Hring," shouted one, "where have you been hiding while the real men were fighting all these weeks?"

"I've been riding with the main army in a civilized fashion, Halbjorn, instead of brawling with a pack of brigands." He jumped from his horse and embraced the shipmaster while the other man, Ragnar, pummeled his back and shoulders. Halbjorn held Hring at arm's length and studied him. "By Loki's unmentionables, Hring, I'd thought you food for the sharks or the Arawaks years back." He surveyed Hring critically. "Except for that red face muff, I'd take you for an Easterner." He referred to Hring's mailed sleeves of silk and his cuirass of lacquered blue-and-gold splints, laced with flame-colored silk— Nipponese armor given to him by Ashikaga. He retained his Norse helm and sword.

"You don't look much like a Viking yourself," Hring observed. Halbjorn was wearing the upper half of an Eagle Knight's scale suit. He had hung a fringe of eagle feathers around the edge of his shield and had abandoned his old sealskin trousers for an east coast loincloth of brilliant green silk. The rest of the Norsemen wore similar motley. Many had abandoned their Norse mail, if they had possessed it in the first place, in favor of the padded cotton or silk armor of the native infantry. Plain steel skullcaps alternated with eagle and jaguar helmets, and brilliant feather cloaks hung from gray-mailed shoulders.

"Can this walking plunder-heap fight at Tenochtitlán?" Hring asked.

"Right now, if you like," Ragnar said.

"You haven't seen the place yet," Hring said. "It'll take the full strength of both armies. By the way, where is the rest of the Viking force? This mangy pack couldn't have taken Tuxpan alone, much less fought off a whole Tenocha army."

"They're out looting, of course," said Halbjorn, "what else? Twenty-five thousand or so Vikings didn't land on these shores to see the sights, you know."

"Come on," said Hring, heading into the town. "You can tell me all about it. Let's find a house where somebody's dinner is still on the table."

"It was hard fighting, after the Tenocha knew we were here in force," Halbjorn said. He was gnawing on a turkey leg and drinking from a bowl of pulque. "The first cities were easy. There were only a few horse patrols at first, and they were nothing. Then the resistance got stronger. After we'd been ashore harvesting for two weeks, the whole Tenocha army arrived and then it was brisk work. Some lost heart and sailed home with their loot, but we'd expected that. The best stayed, and we forted up in the coastal towns. By that time, some of the subject peoples had risen in rebellion and the Tenocha had other worries besides us.

"Oh, by the way," Halbjorn said, "just a few days back, we were joined by a great big bugger of a Skraeling from the south, and he said he knew you. What was his name, Ragnar? Burning-Feathers, or some such."

"Smoking-Crest," Ragnar said.

"That's it, Smoking-Crest. He showed up with a pack of painted savages and some better-dressed ones calling themselves Zapotecas. Sure as Odin hanged nine days, I saw that man hack a Tenocha in two, right down to his saddle, armor and all. And he didn't use an ax, either, just one of those flint-edged clubs some of them carry."

"I know that one, sure enough," Hring said. He went on to describe the disposition of the Mongol army, and deliver Bogotai's instructions. The two commanders pondered this.

"I think your Khan's plan is a good one, Hring," said Halbjorn at length. "Get it all over with in one big battle, then carry on with the serious plundering. The rest may take some convincing, though. Ragnar and I are the leaders, but that only holds as long as we don't push the men too far. There are some of Sweyn's men here, and Christians from the North. They'd turn against us in a flash if we interfered with their business too much.''

''Just get them into the camp near Tenochtitlán for a day or two,'' Hring said. ''By now they should be glad of the rest. I think something can be arranged to make them see things in a reasonable light.''

The massive Norse army, ashine with its stolen finery, sat along the slopes overlooking the plain. In the distance, the great city was a many-hued jewel, the richest unplundered metropolis in the world, and the sight made their palms itch. The smoke of the Mongol camp was faintly visible on the far side of the valley.

''What has the Khan in mind?'' Ragnar asked. He sat among a knot of the Norse leaders along with a few of the new native allies, among them Smoking-Crest.

''He said it was to be an object lesson,'' Hring answered. All around him the Norsemen shouted to one another boisterously, like men at a show.

''Who is this horseback monkey to give us orders?'' said Bengt Gunnarson. He was one of Sweyn's men, the commander of thirty ships.

''You'll see soon enough,'' Hring replied. The men fell silent as a large force of Tenocha began to emerge from a pass in the hills onto the plain below. They were late arrivals, probably a detachment sent to wage a flowery war in the far South. There were at least four thousand of them, cavalry and infantry, turning the flat ground as colorful as a Tenocha feather cloak. Behind them came a force of Mongol horse, moving at a slow walk, quietly herding the Tenocha in front of the Norse camp. The Tenocha halted when another, larger force of Mongols rode from a mountain pass to maneuver into line before them. From deep ravines where they had been hidden, other Mongol horsemen rode until the Tenocha were completely surrounded. They hesitated for a moment, taking stock of their situation. They could see that the Mongols numbered fewer than one thousand. With a great braying of trumpets and conch shells and a beating of drums, they continued their march toward the city. As they approached the Mongols, the cavalry lowered their lances and charged.

Instantly, the air above the Tenocha grew blurred with arrows. The lines of horsemen went down in a heap, horse piling onto horse, man onto man. Within thirty seconds, not a single knight or mount was moving. The infantry formed a hollow square and knelt behind their grounded shields, awaiting the charge of the Mongols. The steppe warriors ambled slowly forward, pouring cloud after cloud of arrows into the massed ranks. By the time the horses were up to the front line, it was all over, and the horsemen dismounted to retrieve their arrows. From the charge of the Tenocha cavalry to the fall of the last arrow, perhaps ten minutes had elasped.

"Not a one of those horseback trolls dead," said Bengt.

"Not one even sweating," Halbjorn added. The noisy banter of the Norse audience had stopped, and a great silence prevailed. After that, there was no more talk of defying Bogotai.

For days, streams of people had been pouring from the city and out onto the plain. The Tenocha were expelling the slaves, the subject peoples, any others who would not contribute to the defense of the city. Interrogations of the refugees had revealed that, besides the true Tenocha, the only subjects to be retained would be those destined for sacrifice. Bogotai smiled at the news. He looked around at the leaders assembled in the mammoth ger he had had erected in the midst of his camp.

"These people have never withstood a real siege, that's plain to see," he said. "It takes more than fighting men to defend a city properly. You need masons and carpenters, and laborers who can haul dirt and patch holes in the walls." He laughed heartily. "It will be amusing to see those splendid knights who know only the sword and lance trying to destroy those causeways! Such masonry I've not seen since I passed through the Great Wall."

A Kerait khan reported that all the tumans were back in after their reconnaissance and looting missions.

"Fine," Bogotai said. "There's nothing to be gained by waiting further. We commence the attack at first light tomorrow. Liu Chi, are your workmen organized?". The Chinese nodded. "Good. If we've failed to force the causeways by nightfall, I will call off the direct attack and we will commence engineering works."

"Hring Khan"—this was the first time Hring had been so addressed—"you and your Norsemen and the Dineh and Navajo will assault the causeway that is carved with feathered serpents. Ashikaga, your bushi love to fight on foot. You will take the causeway carved with skulls." The Nipponese nodded, grinning fiercely, exultant at the prospect. "The native allies, under Smoking-Crest, will attack the causeway carved with that ugly goddess, what was her name?"

"Coatlicue," Hring said.

"Yes. Should the mainland fortress of any of these

causeways prove impregnable, those attacking it will withdraw at midday and go to reinforce the other two." The Khan sat silent for a while, idly playing with the ends of his mustaches.

"Once the causeways have been cleared, the calvary will ride across and into the city. The avenues are broad and straight. It will be like target practice. Some detachments will ride up the sides of the pyramids and fire into the streets below. Others will take the big platforms. Once the streets have been cleared, the footmen will go from house to house, flushing out pockets of resistance." He swept the assembly with his gaze.

"Any man found drunk on the day of battle will be executed immediately. Any man caught looting before the city is declared fully secure will likewise be executed. Any man who seeks to leave the battle without severe wounds will be executed. Physicians will be stationed at the ends of the causeways to examine the wounded. Go now and give your men their final instructions. Tomorrow, conquer in the name of the Kha-Khan!"

The meeting broke up and Hring rode back to the Norse camp, amid a knot of his fellow Northerners. There was some muttering.

"Sounds like they're going to let us do the real fighting while the squint-eyes watch and clap," Bengt said. "They'll let us be killed and then ride in to plunder when all's quiet."

"If you've a better plan, Bengt," Hring said, "the time to speak up was in council. However, Khan Bogotai is always open to new ideas from his subordinates, and if you ride back, he may even now listen to you." Bengt fumed but remained silent.

"Ah, where are the old days," Halbjorn said, "when

people paid us Norsemen huge treasures just to go away? It's sad to see poor Vikings having to work for their keep."

"I'm for home as soon as the fighting's over and the loot shared out," said a one-eyed grizzle-beard from Treeland. "Pretty feathers'll please my wife, and I like gold and jewels as much as any, but there's no beer in this land, and turkey's no substitute for pork and blood sausage." There was a general agreement about this land's lamentable deficiencies.

That night, Hring stood at the edge of the camp, gazing at the city, ablaze with torches. When the wind blew from that direction, it carried the heavy scent of incense, and the reek of the temples. Even at this distance, the overpowering smell of blood could make the horses uneasy. A huge form padded up next to him on bare feet.

"You are restless too, Smoking-Crest?" Hring said. "Tomorrow may see you triumph over your enemies."

"It is in my mind," the Oaxacan said, "that we may have traded one master for another as bad."

"The Khan will demand taxes," Hring said, "but it will be the produce of your lands, not your children. Besides, your land down in the South is mostly mountain and jungle. You will probably never see a Mongol except for a tax official once each year. Of course, you will probably have to stop fighting with your neighbors." He saw the flash of grinning teeth from Smoking-Crest.

"Now, there's a rule that will sit hard with my people. The Zapoteca and the Mixteca think my tribe are savages. Before the Tenocha came, they used to hunt us like monkeys, and we raided them." He sighed. "Well, maybe it's just as well that the Khan will not let us make war.

They would have won, eventually. What are your thoughts tonight, my friend?''

"Over there"—Hring pointed to the city—"are people who befriended me; Two-Earthquake and Nine-Death, One-Reed and Golden-Bells. They made me great among them, and now I am leading men to destroy them. I hate their temples and their bloody rites, but am I any better?''

"They never befriended you, not as I did," Smoking-Crest said. "It was the favor of the gods that they saw in you and wanted to touch that made you important to them. Without that, you were just another foreigner, meat for the gods. Another heart to be ripped out and offered to the sun and the moon, just as a thousand hearts are being cut out this very minute, from the top of every pyramid in Tenochtitlán. They took prisoners on the coast. Some of those hearts will be the hearts of your kinsmen tonight. There will be yellow beards gracing the skull racks tonight. Think of that instead of the priestess.''

Hring nodded at the wisdom of this, but still his thoughts were on the priestess, and on another.

"Tomorrow," Smoking-Crest went on, "I fight on the Causeway of Coatlicue. You, on the Causeway of Quetzalcoatl. We will both be fighting in the forefront, because we are heroes and that is where heroes fight. Often, two heroes do not survive the same battle. Let us meet at the top of the Great Pyramid of Huitzilopochtli. I'll wager my feather cloak against yours that I kill the last Tenocha.''

"Done," Hring said. Smoking-Crest returned to his camp, but Hring remained for a long while, staring out over the plain at the city.

Chapter 14

The Vikings advanced in regular lines toward the small fortress. Hring was in the center of the first line. Flanking him marched Ragnar and Halbjorn. They had eaten a big breakfast before sunrise and then taken their prearranged positions in the dim light of dawn. Row on row of the big round Norse shields fronted the fort when the sun rose. The trumpets brayed the attack just as the drums and gongs in the city signaled the day's first sacrifice of hearts to the rising, newly triumphant god.

Hring raised the war shout and the ranks surged forward against the fort. The fort was a square building of massive stone blocks, its walls twice the height of a tall man and crenellated at top. The gateway leading onto the causeway was bricked up and the top of the wall was lined with Jaguar Knights. When the Norse were close enough, a shower of slingstones, arrows, and javelins commenced. The Norsemen raised their shields and continued their advance.

Hring gritted his teeth as they got to the base of the wall, but no shower of boiling oil, or hot pitch, or melted lead greeted them, and he thanked all the gods he could think of that the Tenocha knew little about real siegecraft. There was little honor in having one's face scalded off, and they were to be spared one of battle's horrors.

Mongol horsemen rode to the edge of the lake and directed an avalanche of shafts upon the battlements, giving the footmen a chance to bring up their ladders and prop them against the wall. Another team of burly Norsemen advanced against the gateway, armed with sledgehammers and a ram made from an entire tree, its tips shod in iron. Hring climbed a ladder, his shield held awkwardly before him, his sword sheathed for the moment. He feared that he might be ignominiously impaled by a Mongol arrow, some of which were barely skimming the merlons of the battlement, but these raised like a curtain as he reached the top of the ladder. A jaguar-masked face appeared over the wall and Hring punched it with the edge of his shield. He heard a cry and felt mask and bone crunch. He got his shield before him just in time to catch a heavy stone which nearly drove him back down upon the man below him, then the stone thrower hurtled past with three arrows through his mask. Hring lunged upward, grabbed the top of the wall with his free hand, and scrambled over onto the battlement. It was covered with dead and dying Tenocha, arrows sticking from their armor in all directions. But, there were more. From ladders at the back of the fort, men were swarming up from the causeway and onto the roof to do battle. Hring took two strides forward to clear a space for other laddermen to mount the wall. A Jaguar Knight charged and Hring picked up a stone from a heap by his foot and hurled it. The man fell back with blood spraying from his mask and now Ragnar was shielding Hring's right side, giving him time to draw his sword. He caught a slash from a long sword on his shield and he swung a short chop at the knight's side beneath his sword arm. There was a meat-cutting impact and Hring twisted his blade free, then did a quick dance to keep his feet free of the tumble of guts that burst forth as the man fell.

A big Viking went howling berserk and threw away his shield, swinging his ax with both hands, clearing a gap in the enemy halfway to the far side of the roof before he was chopped down. Hring, Ragnar, and some others jumped into the gap before the advance could be lost, guarding their flanks desperately until more men fought their way up to them.

Face after face appeared before Hring, and he smashed mask after snarling mask. His shoulder grew weary and he concentrated on defending himself for a while, wielding his sword in short, economical thrusts so as not to tax his strength. The footing was now dangerously slippery with blood, brains, and entrails, and bodies were piled on almost every square foot of the roof. It was a great strain to keep on his feet, but he must stay upright, for a man who falls in battle dies, even though he falls unwounded.

Hring bumped into an obstacle and looked down. It was the parapet of the far wall, not battlemented like the other. They had cleared the roof of Tenocha, but more were still coming up the ladders. Hring leaned out and split an eagle mask but there was another right behind it. Men seized the ladders to push them over, and others cast down rocks.

"Throw the bodies down!" Hring shouted. There was a scramble as men separated the Tenocha bodies from the Norse and hoisted them to the parapet. The hurtling corpses cleared the ladders that had not already been thrown down.

Hring sat down, his back against the parapet, as fresh men arrived with bows, javelins, and throwing axes to rain death on the Tenocha packing the bridge. He gasped for breath, his lungs and sides burning with the strain. Somebody shoved a wineskin into his hands and he pulled at it greedily, then passed it on. The building began to shudder violently and rhythmically as the ram pounded at its portal. A big hand grabbed his shoulder and hauled him to his feet.

"No time to be laying about," Halbjorn said. "The men will be thinking you soft." Holding up his shield against the stones and darts that came from below, Hring surveyed the bridge. It was still teeming with Tenocha warriors, splendid and fearless. They were so jammed together that every arrow and javelin that arced onto the bridge found a man. The dead had no room to fall. The volleys of arrows from shore seemed to be fewer than before. A small Mongol pushed his way through the shouting Norsemen and came to Hring.

"Khan of the yellow-hairs, Khan Bogotai says that his men must now conserve their arrows, or there will be none left to use when we take the city, unless we can get onto the bridge and retrieve some from the bodies there." Hring nodded.

"Tell Khan Bogotai that we'll be through the gate and onto the bridge shortly." He squinted up at the sun, which was near its midday height. How had it gotten so high in such a short time? "We should be onto the bridge before the sun starts to sink. Then you can come get your arrows. We'll have made it safe for you then." The Mongol regarded him scornfully.

"The real killing has not started yet, yellow-hair." He

stalked away, the effect somewhat spoiled by his bandy-legged horseman's waddle.

"Why do they call you that when you hair's red?" Ragnar asked, reaching back to scratch his back. Alone among the Norsemen, Ragnar scorned armor, though he was no berserker. Hring envied his ability to scratch.

"They call us all that. They won't admit that my hair is red." He fended off a viciously barbed javelin. "They think that only their Great Khan and his family had red hair. So my hair is yellow."

"Hm," muttered Ragnar. He picked up a rock and cast it with great accuracy into a gaping eagle beak, opened so that its owner could breathe some fresh air. "I wonder what they make of Ingvar Blackhair?"

"Lucky cast, Ragnar?" said Halbjorn. The pounding below took on a different sound.

"I never miss," Ragnar said. He held his shield before him and leaned far out over the parapet so that he could see what was happening below. Hring and Halbjorn held their shields out to either side to further protect him from missiles. He heaved back to safety. "The ram's coming through," he said.

Already the Tenocha were beginning a fierce attack against the walled-up gate, to prevent the ram from demolishing the barrier and allowing the bulk of the Norse army through. Many Tenocha warriors ran to the breach and thrust their spears through it, seeking to skewer the men on the other side.

"We'll have to go down and keep the breach clear or they'll never get through," Hring said. He looked around. "Who goes with me?"

"This is a matter to consider carefully," Halbjorn said. "I'm not as young as I used to be. Hring, you go first."

Hring considered the problem. They could bring the

ladders across from the other side, but descending they would have to present their backs to the enemy, and that was suicide. He could send for ropes, but ropes required the use of both hands. He would arrive on hostile ground, surrounded by howling Tenocha, with nothing more than a knife in his teeth. No, jumping was the only way. It was a long fall, and the bottom was littered with stones, corpses, fallen weapons and slick with blood. No help for it. He raised his voice. "Sven the Leaper! Hjalmar the Boneless! Ivar Springheels! Come over here!"

The three joined him. True to their names, all were noted jumpers, runners, and tumblers. Hring pointed downward.

"I'm jumping down there to clear a space so the ladders can be lowered and the ram can break through. Are you three with me?"

"A feat like that will be remembered a long time," said Ivar. "Half the skalds of the North are here today. Even if we die, our fame will live forever. I'm with you, Hring." The others nodded vigorously.

"I'll go," Ragnar said. "It ill becomes a man of my good name to let boys attempt such a thing alone."

"We'll follow at a more dignified pace," said Halbjorn, who was marshaling his ladder teams. Hring and his companions stepped back from the parapet a few paces and checked the condition of their gear. Sven stripped off his scaled shirt to land the lighter. They dried their palms and the handles of their swords and axes. Each took a good pull at a wineskin. It was good wine, from the Khan's stores. Each took a firmer grasp on his shield straps. The roof was cleared between them and the parapet, and strewn with sand brought from the shore in a sack by a runner. When all was ready, Hring nodded.

"Now!"

In lockstep, the five strode to the parapet, sprang upon it, and, shields high, stepped out into the clear air beyond.

Hring's stomach lurched up into his throat as he plummeted. He kept his knees loose, his ankles limber. The stone of the bridge slammed his soles and he took the shock with his legs, going into a squat so deep that he was nearly knocked out when his knee smashed into his chin. Miraculously, he kept his feet. Sven was not so lucky. Hring saw him trying to rise after landing on a body.

The Tenocha were so amazed at the sight that the Norsemen had a precious second to recover and defend themselves. Ragnar and Ivar hacked down the men who were spearing through the small breach made by the ram. Hring and Hjalmar attacked the men on the bridge, two against hundreds. Sven was gaffed through the body as he struggled to rise. His abandonment of his armor had proven to be a miscalculation. Ragnar and Ivar now turned to the bridge and the fighting was desperate. There was a rain of missiles from the roof of the fort behind them, and that helped, but the shower of arrows from the shore had trickled to almost nothing.

The four Norsemen tried to force their way into the enemy, seeking desperately and hopelessly to push the immense mass of men back so that the ladders could be lowered. Hring swung his sword in wide arcs, shocked to his heels at each impact, feeling the crunch of bone, the rending of flesh and metal at the end of each blow. There was no room or time for the short chops and thrusts that he preferred, and fighting like this took a toll in fatigue. Not even a berserker could keep it up more than a few minutes.

Ivar went down, blood gushing from the stump of his sword arm, but he wrestled his killer to the slimy stones and crushed his throat with the edge of his shield before he died. Hjalmar took a javelin in his throat and jerked backward, sending a spray of blood jetting high. Hring and Ragnar fought on, scything the Tenocha down in rows. Hring could hear them shouting something. "Seven-Wind! Seven-Wind!" and there was fear in their voices. So they recognized him. And they knew that their gods had turned against them, because their chosen was fighting them. Now Hring and Ragnar were fighting back to back, no longer trying to push back the mass of Tenocha, but merely trying to stay alive, or, failing that, to kill as many Tenocha as they could before dying.

There was a crash behind them, and a loud screaming of war cries, then they were surrounded by howling throngs of Norsemen and Dineh, swinging swords and axes and hatchets. The Tenocha were being pushed back along the causeway. Hring and Ragnar staggered to the waist-high parapet that edged the causeway and sat against it, gasping for breath and checking themselves for wounds. They had surprisingly few. A man tossed them a wineskin as he ran to join the fighting. Hring gulped down a quart at least, then fought to keep it behind his teeth as he handed the skin to Ragnar. In a few seconds, his stomach calmed and he drank some more. A bloodstained man crossed to where they were sitting. It was Halbjorn.

"Really, Hring," Halbjorn said, "I don't know how you won your reputation, since you spend so much of your time in battle sitting about. Here." He dropped a cloth sack between the resting warriors. "You might as well have a picnic while the rest of us are fighting." The shipmaster unshouldered his ax and strolled up the causeway to where the battle still raged.

Hring opened the sack. Inside was dried meat, fruit,

bread, and cheese. Suddenly and surprisingly, he was ravenous. Both men stuffed their mouths with food and washed it down with the wine, which quickly had Hring's head spinning. A Mongol rode through the breach in the fort and reined in before the resting Norsemen.

"The Khan says that you must force the causeway quickly or he will be forced to call off the assault and begin the siege. The sun is getting low, and he does not want to send horsemen into the city after dark."

Hring looked up. It was true. The sun was almost down to the level of the highest pyramids. It seemed only minutes since the assault had begun.

"Tell the Khan that we will not fall back," Hring said. "Not after the fight we've made here, not after losing so many good men. We'll fight all night if need be, and hold the far end until the sun rises again. We'll fight till the last man drops, but we will not give up this causeway." Ragnar grunted agreement through a mouthful of bread and cheese. The Mongol laughed.

"That is just what the Khan said you would answer. Ashikaga and the big native both said the same words."

"Those are men," Ragnar said.

"How is the fight going on the other causeways?" Hring asked. The Mongol stood up in his saddle to see better what was going on where the fight continued a hundred yards away.

"Same as here. They are both a little less than halfway to the city end." The Mongol grinned. "Those Nipponese are always talking about what great hand-to-hand fighters they are. These Tenocha are just as fierce and far more numerous. None of you would be alive now, if it were not that these Tenocha keep trying to take you prisoner instead of killing you." Hring knew that this was true. Even in their desperate plight, the Tenocha could not overcome a lifetime of conditioning to take the enemy prisoner for later sacrifice instead of killing him on the spot. They still acted as if this were a flowery war. The Mongol rode away to deliver Hring's answer, and Hring lurched to his feet. Ragnar flexed his arms and picked up his weapons.

"Just a moment," Hring said. He looked about on the bloody stones of the causeway, bent, and picked up a wooden stick. It was about twenty inches long, hooked at one end. It was what the Tenocha called an atlatl, a spear thrower with which they could hurl their javelins farther and harder than with the hand alone. Hring slid the hooked end under the backplate of his Nipponese cuirass and scratched himself violently. "That's better," he sighed. "I've been wanting to do that since we went up the scaling ladder." He tucked the stick into his belt and picked up his shield and sword. "Let's go."

They strode to the fighting line and continued their endless battle. The sun fell, and Bogotai ordered a rest area constructed on the secured area of the causeway, beyond the extreme range of Tenocha missiles. Wood was brought up for fires, and the tired men could retire from the fighting, gulp a few mouthfuls of wine and hot stew, rest for a few minutes, then return to the fighting. Chinese physicians examined the wounded. If the injuries were severe enough, the men were carried to a camp where they were attended by native allies. The physicians among these were extremely competent in the treatment of injuries.

The battle progressed like a nightmare, with the events of hours seemingly compressed into minutes, and frantic minutes of danger stretched to half a lifetime. As the darkness grew, torches were brought up and set along the parapet of the causeway. The Tenocha likewise illuminated the part of the causeway they still held, which was getting ever smaller.

The city was ablaze with torches, and the pyramids and temples were crested with huge fires against which the moving silhouettes of priests could be seen, methodically cutting the hearts from sacrifice after sacrifice, and in the rare intervals when the din of the battle abated a little, the blasting of conches and trumpets, the thunder of drums and gongs made the night more hideous than did the unending screams of the wounded and dying.

Hring continued to fight, like an automaton, his sword arm rising and falling, thrusting and recovering, his shield arm like a lump of hot lead. As his defense slowed with fatigue, especially in raising his shield, he began to take more blows on his helm. During a lull, he exchanged his light skullcap for a more substantial helm with side pieces that came down over head and neck, almost to the shoulders. Even with that improvement, his head rang constantly, and his vision grew blurred. Once he was carried from the front line, to wake up more than an hour later in the rest area. He picked up his notch-edged sword and battered shield, clapped on the dented helm, and returned to the fight, his clothing in rags, his cuirass showing great rents in its once-fine lacquer work.

The Norsemen grunted with pleased surprise to see him back. They were always surprised to see him return, now. No other man had spent so much time in the forefront except Ragnar. There was little shouting now. The men fought on in grim silence, hoarding their strength. Dineh and Norseman, Treelander and Thorsheimer, Christian and pagan, no man tried to shrink back or demand an end to the fighting. Men had been captured in the coastal fighting, others had been dragged back into the city this very day, and they knew that their comrades were being taken to the tops of those temples to have their hearts ripped forth to slake the thirst of Tenocha gods.

Hring wasn't really sure when the sun came up. He had been fighting as if in a dream for a long, long time. Faces appeared before him and his arm seemed to move and new faces appeared. Sometimes the faces were those of men, more often those of birds or cats or serpents. In a detached fashion, he knew that these were masks, but his mind no longer made that distinction. Eventually the dimness, broken by the lurid glare of the torchlight, was replaced by a pale light, then by a brighter light, finally by full daylight, and they were assaulting the city end of the causeway, forcing their way into the small fort, which the desperate Tenocha had no time to wall up behind the last of their warriors who bravely strove to buy time for their city. There was a last, ferocious struggle in the portal, then the Norsemen were bursting into the city, shouting again, mad with triumph. The shouting stopped when they saw what confronted them. It was a plaza as wide as an entire Norse town, and it was packed with warriors, more than had been able to crowd into the causeway. The buildings all around were covered with men, who began a steady rain of javelins and slingstones.

Hring gaped at the terrifying spectacle, then heard a thundering behind him. "Clear the gateway!" he shouted hoarsely. "Get out of the way!"

The men scrambled to both sides, then the Mongol cavalry were thudding through the gate, plowing into the plaza and shrieking like souls in hell, pouring a veritable avalanche of arrows into the Tenocha host, sweeping the buildings clear of defenders in less time than a man would have thought possible. The Tenocha went down in heaps, unable to strike a blow in their own defense. Their thin shields and fine scale armor was like fragile cloth before the terrible shafts driven by the horn bow of the steppes. More and more horsemen continued pouring through the gateway. The Tenocha were pushed from the plaza, and Mongols rode their mounts up the sides of the terraces and into the broad streets leading toward the center of the city, killing as they went.

"Well," Ragnar said, "I suppose we can rest now." Hring looked at his friend. Miraculously, Ragnar had not taken a single serious wound, though he was covered with nicks and scratches and bruises. It was a tribute to his speed and agility that he could remain so unhurt with only his shield and helm for defensive gear.

"I'd like to rest," Hring said, "but I've an appointment at the top of the Great Pyramid." He began trudging toward the center of the city.

"So," Ragnar said. "We ought to see if we can save any of our people from the priests." He followed Hring, and, one by one, then in groups, so did the other Norsemen, now pitifully few, and none unwounded. Hring waved down a Mongol who had just ridden through the gate and asked him of the other causeways.

"The Nipponese forced theirs an hour ago," the man said. "The native allies were still fighting at the far-end fort last I saw." Then the man was away, eager to join the slaughter.

The Norsemen picked their way along the streets, the bodies and blood making for slow progress. Besides the carnage of the fighting, the sides of all the pyramids had been running with continual rivers of blood for days, and in some of the lower spots, a man could wade almost to his knees. The whole city stank of blood that the tons of burning incense did nothing to alleviate.

"They've all died where they stood," a Norseman said. "I've not seen one run yet," said another.

"Where could they run if they wanted to?" Hring asked. "This is the last of their world, and we've destroyed it."

"The skalds will sing of this forever," said a grizzled Viking. "We've never destroyed a world before. It's like Ragnarok." The group was subdued with fatigue and wonder as they trod the reddened stones of the dying city.

They passed the great ball court, which was crowded with wailing women and crying children. Along its crest, Mongols kept guard as more were herded into the enclosure. For a moment, Hring thought of looking for Golden-Bells, but he knew that she would be at one of the temples, trying to buy the favor of the gods.

The Norsemen gazed in wonderment at the piles and racks of skulls at the pyramid bases. "There can't be that many skulls in the world!" one said. "They must have been taking heads since Ymir died."

The whole city was as colorful as if it were a great festival day. Every man had been dressed for war in his brightest finery, and the streets and terraces and pyramids were a litter of splendid feathers, precious metals, jewels, and brilliant fabrics. Incongruously, the buildings were riotous with flowers. Pots and garlands of bright blooms graced every structure. Beauty and blood were everywhere. Flowers graced skulls and the perfume of incense mingled with the stench of slaughter. The contradictions of the place overwhelmed the band of Norsemen, so that they wandered in a daze, like men suddenly thrust into another world.

They found Bogotai at the base of the Great Pyramid of

Huitzilopochtli. He was gazing up at the mammoth structure, the sides of which were covered with the last defenders of the city. Atop the pyramid, insanely, the priests were still sacrificing captives. The Khan caught sight of Hring and beckoned to him.

"What a slaughter!" Bogotai said, chuckling. "The lake out there is turning pink. Would your men care to share in the glory of the final assault? I'm offering a double share in the plunder to all who participate. Even my Mongols want to dismount and take part."

"I think most of us have had sufficient glory today," Hring said, "but I'll tell my men. I'll go myself, because I made a pact with Smoking-Crest." He told the Norsemen of Bogotai's offer. Predictably, there was much displeasure.

"Those little yellow buggers get a double share for taking this hill when we've been doing all the fighting since sunrise yesterday? I'll go, just to keep them from hogging all the credit." This sentiment, spoken by one, was shared by all but a few who were too sorely wounded to face another assault. Hring delivered their answer to the Khan.

"Good. Hring, you and your Norsemen and the Dineh and other northern tribes will assault the north slope of the pyramid. The native allies will take the south. Ashikaga and the Nipponese will take the east and my Mongols the west. The first man to reach the crest will get a fivefold share." Hring translated this for his men and their eyes glowed with greed.

"There is liable to be fighting over just who reached the top first," Hring said.

"There will be no unseemly brawling among my troops," Bogotai said, cold-eyed. "When the last enemy falls, the battle for this city is ended and we are still under campaign discipline. Anyone who strikes a blow at a fellow soldier will be punished as a criminal. Now assemble your forces at the appointed place. The final assault begins when my drums sound.''

The Norsemen assembled at the base of the north slope. The sides of the pyramid were terribly steep, and inevitably bloody. The defenders would be striking downward, putting the attacking force at a disadvantage. There was no ebullience left in the Norsemen now, just a grim and deadly determination.

The drums beat and the attack was on. It was a slow, strenuous, costly business as the invaders inched their way up the massive pile of stone against the fanatic resistance of the last Tenocha warriors. As they retreated up the sides of the pyramid, their defensive line grew shorter and any gaps were closed. The uphill battle made it impossible for the allies to take advantage of their now superior numbers.

Hring wielded his sword in short jabs beneath the shields of the warriors above him. He regretted not having taken a short spear, which would have been superior for this type of fighting. The swords and macuahuitl came chopping down methodically, managed with the expertise and fearlessness of men bred solely to fight or die on the altar.

Without realizing that the last line had been breached, Hring found himself on top of the pyramid and the battle had broken up into a series of frenzied single combats. He saw Ashikaga scything men down with his long, curved two-handed sword, and Smoking-Crest with macuahuitl and shield, laying about him, shouting war cries. Then Hring was at the altar, where the priests lay dead in a heap. Numbly, he saw the body of Golden-Bells, a great rent below her left breast. She must have been one of the last sacrifices. On the stone sat the Great Speaker, seeming entirely at his ease. In a sudden silence, the Emperor spoke.

"It seems the time has come for the Great Sacrifice. It will come for you, too, Seven-Wind. You were born on the first day of the great year we live in now, and the mark of the gods is still on your brow." He sat cross-legged, his back very straight, and made a sign with his fingers. Smoking-Crest swung his macuahuitl in a horizontal arc and the noble head rolled across the platform and down the steps of the pyramid.

Hring sat on the altar stone and surveyed the city he had helped to murder.

"I owe you a feather cloak," he said.

Chapter 15

The everlasting scent of incense was cloying in his nostrils. He was sick of incense, perfumes, jewels, slaves, feathers, power, all of it. He yearned for the high mountains and broad plains, but those were beginning to swarm with herdsmen and their cattle and sheep and goats. Even the old plains tribes were being organized into tumans and some had taken to living in gers.

"My Khan?" It was the little Chinese, standing by his elbow.

"Hm?" It was annoying, always having these little court functionaries hanging about, snooping and spying. But, he'd be lost without them.

"My apologies, Khan, but the annual report must be signed. You have read it and approve?" Of course he'd read it, or, rather, had it read to him by one of the Chinese secretaries. It gave a careful accounting of the annual tribute sent to Karakorum or Peking or wherever the Great

Khan's court was these days, and a report of the state of the realm. Peaceful, now, after the hard campaigning of the last five years, pacifying the diehard tribes, winkling them out of their mountain strongholds or pursuing them in endless patrols among the dense jungles where horsemen could not go. There had been lengthy forays with his Viking navy among the islands to the east, putting down the eternal forays of the piratical Caribs and Arawaks, who had grown richer and bolder since the shockingly swift collapse of the Tenocha. He smiled at the memory. Those had been good days. That had been real work for Vikings.

He surveyed his realm, the great city of Tenochtitlán. It was as crowded and bustling as ever, though there were no more Tenocha. The vacuum left by their expulsion had been filled by other peoples, just as cultured and now growing as rich.

"My Khan?"

"Oh, sorry." Hring scrawled his name at the bottom of the document, then stamped it with the ink-dipped, carved wooden seal that the Asiatics favored. Hring Khan, Lord of the Flowery Realm, the southern division of the Khanate of the White Horde. All of which was a decorative way of saying that Hring Redbeard, hero and Viking, was a glorified tax collector for the Kha-Khan.

"My Khan," the Chinese said, "the Khan Bogotai wishes to speak with you before he sets out on the new campaign."

Whole hordes had poured in from Asia in the gigantic new ships the Chinese were building for the great eastward migration. Thousands of young warriors had arrived too late for the conquest of the Tenocha Empire. Predictably, something had been found for them to do.

A whole new empire had been found in the continent to the south. The Norse had in the past had only scant contact with that land mass, and then only the eastern shore. This new empire, even bigger and richer than the Tenocha, if the reports were accurate, was on the western coast and extended far inland. It included much grazing plains land such as the Mongols liked, and heaps of precious metals and jewels such as everybody liked. Now, Bogotai was ready to set out on the new invasion, which he had been organizing for the last two years and which Hring and the Norsemen had pointedly not been asked to accompany.

He found Bogotai lounging in his wing of the palace, drinking kumiss and eating raw horsemeat. He looked up as Hring entered and waved toward a cushion. Hring sat and poured himself a cup of wine.

"Esteemed fellow Khan," Bogotai began with his usual heavy irony, "there are some small difficulties in the administration of this, the Kha-Khan's realm, that I would very much like to see eliminated by the time I return next year or the year after." He was quite drunk. It wasn't like him to be so direct. Ordinarily, he made a show of being on an equal footing with Hring, but now he was leaving no question of who was the senior Khan.

"Why tell me?" Hring said. "You know I'm no administrator. I just put my seal on what the Chinese write up. I was a fairly important military governor for a while, but that's long past."

"It was your military authority to which I referred."

Hring had a fair idea of what was coming.

"Your Viking navy has served the Kha-Khan well. However, like most high-spirited men, they are something of a trial in idleness."

"Even so," Hring said, "without them the islanders

would be raiding these shores every year, subtracting greatly from the Kha-Khan's annual tribute.''

"The admiral Halbjorn has done a splendid job of teaching our subject peoples shipbuilding and naval tactics. I think that they will now be able to assume the duties of coast guard. There have been reports that some of your Vikings have been observed descending upon settlements that pay their taxes to the Kha-Khan.''

"There are other Vikings besides those of our navy, Khan,'' Hring protested. "Since so many returned to Thorsheim and Treeland with the loot from the sack of Tenochtitlán, it's like the olden time up there. Each farmer fancies himself a reaver from the old sagas.''

"Then it is time something was done about that,'' Bogotai said. "And, the governor of Tuxpan tells me that the Norse sailors are not keeping the peace.'' Hring gritted his teeth. The Mongols waged war with a savagery surpassing belief, but considered a little brawl with no more than a dozen or so killed to be a serious offense.

"I will speak to Halbjorn, Khan''

"Perhaps it's time for them to return home,'' Bogotai said casually. "After all, they have made themselves unpopular with the natives, and I could not be responsible for any actions they might take to revenge themselves upon the Norsemen while I am away in the South, campaigning for the greater glory of the Kha-Khan.''

"But,'' Hring pointed out, "*I* am responsible for what happens in this province.''

"True. And a sad thing it is to see a great warrior like you reduced to this ignoble administrative post.'' The Khan drank deeply and then fell to studying an incomprehensible mural on the wall opposite him. "Your home, now—these kingdoms of Treeland and Thorsheim—that is a proper setting for a man like you. From all I've heard, it is dense woodland, broken up into hills and valleys. Not at all the kind of land we Mongols favor. We may never go there. Are you never longing to see your old home?"

"Frequently, Khan." He looked the great warlord in the eye to show that he understood and appreciated. "I shall keep your words in mind."

Bogotai gave one of his rare smiles. "Just so."

On his way back to his apartments, Hring gave orders to servants to gather up his goods and load them on wagons. In his bedroom, he belted on his sword and clapped his old, dented iron cap on his thick red hair. He stepped out onto the balcony to look over the bustling city. The great pyramids were as mountainous and solid as ever, but their paint was faded and peeling. They no longer had a purpose now that human sacrifice was forbidden. They were mere curiosities that travelers came from far to see.

Well, Bogotai had been fair, at least. There was room for only one Khan in this realm, and that Khan was going to be a Mongol. The problem might have been solved more easily with a poisoned cup, but Bogotai was giving his old comrade a chance to live, even to win a kingdom of his own. To win a kingdom where he wouldn't be a stranger, as he had been a stranger everywhere he roamed since his youth.

The door of the dockside tavern burst open and the drinkers inside looked up. They were hardbitten Norsemen and most had a hungry look about them. The cruising had been poor, of late. A big, red-bearded man stood in the doorway.

"Halbjorn!" the redbeard shouted.

"Well, Governor Hring," came a voice from the back

of the room. "What brings you to visit our humble town? Poor pickings hereabout, compared with the capital."

"Shut your bearded trap and round up your pirates, all of them. Send word up and down the coast and to the islands. We've worn out our welcome here. We're going home."

"Home?" Halbjorn said. "What for?"

"Sweyn's still on his throne," Hring said. "He's been there too long. We're going to boot him off it and plant me there. Then we're going to take Treeland."

"Damn your eyes, I've been waiting for you to come here and say that for the last three years. What took you so long?"

"I've always been a cautious man," Hring said.

Sweyn's fleet was bottled up in Odinsfell Harbor, surrounded by marshes and difficult to attack. Hring's fleet had struck the coast like a hurricano and ravaged northward, with Sweyn making a poor showing of a fighting retreat. Now the King was jammed against the rune-stone border, his forces dwindling rapidly as men deserted him. He had never commanded much respect, and what little he had was fading fast.

Hring surveyed the ground. He was camped on a rare spot of high ground, overlooking the river. Below him, he could see the smoky squalor of Sweyn's camp. All the good warriors had gone South, and the King had only his hired men to depend on. He smiled in his thick red beard. It was good to be among kinsmen again, even when he was fighting them. It was good to be back in the land of roast pork and strong ale. His thoughts were interrupted when a party of camp guards came to him, escorting a tall, gaunt, white-bearded man.

"This fellow just crossed the river and demands to see you, lord," said a shag-haired youth. "Says he knows you."

"He does," Hring said. "You're grayer than ever, Gudmund. Does my father still live?"

"Dead," said the old housecarl. "Your half brother Thorkel's thegn now, but it's your stepmother who rules. It occurs to me that your outlawry's up now. There's nothing to stop you coming home and setting that aright."

"Presently," Hring said. "First I'm going to kill that King down there, then I'll go North and kill the other one, or drive him from his throne, then we'll see about my half brother and stepmother. The kingdoms have been divided too long."

"Aye. Well, it's been bad times for kings of late, hasn't it?"

The feast had been going on for days, inaugurating the new city of Hringsgard and the great royal hall that crowned it. Built on a high stone platform, the massive timber edifice loomed above the old border where the old rune stones had been thrown down like some great predatory beast. Its eaves could shelter an army and it was roofed with copper instead of shingles.

Along the riverbank, longships and knarrs were drawn ashore or anchored in the deep water. All the nobility of the reunited Kingdoms had come to pay their homage to the hero of the age, Hring Redbeard; Sea King, Champion of the Great Pyramid, Sacker of Tenochtitlán, Conqueror of the Two Kingdoms, King of the Wood.

The man who held all those titles belched contentedly as he lowered his drinking horn. Foam flecked his flaming beard. He sat on one of the two thrones he had looted from two palaces. On his head was the crown of Treeland. Across his thighs lay the great sword of Thorsheim. The long tables down the length of the cavernous hall were lined with thegns and ladies, Viking captains, Skraeling chieftains, Moorish merchants, even a Mongol ambassador or two. A scowling knot of Christian priests sat at one table, uneasy now that their church was no longer the established faith of a kingdom. Hring smiled at their discomfiture. It seemed as if every noble had brought along a gaggle of unwed daughters. Hring smiled at that, too.

The great door a hundred yards from where Hring sat opened for a moment, and someone came in. People had been coming in and going out for days, and the King paid no attention. A small, lone figure came walking down the long corridor which ran from door to throne. A pool of silence spread as the lonely figure passed with slow but springy tread, and Hring looked up. His heart sank but beat faster as he made out the gray homespun dress, the arm-thick yellow braid.

She stopped at the foot of the dais. Her glacial eyes regarded him from under level brows, expressionless but somehow mocking. She had not changed at all, unlike Hring, who had been little more than a boy when he had last seen her, and was now a warrior and king in his prime; a hero. He stood.

"Greeting, priestess," Hring said.

"I always said you had the makings, Hring," she said. She looked at the empty throne beside the one he had been sitting on. "You'll be needing a queen."

Hring descended the dais steps and stood, looking down into her eyes. He turned and faced the thrones, holding out a massive, red-furred, gold-banded arm. She took it. "I knew you were a queen the day I first saw you, witch."

They walked up the steps, to a chorus of shocked gasps, which turned to shouts of outrage when Hring seated Yngva on the throne. He reseated himself on the other and picked up his horn. Servants ran to bring the Queen food and drink.

"Is your knife still sharp?" Hring asked.

"Sharp enough for its task," she answered.

Epilogue

The wind had a sharp edge. It would not be long until mid-winter, Hring thought. Not that it would be much of a mid-winter feast, what with the poor harvests of the last few years. He yawned and stretched stiffly, his joints cracking loudly, as they had been doing for years now.

He splashed water in his face from a basin, and looked at his countenance in the looking glass above it. Gods, but he was getting gray. Hardly any red left in hair or beard. Reasonable enough, really. He tried to calculate his age. Fifty-two, or thereabouts.

And, who would be coming to the feast that he wanted to see again, anyway? Ragnar was gone these many years, somewhere out West, buried in the mountains he loved. Halbjorn dead three years past. The old pirate had died in his bed of all places, surrounded by his grandchildren. And Halvdan—gods, but it had been a long time since he'd thought of Halvdan. Sudden, unaccustomed tears filled his eyes as he thought of the man who had been more than a brother to him.

Well, he was alone, now. Yngva had died bearing their last child. What a woman she had been, as bloodthirsty in bed as ever he had been on the battlefield. He still bore the scars. As fine a queen as he could have wished, too, and it hadn't hurt that the people had feared her more than him. Her last words still disturbed him, sometimes; "You will know the time when it comes, red man," she'd said.

He stretched his arms as he tried to set his mind to the business of the day. At least his back no longer pained him. He chuckled at the thought of how that had come to be. A few years past, at Yule, it had been, and he'd been telling for the thousandth time of his one-man fight atop the pyramid. He could see the disbelief in the eyes of the young people, to whom he was a hero of the olden time, a name from an old saga, not a real man at all. He'd felt a sharp twinge in his back, just below the shoulder, and the sharp obsidian blade had cut through skin and tunic and dropped to lie bloodily upon the table. The looks on those faces had been among the great triumphs of his life.

It suddenly came to him that there was nothing he wanted to do today. Come to think of it, there was nothing he could think of that was worth doing from now on. Then it came to him. He laughed aloud. Going back to the looking glass, he pushed back the heavy fringe of hair that had covered his brow for many years. There was the mark, just as she had traced it so long ago, visible to him now for the first time.

"You win, Yngva," he said, smiling.

He packed a few items in a bag and went down into the hall. A big red-haired young man was sprawled on a bench, his arm around a big hunting dog. Hring kicked him awake. This one was also Hring, called the Young, to distinguish him from his father.

"Off the bench, boy," he said. "You'll be sitting on the throne now." He jerked a thumb over his shoulder at the high chair.

"Are you going to be away?" the youth said, yawning.

"That is right. You can be kinging it now."

"You won't be gone long, will you? Guthlaf Halbjornson and I are planning to go a-viking in the spring, down among the isles."

"I'm not coming back. You're King for good now."

"What are you saying?" said the boy, shocked.

"It can't be helped," Hring said. "It comes of being born with red hair and a destiny to be king. But, I'm King of the Wood, too, you see. That's a more important kind of king."

"I don't understand," said Hring the Young.

"No matter. It may happen to you, too. If so, you will fight it as I did, but it will do no good." He clapped his arms around his son. "Well, farewell, lad. You will start well, at least. The harvest will be the best ever next fall." He turned and strode toward the stable.

The grove was just as he'd remembered it. These ancient trees didn't change appreciably in the lifetime of a mere man. The only thing missing was the sight of the dangling forms swaying in the breeze. Next to the great central oak lay a gray, slablike stone. Hring dismounted and walked to the stone. He looked about. The light was failing, early as it was. The days would be growing longer now, because it was midwinter day. He caught a hint of movement at the edge of the clearing.

The young woman in the gray dress caught at his breath,

so much did she resemble her mother, save for the reddish glints in her hair. As she came closer, he saw that she was not as young as she first seemed. But then, all that breed concealed their years well. This one had been conceived on a night he remembered well, more than thirty years ago. He bowed a brief greeting, but her eyes remained steady and her expression never changed.

Hring lay down and stretched himself out on the stone. As the woman came to him with the knife in her hand, it seemed to him that it was the most comfortable bed he had ever lain upon.

CONAN

- ☐ 54238-X   CONAN THE DESTROYER $2.95
     54239-8   Canada $3.50

- ☐ 54228-2   CONAN THE DEFENDER $2.95
     54229-0   Canada $3.50

- ☐ 54225-8   CONAN THE INVINCIBLE $2.95
     54226-6   Canada $3.50

- ☐ 54236-3   CONAN THE MAGNIFICENT $2.95
     54237-1   Canada $3.50

- ☐ 54231-2   CONAN THE UNCONQUERED $2.95
     54232-0   Canada $3.50

- ☐ 54246-0   CONAN THE VICTORIOUS $2.95
     54247-9   Canada $3.50

- ☐ 54248-7   CONAN THE FEARLESS (trade) $6.95
     54249-5   Canada $7.95

- ☐ 54242-8   CONAN THE TRIUMPHANT $2.95
     54243-6   Canada $3.50

- ☐ 54244-4   CONAN THE VALOROUS (trade) $6.95
     54245-2   Canada $7.95

Buy them at your local bookstore or use this handy coupon:
Clip and mail this page with your order

TOR BOOKS—Reader Service Dept.
49 W. 24 Street, 9th Floor, New York, NY 10010

Please send me the book(s) I have checked above. I am enclosing
$_____ (please add $1.00 to cover postage and handling).
Send check or money order only—no cash or C.O.D.'s.

Mr./Mrs./Miss _____

Address _____

City _____ State/Zip _____

Please allow six weeks for delivery. Prices subject to change without
notice.

ANDRÉ NORTON

<table>
<tr><td>☐</td><td>54736-5
54737-3</td><td>GRYPHON'S EYRIE</td><td>
Canada</td><td>$2.95
$3.50</td></tr>
<tr><td>☐</td><td>48558-1</td><td>FORERUNNER</td><td></td><td>$2.75</td></tr>
<tr><td>☐</td><td>48585-9</td><td>MOON CALLED</td><td></td><td>$2.95</td></tr>
<tr><td>☐</td><td>54725-X
54726-8</td><td>WHEEL OF STARS</td><td>
Canada</td><td>$2.95
$3.50</td></tr>
<tr><td>☐</td><td>54738-1
54739-X</td><td>THE CRYSTAL GRYPHON</td><td>
Canada</td><td>$2.95
$3.50</td></tr>
<tr><td>☐</td><td>54740-3

54741-1</td><td>MAGIC IN ITHKAR Edited by
André Norton and Robert Adams Trade
</td><td>

Canada</td><td>
$6.95
$7.95</td></tr>
</table>